# READY OR NOT

# READY OR NOT

## by Norma Johnston

*Funk & Wagnalls Company, Inc., New York*

*Other books by the same author*

THE WISHING STAR

THE WIDER HEART

This one's for Lois—
good critic and good friend

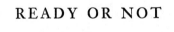

READY OR NOT

# CHAPTER

# 1

NEW YEAR'S DAY in 1861 was wet and dark. The wind was high, steel-sharp, and bitter cold. But it was no more bitter than Carlie Benson's mood. She swung the horse between the iron gates at the entrance of the curving driveway to Beaufort, jerked on the reins, and sat back, breathing deeply.

It was her fifteenth birthday, and she had never, she thought passionately, been more desperately unhappy in her life. Her list of grievances was as long as the catalogue of her sins, and they were many. She contemplated them grimly now before going in to face her family's wrath.

She had taken Midnight, her brother's horse, without permission—a thing Ben had expressly forbidden. Not only was she not sidesaddle—she was riding bareback. She had borrowed her sister Laura's fascinator to throw over her head, since she could not find her own, and had lost it somewhere in the woods. She was not, of course, supposed to be riding alone in the Franklin woods at all, particularly not in the wind and rain. Worst of all, she had lost track of the time. She had got home so late that the Bensons' famous New Year's Open House was already under way. She had the choice of going in the front way and risking being seen like this—hair tumbling down, her wet dress hoopless and bedraggled, a jagged scratch from a low-hanging tree branch across her face—or she could go in the back door and almost certainly encounter her mother or Laura in the kitchen.

Rain beat through the bare branches of the maple trees and ran inside her cloak, reminding her uncomfortably that she could not stay out here forever. First, however, Midnight must be returned to the barn; he must be dried off, groomed, and fed. Carlie did not mind these chores; Ben had taught her that it was part of the responsibility of the rider and they had often done these tasks together in the old days. But she and Ben seldom did anything together now.

Reminded of her grievance, Carlie pressed her lips together tightly. She started Midnight down the path to the barn with such a rough jerk that he flung his head and rolled his eyes wildly.

"Poor Midnight! It isn't fair to take it out on you. At least you still treat me the same!" Carlie leaned forward, pressing her face against his sable neck. Her eyes brimmed suddenly.

Tears were Laura's weapon. Carlie was too proud and too stubborn to let them show in public, but now, alone in the darkness, they ran down her grimy cheeks and onto Midnight's neck, making her feel bitterly ashamed. Ben didn't cry. Papa didn't. Tears were a female weakness, pointing out inexorably that Mama and Laura were right. The time for the parting of the ways had come.

It had been coming for some time, although Carlie had been too blind to see it . . . or too stubborn. Ben was no longer eager to have her share his escapades or dreams. Papa, instead of laughing at her exploits as he used to do, had been reproving . . . or, worse, had had a sad look as if he were aware of things she couldn't yet see. Even Paul and Oliver were no longer willing to let her weave them fanciful games and tales of derring-do. Her ability to fascinate them was faltering; the old enchantments no longer held. Six-year-old Oliver wriggled his fat little body away from her grasp, and Paul, lean and solemn at nine, had informed her bluntly, "You're too big."

It had come to a head this morning.

She had awakened early, a sense of expectation stirring in her heart, rising through the restlessness that was there so often lately. The bright optimism of the holiday season was still in the air, filling her with a sense of hope. She had dressed in the old bottle-green merino she still loved, although it was now growing small. Downstairs the table had looked as it always had at birthday breakfasts in the past, laden with be-ribboned gifts, surrounded with family, with expectation, with love.

The gifts, too, had followed the patterns of the past. A leather bookmark painstakingly hand-tooled by Ben. Less-carefully handmade objects from Paul and Oliver. A book from Laura. From her mother a tiny turquoise finger ring that had been Grandmother Rutledge's.

Her father's gift, as usual, she opened last, for his was always special, reflecting the particular closeness that was between them. She had ripped off the tissue and ribbons, lifted the cover—and stared at the contents in despair and disbelief. It was an ornate wicker sewing basket, tufted in satin, filled with delicate silver equipment. And the last thing in the world, Carlie thought bitterly, that Papa should have thought I'd want! He knows I hate fancywork!

The tears she so despised welled up suddenly, and she had stared at him through them in bitter hurt. Her father, looking bewildered, had turned to her pretty red-haired mother.

"I don't understand. The clerk in the store assured me it was the very thing for a young lady."

*Young lady.* There it was in words. Suddenly, with an unexpectedness that shocked even herself, Carlie's arm had swept out, knocking the basket to the floor.

"*You, too?*" she had shouted in bitter accusation. "Why can't you let me be!"

She had pushed her chair back so abruptly that coffee flew from cups. She had run upstairs to her room, banged the door behind her, and thrown herself across the bed. After awhile someone had knocked on the door.

"Go away!" she had shouted, and for once whoever it was had had the tact to do so. It was shortly afterward that she had risen, flung her old blue cloak around her shoulders, and taken Laura's fleecy scarf in place of her own. She had crept down the back stairs and out to the barn. Secure in the knowledge that old Daniel, the slave Mama had brought with her from Carolina, was in the hencoops gathering eggs, she had eased Midnight out of his stall and turned him into the bleak wildness of the woods behind the neighboring Courtins farm.

"I had to do it," she whispered to Midnight now and heard him whinny in sympathy. "If I hadn't gotten out, I'd have just exploded!" Her temper outbursts, always spectacular, had become increasingly frequent of late, and although she would never have admitted it to Mama or Laura, they were another thing of which she was bitterly ashamed. More than anything she wished for Papa's calm control. Mr. Benson, too, could often flare with righteous anger, but he let the fire spill out only in his writing. He himself always remained poised, courteous, and gracious, as a gentleman should.

Gentleman. There was respect in the word. Not so in its opposite number.

"Young *lady!*" Carlie said scathingly, throwing into the

words all the helpless fury at her command. It was all right for some people. Mama was a Southern gentlewoman in every sense that the term implied. And Laura—who knows it full well, too, Carlie thought—was the very epitome of a fashionable young lady. It might not be so bad, being a young lady, Carlie admitted unwillingly, if she looked like Laura. But she did not.

Laura at eighteen was alluringly fragile-looking. Carlie, if she was what novels would describe as "slender as a willow sapling," had a sapling's toughness, too. Laura's hair was like spun-gold and smooth like Mama's. Carlie's was merely light-colored, and it curved in a cowlick that she loathed. Laura's nose, like Mama's, was Grecian; Carlie's was tip-tilted. Laura's eyes were like serene blue summer skies. Carlie's own eyes were gray as slate; they were often glowing, frequently mutinous, and occasionally sullen, but they were never, never serene.

As for her chin—on Papa, that same chin was considered indicative of strength of character. But when Mama referred to Carlie's, she just sighed, and Laura, who never wasted tact on the family, said bluntly that Carlie was "stubborn as an old mule."

If she had to take after Papa, whom she adored, why couldn't she have been born a boy! When Ben did the very things that brought upon her so much censure, he received only mild reproof.

It had not always been so. Once she and Ben, only a year and a half older, had roamed the woods together, read Papa's adventure books together, and listened enthralled to Papa's stories of the part their mother's family had played in founding the country. The three of them had been a tight, closed circle, united by their impulsiveness, their idealism, their creative yearnings. They were all what Papa called "restless dreamers."

[ 7 ]

Those dreams might still come true some day—for Ben. Never for her. When girls grew up, they were supposed to take a back seat to their menfolks, to be content with running a household, doing fancywork, and raising children.

Carlie breathed a deep, angry sigh. How could anyone in his right mind expect her willingly to act a simpering fool like Laura, flirting and mooning over her beau Peter Van Dirk. Carlie had never been able to understand either how Mama, gay and beautiful Mama, could be content with the endless cooking, cleaning, sewing, and raising children. Then the sense of justice Papa had instilled in her rose swiftly, and she felt ashamed. She loved Laura, despite her coquettish ways; she loved helping with Paul and Oliver. And Papa had always considered Mama's fine mind one of his greatest joys.

"But it's not enough for me!" Carlie's eyes shut tightly and the feeling of helpless resentment rose again in her chest. She would not—could not—compromise; that sort of life was as alien to her as Beaufort itself was alien to its surroundings.

She looked back at Beaufort now and felt her heart grow quiet. Like all the Bensons, she had a passionate love of her home. It was a replica of Mama's girlhood home in Carolina, and with its tall white columns reaching up a full three stories to the portico, it was like a swan among chickens in contrast to the low rambling Dutch-style houses that dotted the rest of the small New Jersey town. "Benson's Folly," the neighbors had called it when Papa built it for his Southern bride. It was regarded now with amused affection as an understandable idiosyncrasy on the part of otherwise normal people, and even the scoffers dropped in unexpectedly at any hour of the day or night. Mr. Benson commented ruefully that Beaufort was patronized even more than the Franklin Inn, where townsfolk gathered to discuss the increasingly explosive political situation.

Mr. Ryerson, the parson, had recently been making quite a

fuss about the Inn, and so the impromptu discussions had switched to Beaufort. Because Mr. Benson was the publisher of the *Bergen Journal,* he wanted to keep a weather eye on local political feeling. The family was hoping half-heartedly that politics would not crop up today to spoil the party.

Carlie, remembering the party, felt depression settle on her again. She would have to go in sooner or later to face the music, and as she grew older, she was becoming increasingly aware that postponing such things only made them worse. One step forward in growing up, she thought wryly, although she was uncomfortably conscious that her flight today would be held as proof that the growing process had not yet begun.

*When will you learn that you can't run away from things?* She could hear Papa's sad voice so plainly. Once Papa would have sympathized with her impulse, she thought, but not any more. And that for Carlie was the bitterest pill of all.

She realized suddenly that Midnight was no longer moving; they had reached the barn and he stood patiently waiting. She slid down from his back just as the door opened, lantern-light fanned across the snow, and a wizened, ugly, black face peered out at her.

"Ain't you got no more sense than to race that critter on a day like this?" Daniel held the lantern higher and scowled at her, and Carlie grinned back at him in complete accord.

"I only raced up the drive, and Midnight loved it." The horse whinnied and nuzzled her ear gently, and she reached up to pat his nose. The familiar sounds and smells of the barn enveloped her as she led him in. This was her refuge, one of her special havens, to which she ran whenever things went wrong.

Daniel was a haven, too. He had a wooden leg, a gold tooth, and a gold earring in one ear—proof, he insisted, that he had been a chieftain's son. No one quite knew; long ago he had come from Africa on a slaving ship. And he considered not only Carlie, but Mama too, to be still little girls in need of his especial guidance.

"Yer Ma's fit ter bust you," he said now, scowling in a way that was supposed to be ferocious but succeeded only in being fond. "And so's Benjamin, when he found out what you'd done. You run now and make your peace. I'll put the nag to bed."

"Thanks, Dan." Carlie flashed him a swift grateful smile and raced up the path, holding her skirts high to avoid the icy puddles. Behind the lilac bushes by the kitchen steps, she paused to reconnoiter. She decided on the front door as the lesser of two evils—Mama, for all her gentleness, had a sharp tongue when roused—and picked her way around the side of the house, ducking low to avoid being seen from the tall windows.

Perhaps, she thought hopefully, she could loiter on the veranda till the front hall was empty. The ladies usually gathered in the further of the two double parlors, since it was closer to the kitchen and hence warmer. If the conversation had become too fiery, as it usually did these days, Papa would have ushered the gentlemen into the library for their port and cigars behind closed doors. She might then, she hoped, be able to reach her bedroom unobserved.

She opened the big carved door cautiously. Yes, the front parlor was deserted. The sounds of teacups being set on saucers and soft laughter came from the room beyond. The sound of raised voices came from the library.

"Discipline, that's what the South needs, discipline!" That was Uncle Henry Demarest, sounding his oft-repeated theme. "Not a democracy, an autocracy!" That was Mr. Pryor, his voice showing he was growing red-faced and choleric. Then Mr. Benson's calm, "Gentlemen, this is a party! To the New

Year—and the new administration!" Then the clink of glasses, and a reference to Mr. Lincoln, and somebody's angry snort.

The library's double doors were closed; the coast was clear. Carlie slid inside, shut the door noiselessly, hung her cloak on the stand, and sprinted for the stairs. She could just see through the arch of the back parlor. If only Laura—or, worse, Mama—would not turn around! Her rain-wet skirts, too long without the hoops, slapped at her feet, and she swept them up impatiently. Then, out of nowhere, came a chuckle, close at hand, definitely male.

Appalled, she stared over the banister at the lower hall, straight into the blackest eyes she had ever seen.

The boy—or young man, rather, for he was at least seventeen—was a stranger. He was tall and had even white teeth and very straight black hair, and his eyes, meeting Carlie's horror-filled ones, held an unmistakable twinkle.

For a second she stood there, frozen. Then, crimson with embarrassment, she dropped her skirts and plunged blindly up the stairs—only to have her long skirts suddenly tangle underfoot and to find herself rolling, head over heels, down the long flight of stairs.

There was a scream, not hers, from somewhere far away. There was a clatter of china, a swift scraping of chairs, and people pressing close. Mama was there, her face pale above her new green brocade gown, her eyes dark with fear. Embarrassment mixed with concern in Laura's blue eyes. Uncle Henry looked shocked. There were her own friends, whom she was supposed to be helping entertain—gay, dark-blond Emily Garrison, and the gentle Courtins girls. And Emily's brother Tom and hot-tempered Joe Pryor—they had been boyhood friends of Ben's, but lately, since their parents disagreed on politics, they had grown apart.

Carlie did not know where to look. For a moment she lay still, the breath knocked out of her, conscious of a general aching, and of two things more. One was the stranger, bending over her, his handsome face concerned. The other was her father, looking at her with an expression that made her drop her eyes. "I'm really all right," she whispered. "Just a bit breathless."

Her father looked her over slowly and carefully. Then he said, "Carolina, go to your room." Mr. Benson's voice was very quiet, and his use of her full name brought home to Carlie, more than anything else, the depth of his disappointment in her.

# CHAPTER

## 2

HAVING REACHED THE REFUGE of her room, Carlie slammed the door. This childish action made her feel somewhat better, but not all the slammed doors in the world could shut out the remembrance of the look on her father's face. Of all the people in the hall, only Carlie had seen that look, and it had moved her far more deeply than any words could have.

Her conduct today had been for Papa as complete a betrayal as his gift of the sewing basket had been to her. She knew this quite suddenly and clearly, and she knew, too, that his disappointment in her was surpassed by her disappointment in herself.

I don't know what gets into me, she thought. It was no wonder Papa no longer seemed to understand her. She didn't even understand herself.

She moved toward the bureau, caught a glimpse of herself in the mirror, and went cold with shock. The skimpy dress, rain-soaked and hoopless, clung to her body tightly, revealing curves she hadn't known she had. To have appeared like this, before all her parents' friends—and before the stranger! Unbidden, the memory of his twinkling black eyes rose before her.

How she must have looked! Like a naughty child—no, *not* a child! Face flaming, she ripped off the dress and flung it to the floor. She would never wear it again. She stared at herself in the mirror somberly.

"Skinny!" she jeered at the reflection. "Skinny! Gawky!" Her face was as black as a chimney sweep's, she could see bruises forming on her arms, and her petticoat was torn. She ought to repair the damages and go downstairs gracefully, but she did none of these things. She threw herself full-length across the bed and stared out of the window at the dark sky.

Presently she heard a soft tapping at the door. "Go away," Carlie called, not turning.

"It's Bess," a gentle voice said. "May I come in?" Not waiting for an answer, her cousin Bess Demarest slipped inside, shutting the door behind her.

Bess was the same age as Carlie, but so small and timid that she seemed a full two years younger. Her mother, who had been Mr. Benson's sister Elizabeth, had died four years ago and since then Bess had been more hesitant than ever. She was not shy with Carlie, though. She came forward now, her sweet pointed face concerned, and sat down on the edge of the bed.

"Carlie? What's wrong?" Bess's taffeta dress rustled as she leaned forward. "Are you hurt? Your father's worried. You took such a tumble!"

"I'd be all right if people would just leave me be!" Carlie said ungraciously. She sat up and pulled the rest of the pins from her hair.

Bess changed the subject tactfully. "I've brought your birthday present." She offered a small, tissue-wrapped package. "Many happy returns."

"Not of this one. This has been one—dickens—of a day!"

The package contained a velvet-covered journal. "For you to write in," Bess explained, her soft voice breathless. Bess, who had no ambition beyond getting through each day peacefully, admired almost with awe her cousin's wider dreams.

"I'm not going to write any more." Carlie stared at the gilt letters on the journal's cover. "What's going to happen to me in 1861 that will be worth writing about?"

"Lots of things. Maybe even a war. Pa thinks there will be."

"I wish there would be a war," Carlie exclaimed suddenly. "I wish I could run off and join and do something important like John Rutledge in the Revolution." Then her energy evaporated as swiftly as it had come. "What's the use? If we had a war now, I'd still have to sit home and be useless." She looked at Bess's shocked face, bent down and kissed her impulsively on the cheek. "Thank you, hon. You run on down. I'll get dressed and come like a proper miss, I promise."

After Bess had left, she worked swiftly, washing with cold water from the pitcher and brushing her hair with vigor, wincing as she did so for her arms and shoulders were beginning to ache. She pulled out the taffeta dress Mama had insisted on making her last fall. It was the same blue-gray as her eyes, and Mama, with surprising understanding, had left it perfectly plain. Just bishop sleeves, narrow at the shoulder but growing wide before being gathered in elbow-high; a round neck, low cut, but finished with only the narrowest of self-folds; the skirt untrimmed although ridiculously long and full. Even over her widest hoops it trailed the ground. She turned to face the mirror, and stared. In the new gown, she looked . . .

"I look like Laura!" she breathed aloud.

No, not like Laura. Laura would have been in frills and

ruffles, her head coquettishly on one side. Carlie's own head was tilted back by the weight of her hair, caught at the nape of her neck in a velvet snood. Her eyes, still smoldering, glowed like the highlights in the changeable taffeta, and above the wide folds of the skirt her waist looked unbelievably tiny. Tinier than Laura's, Carlie thought with a flash of uncharacteristic satisfaction.

For the first time she felt the sense of strength that comes from looking well. It was a kind of armor. But all the same, when her hand reached the doorknob, she felt a shakiness that had nothing whatsoever to do with her headlong fall. It would not be easy, going downstairs, facing a sea of disapproving faces . . . facing Papa to apologize.

"Don't be a ninny!" she told herself sternly. "You're acting like a silly female!" She took a deep breath, flung the door open, and started down the stairs.

The heavy skirts and the ache in her back made her move slowly. She noticed with acute relief that the front room was still deserted. Then, as she reached the bottom step, an arm was held out and she looked up, startled, into smiling black eyes.

"I thought you might be in need of a strong right arm—or left one, rather." He intercepted her swift glance around the empty hall. "The ladies are in the back parlor, sipping punch. The men are in the library, dissecting Old Abe."

"Wouldn't you rather . . ."

He shook his head. "I hear enough politics in New York and at Judge Zabriskie's office. I'm his new clerk. Bradley Otis Sturdevant, III." He flashed a charming, one-sided smile. "Brad, to you." He steered her into the front parlor and held a big chair out before the fire. Carlie sank into it gratefully. She couldn't quite look him in the face; she stared into the dancing flames as he reached into the niche beside the fireplace and produced two cups of punch and a plate of cakes. "I also thought you'd need some sustenance before you braved the lions."

"You're . . . very kind."

"No, just guilty. It's my fault you're in trouble. I never should have laughed."

"It's not your fault." Carlie took a deep breath and met his eyes directly. "It's not because I fell that I'm in trouble. That was just the final straw!" The words, meant to be light and casual, came out with unexpected vehemence. She colored and looked away.

"Want to tell me about it?" Brad's chaffing manner vanished, and he pulled a chair up opposite hers. His deep musical voice was unexpectedly gentle. "Sometimes it's easier talking to a stranger."

"There's nothing to tell." Carlie looked at her hands. "I've just been—behaving like a fool, and I can't seem to stop. It's terrible, to know you've hurt people and not be able to do a thing about it."

"I know." Brad's tone was so sober that she glanced up, startled. Then he grinned disarmingly. "This is your life story, not mine!"

"Sounds like one of those trashy novels by Adelaide Somerville!" She laughed shortly, and for no reason she could see he looked amused.

"*The Trials of Carlie Benson?*" His tone was light, but his eyes were compassionate. "It sounds serious. Is there anything I can do?"

"There isn't; nobody can. Except myself, and I . . . don't want to." His interest and his obvious concern, two qualities she had been sorely needing lately, were comforting. Unexpectedly the words she had been longing to say to Papa burst out with passion. "When you have so much life inside of you, it's as if . . . Well, if it doesn't get out—if you don't use it—you die inside. I want to be more than a bystander to life!"

It was true, what Brad had said about its being easier to talk to a stranger. The quietness of the room and the crackling flames had woven a curious intimacy between them. Then Laura appeared in the archway, and the spell was broken.

"Mr. Sturdevant! We've been neglecting you, I declare!" There were times when Laura, born in New Jersey, was more Southern even than Mama. She came forward now, all frills and laces, holding out both hands to Brad, who rose politely. "Come let me give you some punch!"

Head tilted, her hoopskirts swaying, Laura smiled provocatively, and the sight drove Carlie out of her momentary confidence back into the insecurity Laura always caused. But to her surprise, Brad's tone showed only gentlemanly courtesy, nothing more.

"Thank you. Miss Carlie and I have already had punch."

Laura flashed Carlie a sharp glance. "Carlie, Papa's waiting for you. Mr. Sturdevant, the gentlemen have joined the ladies. Will you come?"

Brad smiled noncommittally, and Laura glided out, trailing the scent of her sweet cologne. Carlie stared across the hall. The library door had opened and the men were moving out to join the ladies. But Mr. Benson had lingered, and Carlie could see him standing by the window, looking out. Now was her chance to speak to him alone, but she felt that strange mixture of resentment and self-loathing descend again, and for a second she fought an insane desire to bolt and run.

"Carlie?" Brad was standing behind her, his hands on the high back of her chair. Unwillingly she felt herself rising to her feet, and he came to face her, touching her shoulders lightly. "I don't know what's the matter, but I do know this. It's the things we run from that hurt the most."

For a second they looked deep into each other's eyes. Then

she stiffened her shoulders and crossed to the library door. When she looked back, she saw Brad still watching her, standing before the fire.

She straightened up as tall as she could, raised her chin, and stepped inside, closing the door behind her. Then she looked into her father's eyes, and all the proud and defensive things she planned to say suddenly fled. She rushed over and sank into the chair opposite her father's desk, her hands clenched tightly. "Papa, I'm sorry! I didn't mean to embarrass you and Mama. And I didn't mean to stay out late and forget the party. I'm so sorry!"

"You always are, Carlie, when it's too late."

Quite suddenly tears welled up and she averted her face. Mr. Benson came around and sat on the edge of the desk, and for a moment she thought he was going to reach out and rumple her hair as he had often done when she was little. "Are you all right, Carlie?" he asked gently.

Carlie nodded, unable to speak, and for several seconds there was silence. She expected him to say something about her rudeness that morning, the worry she had caused, and her humiliation in the hall, but when he spoke at last it was something quite different.

"I wasn't going to speak of this till later, for there isn't time to discuss it now with our guests waiting. But it's been on my mind for some time, Carlie. How would you like to take a trip?"

"A—trip?"

"To South Carolina. Your mother's relatives have been asking for a long time to have one of you children come for a visit. We've never wanted to let one of you go for so long a time, but now I think perhaps it would be wise for you to go."

"Papa!" She stared at him in stunned disbelief.

"You always do want to run away from things, Carlie, so

you might as well really travel." Mr. Benson gave her a very faint smile, but she was too shocked to see the humor.

"Papa, you couldn't, you wouldn't, just cast me off! If you send me away from Beaufort, I'll die!" She was sounding like one of those trashy novels she'd mentioned, but she was too worked up to care. "Papa, I didn't mean to be rude this morning! I'll apologize. I'll apologize to everybody, only can't we just go on the way we were before?"

"That's just it, Carlie. Things never stay the same." He handed her a handkerchief and looked away tactfully while she dried her eyes. "That's one of the things you haven't learned, any more than you've learned that you cannot run away from unpleasantness, as you tried to do this morning." She started to speak, but he held up his hand. "You do, Carlie—it's exactly what you do. And one of these days you're going to reach a point where you realize you can't run any more, where you've got to turn around and dig in your heels and fight."

For a second he sounded as if he were speaking more to himself than to her, but the significance was lost in her burst of words. "That's what I'm trying to do! I thought you'd understand. You always taught us that self-expression was necessary for creative people. Why does it have to be different for me just because I'm a girl? Is *this* the kind of democracy we live in?"

"Carlie, Carlie! What you're talking about isn't democracy. It's anarchy!" Mr. Benson laughed and then turned serious. "True creativity doesn't consist of being without rules and boundaries, but of achieving fulfillment within those bounds. I think you may find this easier to learn if you're away from familiar surroundings for a while!"

"Papa, please don't send me off! I'm trying, truly I am!" Carlie leaned forward impulsively, her eyes filling. "I put on the dress Mama made me. I'll be ladylike and prissy and say

[ 20 ]

'Yes, Ma'am; no, Ma'am' till it chokes me. Only please don't send me off!"

"Oh, Carlie!" Mr. Benson was looking at her as if she were no older than Oliver, and suddenly, in one of her abrupt reversals of feeling, she felt that way. Here she was, humbling herself, begging and pleading like a little girl teasing for a doll! She stood up as stiffly as the hurt back would allow and lifted her chin.

At the familiar sight, Mr. Benson's eyes softened. "Carlie, I feel sorry for you. You have a tough row to hoe, and nothing but your own heart can tell you how. As for the trip South, we'll let the matter drop until I have discussed it with your mother." He turned back toward the fire.

She was being dismissed, as if she were a child. Her head jerked up. "That's it! One minute you expect me to be an adult, and the next you treat me like a baby! And you say I'm changeable! Maybe it's not all my fault!" Eyes smarting but head up, she stormed out of the door, banging it behind her. She collided with Laura in the hall outside.

"Carlie, what's the matter?" Laura put out a quick hand to hold her. "Honey, it can't be that bad!" She pulled a lace-edged scrap of linen from her bodice and dabbed at Carlie's eyes. "Papa will get over it. You just ought to learn to handle him better. And your new beau's still waiting for you." Laura flashed a glance of tender amusement toward the front parlor. "I think that's rather sweet."

Laura's words ruined for Carlie what had been the one bright moment of the day. "New beau . . . sweet . . ." To Carlie, it cheapened a relationship that had just begun. She stared at Laura out of resentful eyes, then wrenched herself free and fled up the stairs. She rushed into the darkness of her room, not bothering to shut the door, and once again threw herself across the bed.

"Carlie, dear." There was a whispering of silks, and her

mother sank down beside her. Mrs. Benson's cool cheek was pressed against Carlie's feverish face, and her green brocade, crushed against Carlie's heaving shoulders, gave off the faint familiar scent of lemon verbena.

"Why, Mama?" Carlie twisted over to look up at her mother's face with anguished eyes. "I don't want to be like this. It would be so much easier if I were like you and Laura. I don't want to fight everything, but I just can't seem to help myself!"

"Poor Carlie!" Her mother's voice was full of infinite wisdom. "It's so easy for the ones like Laura. But you and Ben, you're such restless dreamers. You fight with life so, Carlie. And you haven't yet learned how to make it bless you." She bent and pressed her lips against Carlie's forehead, paused for a moment looking down at her, and left.

Carlie lay there in the darkness, the rigid steels of her hoopskirt crushed beneath her, the harsh stays of her corset jabbing mercilessly into her aching back. The wan light coming from the hall threw the shadows of the bedposts against the walls like bars. Like a prison, she thought bitterly.

She was in a prison, not of her own making, and it was for life. It was worse for her than for the slaves everybody was making such a fuss about down South. At least some of them managed to run away to freedom. For her there could be no escape.

## 3

URING THE NIGHT, the rain turned to snow. It fell steadily all the next day, and by evening the drifts were
higher than Beaufort's four front steps. The following morning, Ben, going out to the barn to feed Midnight, had to wade
through drifts waist-high. School, which was supposed to
resume that day, was postponed until the following Monday.

It was a strange, restless week. Paul and Oliver, kept inside
by the storm, were in continual trouble. The Wednesday-
evening prayer meeting was cancelled, and Laura, who'd been
attending regularly because Peter did, took out her disappointment by being waspish. And over and above everything else hung the threat of Carlie's banishment to South
Carolina.

The matter, as Mr. Benson had said, was dropped, but it
gathered weight by the very fact that it was not mentioned.
Her parents had discussed it, Carlie knew; more than once
she felt her mother's eyes on her, anxious, loving, worried.

Her parents did not know what to do with her. She knew it
as clearly as if they'd put it into words, and the thought made

Carlie a little sick. Once she would have relieved her tumultuous emotions by running through the woods, by losing herself in Papa's books, or by talking to Ben. But the storm and her determination to act decorously kept her inside; the vicarious fulfillment of novels was no longer sufficient; and Ben was still so angry over her taking Midnight that he was barely speaking to her.

She wrote pages in the journal Bess had given her, but when she read them over, they filled her with disgust. And no amount of writing could take away the sting of being sent away because she did not fit in.

"Misfit!" she thought bitterly, staring up at the canopy over her head in the long hours of the night. Was it, after all, entirely her fault? Why had Papa encouraged her, along with Ben, to think, to read, to argue?

She turned restlessly in bed, trying not to waken Laura, who was sleeping soundly beside her. But no matter how she tried to shift the blame, one fact remained. She was proving a disappointment to Papa, whom she loved.

There was no running away from that.

*It's the things we run from that hurt the most.* The words came back to her out of nowhere and with them came a memory of compassionate black eyes. She had carefully avoided thinking of that talk with Brad; Laura's putting it on the level of a boy-girl flirtation had made her feel self-conscious.

She wished she could talk about it to her father or to Ben, but Mr. Benson was preoccupied, shutting himself in the library for hours on end. Ben's thin dark face, crowned with a thatch of brown hair so like their father's, was closed as only Ben could close it, and Carlie was too proud and too stubborn to break the silence.

To Bess alone could Carlie pour out her misery when she and Uncle Henry came for dinner on Saturday night. This was a once-a-month ritual, and Carlie's pleasure in seeing Bess was always marred by the necessity of sitting through the formal meal with Uncle Henry. He always acted as if he did not quite like them; he regarded Mama's Southern tact and charm as flighty and artificial; and he particularly, Carlie realized uncomfortably, did not approve of her.

Usually it was Bess who whispered her woes and Carlie who listened. Tonight, upstairs with the door shut, it was Carlie who poured out her troubles and Bess who sat holding her hands, making small sounds of compassion. Bess might never fully comprehend Carlie's stormy nature, but her sympathy was comforting.

"They wouldn't just send you off, particularly now!" Bess was shocked.

"Oh, yes, they would. For one thing, Papa doesn't believe there's going to *be* a war. Probably they wouldn't care even if there was." She was being unfair and she knew it. "Oh, Bess, if only somebody could tell me what to do! If there were just some kind of pill you could take and wake up in the morning middle-aged and content!"

"I don't think there is any easy way." Bess's face looked wistful. She picked up the journal, which Carlie had let her read. "Couldn't you show this to your father? You write so well . . . all the things you can't say. Maybe then he'd understand."

"I'd die first." Carlie shook her head. "All I can do is just . . . dig in my heels and refuse to go!" Bess's eyes grew enormous at the very thought of such defiance, and Carlie's bravado collapsed like a pricked balloon. "Who am I trying to fool? It would take a miracle—or the end of the world—to get me out of this."

They went down to dinner in somber silence.

Mrs. Benson was flying around the kitchen in the anxious abstraction Uncle Henry's visits always caused, and Laura, who was going to a dance at Ramsey's Hotel later with Peter, had an apron tied over her prized silk dress. Uncle Henry, eyeing it as they sat down, had one of his usual dour comments.

"Not much future in that, him with a small farm and a widowed mother to support. You're too flighty for a farmer's wife."

Mrs. Benson sent Laura a warning glance, but Laura was too happy tonight to take offense. "When it's time to wed, I'll find me a beau who can support me in style. But for now, Peter's a good dancer, he's crazy about me, and that's what counts." She gave her curls a saucy toss, and Mrs. Benson hastily asked Uncle Henry if he'd like some more Southern fried chicken.

"Might be better for you to play down the Southern angle." Uncle Henry gazed at the chicken distastefully. "From the looks of things we're fast approaching a showdown, and if it comes, a lot of folks are going to be asking questions about some other folks."

Mrs. Benson's green eyes shot sparks, but Mr. Benson broke in calmly. "Now, Henry, don't be an alarmist. Old Buchanan's not going to do anything drastic during his last months in office, and for all we voted for Douglas, I don't think Mr. Lincoln's about to start a war."

"War or no war, there's been too much dissension hereabouts since before election." Uncle Henry looked at Mrs. Benson directly. "Those of us who were bred here know where we stand, but we wonder about the others. Particularly those with power, like the county press. Especially when they're likely to be influenced by outsiders."

Carlie, who'd been lost in her own private problems, looked up quickly. Ben's eyes had narrowed. Mrs. Benson's face was white, but her voice was quiet.

"I agree with my husband that the press should be impartial. As for myself . . ." Her voice shook slightly. "I love the South. It would break my heart if we became estranged. I pray God the need for taking sides will never come. Now, Henry, if you're quite finished, shall we have coffee and cake in the parlor?" She turned to Bess, who'd shrunk back in her chair. "My dear, will you help me serve?" She rose with a rustle of taffeta and Bess followed.

Carlie went out after them and closed the kitchen door behind her. "Well, I never!" she exploded angrily. "Bess, I'm sorry, but he makes me so mad! Mama, how could you let him talk to you like that?"

"He's our guest and our kinfolk, Carlie, and he has a right to his own opinion, as do we." Mrs. Benson went on cutting cake with even precision, but her hand was shaking. Bess had pressed up close, her brown eyes enormous, her soft voice breathless.

"Aunt Clarissa, what *would* you do, if something happens the way Pa thinks?"

"I . . . don't know, Bess." Mrs. Benson flicked a sudden glance at Carlie. "I guess I'm like my daughter. I want to run away from facing that until I really have to."

She picked up the silver tray and carried it into the parlor. Carlie, following with the plate of cake, knew that she had grown up more than she had dreamed. When she was little, it had never occurred to her that parents, too, could be uncertain. Now, the knowledge that they could be was frightening.

That Sunday, the first of the New Year, it was bitterly cold, so cold that the water in the bedroom pitchers was solid ice. But the sun was shining, and with it everyone's spirits seemed to lift. In the kitchen, flames danced cheerfully in the big black stove and bubbling coffee sent forth a spicy fragrance. Paul and Oliver were jumping around like clumsy elves in their long red underwear. Carlie began to pull on her clothes inside her flannel nightgown.

Ben staggered in the back door, his arms full of kindling and his breath making frosty clouds before his face. "The snow's three feet deep outside the woodshed. I had to dig my way in."

Oliver looked up hopefully. "Maybe we can't go to church."

"Hate to disappoint you, but I think we can. Pa's getting out the sleigh." Ben ruffled Oliver's blond head. "A little church won't hurt you."

"Parson Ryerson talks too long," Paul volunteered.

"Don't criticize the parson," Mrs. Benson said automatically, ladling oatmeal into flowered bowls.

"But he does," Paul insisted, caught his mother's eyes, and subsided. Ben grinned.

"For once the lad's right," he whispered to Carlie, and her heart rose. It was the first friendly remark Ben had made to her in a week. And Mr. Benson, stamping in to announce that the sleigh was waiting, was also in high spirits.

The first clear day had brought everyone out. When the Bensons started for church, the road was already dotted with sleighs large and small, and even Mr. Pryor's big work sled, pulled by two patient oxen. From the back of it, Joe and his brother were pelting passing vehicles with snowballs.

Paul scooped up a handful of snow and shaped it expertly. From the front seat, Mr. Benson flashed him a warning glance.

"Not on the Sabbath, young man."

"Aw!" Paul said aggrievedly and contented himself with dropping the icy lump inside Ben's muffler. Ben turned with a howl.

"Wait till I get you after church!"

"Can't. It's the Sabbath," Oliver said virtuously, and Mr. Benson roared with laughter.

"The devil can quote Scripture with a vengeance!" He slapped Midnight with the reins.

The small stone church was crowded, and the new stove radiated a comforting warmth. New bonnets and Christmas-present tippets and muffs appeared in abundance. Uncle Henry was in his customary seat among the Consistory in the Amen Pews up front.

"Where he can glare at everybody, the old goat," Ben muttered grimly, pinching Oliver who was squirming under Uncle Henry's forbidding stare.

Carlie stirred restlessly, staring out of the window. Brad Sturdevant was sitting next to the Judge in the Zabriskie pew. She had found herself staring at him involuntarily, and their glances had met. He had nodded cordially, but she had flushed and hastily looked away. The sun, shining through the branches of the ice-sheathed trees, sent rainbow prisms dancing, and the wind made the icicles clink together like fairy chimes. It was doubly hard, on a day like this, to sit decorously listening to the Reverend Ryerson's dull sermons. Then suddenly she realized that this was *not* just another sermon.

"I tell you, brethren, slavery is a wicked evil, and unless it is destroyed, it will bring the end of the world!"

There was a sharp gasp from the congregation. Several families in the valley, like Mrs. Benson, owned one or more slaves; much of the county had favored Breckenridge, the Democratic candidate, in the national election, and Breckenridge himself had declared that in Bergen County people thought and felt as they did in North Carolina. Almost no one, with the exception, of course, of Uncle Henry and Mr. Garrison, backed Lincoln. In church, the minister, knowing this, had avoided the touchy subject of slavery before. Now, however, he plunged in as if he didn't even care. His iron-gray beard fairly bristled with wrath and his eyes were glittering. He pounded the Bible with his fist.

"Woe unto you, scribes and pharisees, hypocrites, who try to lay up treasures on this earth through the slavery of other human beings! Verily I say unto you, they shall have their reward!"

The church was tensely silent. Up in the Amen Pews, Mr. Pryor's face had turned a dull angry red and Uncle Henry's was sternly triumphant. Carlie saw Ben's head jerk upright, and she felt her mother's back grow rigid. Reverend Ryerson thundered on.

"Think you that the Lord is sleeping? That He will not judge you for the evil in your midst? It is not enough for us not to own slaves ourselves! I tell you, brethren, as long as we countenance this sin upon our land, so long is the guilt on our souls. We must pluck out this evil in our midst or we will bring down the wrath of God upon our heads!"

He slammed the Bible shut and announced the closing hymn. Church was over.

Before the hymn was half-finished, before even the benediction, the church erupted with excitement. Uncle Henry was pumping the minister's hand, and Mr. Pryor, red-faced and choleric, was demanding an immediate meeting of the Consistory. Mrs. Benson sat down suddenly, her hand pressed against her bodice, and Mr. Benson was pushing his way toward the men, with what the family called his "reporter's expression" on his face.

Carlie saw Bess sitting tense and silent on the far side of the church and went over to her. "What happened?" she demanded.

Bess put her hand to her lips and pulled Carlie down beside her. "There was a Consistory meeting at our house the other night," she whispered. "Pa and Mr. Pryor had a row, a bad one, over Mr. Lincoln. I could hear them clear upstairs. When the parson tried to soothe them, Pa told him maybe it was time he showed his own colors, since he'd been too namby-pamby to do so up till now. The parson said all right, he would; he'd start the new year right by saying what he really thought, only he wouldn't be responsible for what would happen." She looked at Carlie out of troubled dark eyes. "That's why Pa was so . . . rude to Aunt Clarissa yesterday. He keeps saying the time has come for folks to choose."

Carlie's eyes turned involuntarily to the Benson pew. Her mother was sitting perfectly still, staring straight ahead, her expression unreadable, her hands clenched tightly.

The time for folks to choose . . . What had Mama said? *I pray God the need . . . will never come . . .*

"Come on," Carlie said abruptly, "let's go outside." She stood up, dragging Bess with her, feeling as if she had to get back to the bright fresh sunlight or she could not breathe.

Outside in the street, the atmosphere was explosive. No one had yet made a move to start home. Far up the road, a large man appeared, galloping on a big white horse. Reaching the church, he swung himself down, tossed the reins to the nearest boy, and pushed his way through the crowd to the minister's side.

Bess's eyes widened. "It's John Haring, the hand-loom weaver." They edged up close.

The minister had turned and raised his hand for silence. "Brethren, the wrath of God has come! The Union is dissolved!"

For a moment, there was frozen silence, but the whispers grew as the paper passed from hand to hand. "The South's seceded . . . South Carolina . . . let them go . . . they won't let them . . . this means war . . ."

Deep within Carlie, the first reaction was one of joy. *Now they won't be able to send me South . . .* Then she saw her mother, standing rigid in the church doorway, and her head cleared sharply.

*I pray God . . .* her mother had said. And now the time had

come. Mr. Benson, breaking away from the men, moved toward the doorway, and Mrs. Benson put both hands out
toward him, blindly, instinctively, as Carlie sometimes did.
Carlie saw them look deep into each other's eyes.

Around them everything was in an uproar. Ben was standing with some of the other boys. Tom Garrison swung his fist
at Joe Pryor. Bess was trembling. Uncle Henry's eyes glit-
tered. "President Buchanan will never let them get away with
this!"

Mr. Pryor snorted. "That nincompoop won't have the
gumption to do a single thing!"

"Sir! The man you call a nincompoop is the President of
the United States!"

"Then, sir, I do not blame the states for dis-uniting!"

"I am sure the whole matter will be settled amicably," Mr.
Benson put in quietly. "I doubt that it will come to war."

Mr. Pryor glared at him. "Sir, you astound me. I thought
your sympathies were Southern."

"I am also an American," Mr. Benson said evenly. "I trust I
can be both."

Uncle Henry shot him a level look. "Not any more, Richard. Not any more."

Carlie, feeling Bess's cold hand slide into hers, felt a shiver
down her spine. She fought an insane desire to cry out something she had often said as a child: *Put it together again.* She
had said that when toys were broken, when things went
wrong, when she wanted life to be as it had been before. But,
as Papa said, things never stayed the same.

*Put it together again,* her heart cried out. Let things be as
they were. Even if it meant being back in Papa's bad graces,
even if it meant being sent away. It would take a miracle to
prevent that, she had said . . . or the end of the world. To
Carlie, remembering the look in her mother's eyes, it seemed
as if perhaps the latter had, indeed, come.

# CHAPTER

## 4

I T WAS STRANGE the way something that had happened so
far away could affect them all here in this little northern
corner of New Jersey. And it *did* affect them. It was as if
something unspoken waited to be said.

Mrs. Benson moved through her accustomed tasks with an
odd faraway look on her face that made Carlie feel confused
and vaguely fearful. Mr. Benson stayed late into the night at
the Hackensack newspaper office. Frequently, when he returned, there would be men with him. Carlie, lying wakeful in
bed in the room above the library, would hear a deep murmur
of voices rising through the register in the floor.

Mr. Benson's *Journal* was sticking to strictly factual reporting, but the other Jersey papers were less impartial. The
*Paterson Register* had come out broadly for the South. John
Haring brought these other publications into town on Saturday nights and distributed them at the Franklin Inn. The ar-
guments grew fiery and carried over into the churchyard on
Sunday mornings, for the entire congregation had become
involved in the political fight.

It had started, of course, with that Sunday sermon, followed so dramatically by the secession news. The minister and the congregation had been at variance for some time. Now some members were threatening to leave, while others were demanding the minister's own resignation. And it did not help matters that on the Consistory were such widely-opposed partisans as Uncle Henry and Mr. Pryor.

"Pig-headed," Ben described them to Carlie bluntly, one Sunday late in January. They were sitting in the library in the twilight as they had so often before—he in Papa's big leather chair, she down on a pillow on the floor before the fire. This was one good thing to have come out of the whole mixed-up month, Carlie reflected. Ben's intense imagination and idealism had been stirred. He needed someone who would listen, and because their father was seldom home, he had turned to her.

Carlie was too grateful to be proud. She pulled her feet up close now, locked her hands around her knees, and listened until Ben ran out of epithets for the two stubborn men.

"Papa says the North and South are very much like Uncle Henry and Mr. Pryor," she said thoughtfully. "Each one so sure he's right, and each one unwilling to unbend even a little."

"Well, they'd better bend soon," Ben said grimly, "or we'll have our own private and particular war right here in Franklin. You know that Mr. Pryor and two of the other deacons have stayed away from church for the past two Sundays. There's a Consistory meeting on Tuesday, and Uncle Henry's going to try to have them suspended."

"Where did you hear that?"

"Around," Ben said ambiguously. He thrust a log into the fire, his face darkening. "The power of the press!" he burst out. "Why doesn't Pa come out and take a stand? Maybe that would keep folks from being swayed by Mr. Pryor."

"Papa thinks the press should be impartial."

"How can it? Breaking up a country is *wrong*. Why can't he come right out and say it?"

"Maybe he doesn't want to . . . because of Mama." Carlie didn't dare to look at Ben; she stared at the flames and felt her fingernails dig into her hands. "Ben, you know what she's looked like lately. It's just as if somebody'd died."

Ben snorted. "You sound like Bess, looking for bogeymen in corners. . . . Somebody's at the door."

"I'll go." Carlie stood, glad of something to do, for her thoughts were wandering down dark corridors she didn't want to see. She opened the door and looked up into Brad Sturdevant's cheerful grin.

"Hello. I see you survived." He smiled again at her blank expression. "The lions, I mean, on New Year's Day."

"Oh . . . yes." She had almost forgotten, but now, remembering that day, she blushed.

"Mercy sakes, let the poor fellow in. It's freezing out." Ben had followed her into the hall.

"I've a message for your father. Some of the county leaders are meeting at Zabriskie's, and the Judge would like to have him come." C605317 **CO.** SCHOOLS

"He's next door at the Courtins' house with Mama. I'll go get him." Ben picked up his coat, looking as if he too were grateful for activity. He vanished outside, slamming the door behind him, but Brad lingered.

"Would you . . . like to warm yourself a spell before leaving?"

"Thanks, I would. It's nasty out." He followed her into the library and sat in the leather chair as she dropped down onto the pillow and searched self-consciously for conversation.

"What do you . . . think of the political situation, Mr. Sturdevant?"

"Brad," he corrected. "I thought we were friends by now. As for politics, I think they're a mess, and I'd rather just

[ 35 ]

forget them." He looked at her mischievously. "How's your own internal political situation?"

"At a truce, a silent one. I was supposed to be sent South to learn to behave, but I guess that's off now." Unconsciously she sighed.

"Here, let's change places." He knelt down beside her on the floor. "You look tired to death."

"I guess it's just a blue day." Unexpectedly her eyes filled with tears. She dropped her head down against her knees and stared at the fire.

"I always seem to come at the wrong time." Brad's voice was gentle.

"Everything seems so strange." As before, he had some magic that made her words come freely. "Papa's trying so hard to stay impartial, but folks just won't let him. And Mama . . . she's from Carolina . . . I don't know what she feels."

"It's always hard, when your mind directs you one way and your heart another."

Carlie looked at him gratefully. "That's it, exactly. I think Mama's mind *is* for the Union, and it's just . . . why!" She stared at him, startled. "It's the same with me, isn't it? My mind knows I ought to be a certain way, but my heart won't let me."

There was something so comforting about talking to Brad. With Ben, even though he was older, it was he who poured out his thoughts and she who listened. Brad listened to her thoughtfully, offering quiet, clear-cut suggestions. He was, she had learned, eighteen. He was living with the Zabriskies as the Judge's law clerk for a year before starting college.

He probably thinks I'm all of eleven, she decided. But his words, when she walked to the door, disabused her of the notion.

"I'd like to call again, if I may . . . even if you don't happen to need a father confessor!" He looked past her into the library, with its ceiling-high bookshelves, its big workmanlike desk in the center, the piles of papers, the stands of pens. "It reminds me of home. My mother's a writer, too." His eyes were mischievous. "She's that Adelaide Somerville you once mentioned."

"She's . . . *oh!*" Carlie turned scarlet.

" 'Trashy novels'? Some of them are! But she writes other things, too. I'll tell you about them sometime. I think you'd like them." He smiled, bowed, and backed out the door, leaving Carlie filled with confusion.

Sunday tea that evening, usually the cosiest time of the week, was still and strained. Mr. Benson, coming in late from the meeting, was in one of his silent moods and so was Ben, jackknifed into a tall chair by the fire, his chin propped gloomily on his knee. In the dim light from the lamp on the center table, Mrs. Benson's face looked unhappy and tired. She pulled the crocheted shawl up closer around her shoulders.

Mama's still not used to these Northern winters, Carlie thought. She rolled over on the hearthrug and stared moodily into the sputtering coals.

"Oh, for mercy sake!" Laura shut her book with a snap. "Why is everyone getting so depressed because of a lot of old things happening way down South? It's not as if it's going to affect us here!"

"The wisdom of youth," Mr. Benson murmured wryly.

Carlie sat up as Laura, looking nettled, started upstairs with a swish of petticoats. Mama reached a slender hand across the table.

"A bad session, dearest?"

"Rather." Mr. Benson raised his eyebrows briefly. "Garry Ackerman and his crew are all for appeasement. If war comes, the wind will change, of course, but for the moment it's very much down-with-Lincoln, and they thought they could pressure the paper to swing along. And, of course, Henry's hammering away from the other side."

"Then why don't you do something?" Ben's long legs swung suddenly to the floor. "Why do you have to stay in the middle so everybody thinks you're scared to take a stand?"

"Benjamin!" Mrs. Benson's eyes shot sparks and Mr. Benson put up his hand.

"No, Clarissa. Ben, I don't know how to explain it to you because I find it hard to put into words. I only know a newspaper must remain impartial."

"The *Paterson Register* doesn't think so," Ben said stubbornly.

"They must do what they think is right, and so must I. So must we all," Mr. Benson added quietly. "You and I know how easy it is to let emotion cloud out logic." His glance included Carlie, and she moved silently to a chair by the table. "It is difficult for us to make sure that our knowledge of the right, however hard it may be, is not obscured by sentiment or emotion."

He was speaking to Ben, but he was looking directly at his wife, and after a moment she rose in a swirl of skirts. Returning with a letter, wrinkled as if it had been much read, she laid it on the table.

"It came last week." Mrs. Benson's face was without emotion.

Carlie held her breath as Mr. Benson glanced at the postmark, quirked his brows, and began to read.

" 'My dear cousin,

" 'You must forgive our not answering more promptly your New Year's letter, but you will understand for what sad reason the delay has been.' "

Carlie flashed a swift glance at her mother, but Mrs. Benson was leaning back in the chair, her eyes closed as if she felt exhausted.

" 'You ask if your daughter may come here for a visit. She is welcome, you all are welcome. You and your child are our kin, Clarissa, whatever happens, and we both know that our Beaufort here will always be your home.' "

For a second, a breath of cold air seemed to descend on the shadowy room. Mr. Benson put down the unfinished letter. "Would you like to go, Clarissa?" he asked quietly. "You haven't been back home in some time, and there's no telling when you'll have the chance again."

*Perhaps never* . . . The words, unspoken, were in everyone's mind. Mrs. Benson stared at her husband. Suddenly, shockingly, she began to cry. "I do not want to have to choose!" She pressed her hands up hard against her face.

"Mama!" Laura, halfway up the stairs, ran down to her. There was no answer, and after a second Laura straightened, picked up the teacups, and started out. Ben was already steering the boys, open-mouthed with astonishment, toward the kitchen. Carlie gathered up the tea things and followed, feeling as if the weight of the heavy silver tray were nothing compared to the one that lay on her heart.

In the kitchen, Ben was thrusting logs viciously into the stove, while the children, sobered by things they did not understand, sat around the kitchen table stiff as dolls. Laura, her lips pressed together in a thin straight line, got out the dishpan.

"Ben?" Paul piped up suddenly. "What's 'tarred and feathered'? Neddy Garrison says that's what his brother says'll happen to Mama."

Ben slammed the stove door so hard that the stovepipe rattled, and Laura swerved sharply. "Where are you going?"

"To bash Tom Garrison's head in!"

"*No, you're not!*" Laura's eyes were black and her voice,

for all it was almost a whisper, came harshly. "Do you want to make things worse for Mama than they are already? Until you learn some tact, you keep hands off!" She turned to the shocked children, her voice deliberately gay. "Off to bed, chickens, and maybe sister Carlie will tell us all a story!" She shooed them competently up the back stairs, but once the boys were in their room, she leaned her head against the wall of the upper hall.

Carlie, sliding an arm around her sister's waist, could feel her trembling. "I can take it from here," she suggested. Supervising the boys' unwilling washing kept her busy for a time, but once she had them bundled into bed, anger choked her.

In her room, she found Laura already in bed, face hidden in the pillows, and Carlie crept in beside her, grateful for her nearness.

When she awoke, the room was dark and sleet was beating against the windowpanes. Dimly she realized that the pillow next to hers was empty. "Laura?"

"Hush!" Laura's whisper came sharply. She was huddled on the floor by the register, her face strained. Carlie knelt beside her, shivering.

"What's the mat . . ." she began, and Laura put her hand up swiftly. Through the grating of the register voices came clearly from the room below.

". . . have told you, Henry, that I will not allow the paper to become a partisan mouthpiece." Mr. Benson sounded very tired. ". . . told Garry Ackerson the same."

"You did meet with them, then." Uncle Henry's voice was cold. "Tom Garrison reported it to me, but I did not believe it."

*Spies*, Carlie's mind registered blankly. Yesterday they were our neighbors, our friends. She listened numbly to

Uncle Henry's voice saying words she could scarcely believe were real.

"I am glad that my wife is not alive to see her own brother seduced by the poisonous wiles of a traitorous woman."

"Henry, you go too far." Mr. Benson's voice was very quiet. "I've stood silent up to this, but now you owe an apology to all my house."

"That, sir, you'll receive when your own actions prove me wrong. This house! Take it and all in it back to that accursed section where it belongs! I never want to set eyes on it again!"

The door slammed sharply.

"What's happening to us?" Laura's eyes filled with tears. She put her head down suddenly as Mama had done. Carlie, holding her tightly as if she and not Laura were the elder, echoed the question.

Dimly she could hear the sound of Papa locking the heavy door. Once it had been a comforting sound, as if he were locking out all the troubles of the night.

# CHAPTER

# 5

T HERE WAS NO MENTION at breakfast of Uncle Henry's visit. Mr. Benson left very early for his Hackensack office. Mrs. Benson, stirring oatmeal over the glowing stove, was determinedly cheerful.

For the first time, Carlie envied Laura for no longer having to go to school. It was difficult to go out, head up and smiling, into the glaring icy brightness of the day, with Paul and Oliver scuffling about her like happy puppies. Doubly difficult to sit in the stuffy closeness of the schoolhouse, conscious all the while of Tom Garrison and Joe Pryor sitting on the boys' side across the way. She knew without looking that Ben, seated by circumstance between the two of them, was glowering.

Usually at noon, she took her basket up to the stove with the two Courtins girls and Emily Garrison. Today she ate in chilly solitude at her desk, conscious of covert whispering and staring. She lifted her chin. Let them stare! They had always thought her queer, and if they talked about her, perhaps it would keep their minds off Mama.

She had always rather liked Emily Garrison, but today she found herself almost hating her, and she was shocked at her own emotion. She wished fervently that Bess were still in school, but Bess had not come for two years now. Uncle Henry thought education for women a dangerous waste of time.

When school was dismissed at four, Ben struck out immediately and alone, not waiting for the others. Carlie, bundling Paul and Oliver into overshoes and coats, looked after him enviously. She jerked Oliver's muffler sharply. Then, seeing his small bewildered face, she was immediately repentant.

"You boys run on ahead," she told them when they reached the corner by the general store. She would buy them some penny candy, and some lemon drops for Mama. Poor Mama—in her own unhappiness she'd been forgetting that Mama's heartache was the worst of all.

It was some moments before her eyes became accustomed to the stale dimness of the cluttered shop. Then, to her joy, she spied a small familiar figure.

"Bess, I'm so glad . . ." Carlie ran toward her, then stopped abruptly. "Why, what's . . ."

Bess had given her one frightened look, seized her bundles, and without even speaking run outside. Carlie stared after her dumbly, too stunned to move. Then she rushed toward the door, not seeing anything until she crashed against someone tall, and hands gripped her arms.

"Whoa, Miss Mercury! Where's the fire?"

She was barely conscious that it was Brad. "It's Bess, my cousin . . . she didn't even speak . . ."

Brad glanced at the two Courtins girls, whispering by the candy counter, at Mrs. Garrison looking at calicos, and came to a swift decision. "This is no place to talk. You run up to the Judge's house. Mrs. Zabriskie will give you tea. I'll go

[ 43 ]

fetch Bess." He smiled and nodded as if they'd been having just a casual conversation, tipped his hat, and hurried out.

As she climbed the hill against the wind toward the old Zabriskie house, Carlie saw children laughing and shouting on the pond. How far away it seemed! Less than a month ago she had sobbed and moaned that she didn't want to grow up. Now it seemed that she was being forced to do so, whether she would or not.

Tall, gentle-faced Mrs. Zabriskie took her cloak and bonnet without question, showed her to a seat before the colonial fireplace, and poured tea into delicate china cups. Carlie sipped hers silently, grateful that her hostess did not force conversation. Soon the door opened, and Brad appeared, ushering in another, smaller figure.

"Carlie, dear!" Bess ran toward her, hands outstretched, as Brad and Mrs. Zabriskie discreetly slipped away. "I shouldn't have come. It will be terrible if Pa finds out, but I couldn't just not tell you."

"Tell me what?" Bess's hands were cold as ice and Carlie held them tightly.

"That I'm not to speak to you again, not ever." Bess's eyes were enormous as Carlie pulled her down into a chair. "When he came home last night . . . it was so late . . . he made me get up, and he told me. Carlie, he's been angry before, but never like this. He said . . . I can't tell you what he said . . ."

"I know," Carlie said.

"And then he said . . . I'm not to see you again, you or Aunt Clarissa, or any of you . . ." Her thin body shook with sobs.

"Perhaps Bess would like some tea." Mrs. Zabriskie came in, her eyes compassionate, carrying a steaming pot. Bess looked frightened.

"Oh, no! I have to get back before I'm missed. Carlie, I'm

so sorry!" She pressed her hand against her mouth and bolted out.

"Then perhaps you and Brad?"

Carlie shook her head blindly. She did not want to speak, not even to Brad; if she did not get outside quickly, something would explode. She pulled the cloak Brad held for her around her tightly and hurried out, not even waiting to put on her bonnet or her gloves.

The harsh wind stung her face, bringing tears to her eyes as she rushed downhill. She ran the half mile through the purple dusk and burst in, breathless, to find the family at the dinner table.

"Carlie, what's the matter?"

"Papa, Uncle Henry . . . Bess . . ." She held onto the back of a chair, half sobbing, and the words tumbled out. Before she was halfway through, she knew she ought not to have told it, not like this, but she could not stop.

Mrs. Benson's face was gray. "Perhaps I *should* go away. You and the children cannot live like this."

"Why, the old . . ." Ben's face was dark with fury. "Why can't she just tell him she won't do it?"

Nobody bothered to answer that ridiculous question. Bess was so vulnerable. It was worse for Bess, Carlie thought, than for herself; she at least had all her family. For a second, she almost wished a real shooting war, the thing everyone feared, had come. Then, at least, the fighting was open. This was subtle, insidious.

"Why, Papa?" she burst out. "What makes people be like this?"

"Carlie, I wish I knew." Mr. Benson picked up his fork and resumed eating with a calmness that fooled no one. After a minute, Carlie too sat down and forced herself to swallow food. They did not speak of it again until Laura began to clear the table and Mrs. Benson went to the kitchen to bring

[ 45 ]

in dessert. Mr. Benson looked up, fixing Carlie with level brown eyes.

"It is often hard in times like these," he said slowly, "to see any reason for seemingly senseless things. All I can say to you is what a far wiser man than I said long ago, that now we can but 'see through a glass, darkly.' Also that 'charity endureth all things.' " His gaze moved meaningfully to Ben. "I am asking you both for your solemn word that you *will* endure without retaliation. You will simply have to take it on faith that if you don't, you would do more harm than good. Your uncle is a just man, no matter what else he is, and one day he may realize he has been wrong."

"It could take twenty years!"

"It could," Mr. Benson agreed evenly. "I did not say it would be easy."

It came to Carlie that her father was testing them, wondering how far they would measure up. She saw Ben's lip thrust out, and she spoke quickly.

"I promise, Papa." She reached her hand out across the table, and her father grasped it.

"Heck," Ben said gruffly, as she'd known he would. "If she can do it, I can." Their hands joined in a tight family circle.

It was easy to make a promise in the flush of loyalty and family devotion. It was hard to abide by it under the day-by-day barbs and petty thrusts that followed. More than once Carlie saw Ben's face grow dark from some whispered taunt of Tom Garrison's, felt her own face flush and her chin grow rigid under the sidewise glances of the girls.

At home it was somewhat easier. Mr. Benson began coming home earlier nights, bringing a book by the English author Charles Dickens, which he read aloud: "It was the best of times, it was the worst of times. It was the spring of hope, it was the winter of despair." They walked the streets of Revolutionary Paris with Sidney Carton.

[ 46 ]

After the first session, Laura withdrew, shuddering. "How you can listen to those horrible stories is beyond me," she said plaintively on Sunday night when Carlie came upstairs. "I can understand Ben's liking them, but they'd make me faint!"

Carlie, her thoughts still on the dark byways of Paris, shook her head. "I wish I lived in a time like that," she said bemusedly. "Even if it was dangerous. At least people *did* things then." She flung her flannel petticoat to the floor. A month had gone by now since the secession news had come, and this constant waiting for further developments was getting on everybody's nerves.

She pulled her nightgown on and crawled into bed, but she was too restless to sleep. She lay awake, arms locked beneath her head, hearing Laura's soft breathing, the clatter of Ben getting ready for bed in the room next door, and presently the soft whisper of her mother's hoopskirts as she came upstairs. Downstairs, in the library, a fire still crackled, as though Mr. Benson, too, was too full of thoughts for sleep.

In the upstairs foyer, the grandfather's clock ticked like a comfortable sentinel. The familiar night sounds of the house were reassuring and Carlie's eyes grew drowsy. Then suddenly they widened as other sounds intruded. The thud of horse's hooves on the drive—a muffled "whoa"—footsteps coming rapidly up the steps—the front door opening, then closing.

Carlie sat bolt upright. Another sound, the library door this time. Then, from the register, the faint sound of rapid voices, one of them Papa's, too indistinct to be understood. Carlie flashed a glance at Laura, but Laura was still sleeping soundly. After a second, she heard creaking in the upper hall. She slid out of bed, tiptoed to the door and peered out into blackness.

"Ben, what . . ." The swift jerk of his hand silenced her, and she crept out to crouch beside him at the top of the stairs. The lower hall was lost in shadows. Drafts from the front door and from the doors opening onto the foyer's balcony cut through her nightgown. Quite suddenly, her heart was pounding.

"Who is it?" she whispered, and Ben shook his head.

"I thought it was Mr. Baldwin from the paper, but I'm not sure." His response was barely audible. They strained their ears, then the library door opened, and they shrank back from the arrowing light. There was a glimpse of the back of a man's head as he went out the front door, shutting it silently. The light in the library went out, and Mr. Benson came rapidly up the stairs.

"Carlie, Benjamin!" He stopped abruptly. "What are you children doing up? Get to bed at once." His voice was so stern that they melted into their own rooms without daring a response. Carlie crept into bed, shivering. Laura, stirring in her sleep, flung an arm around Carlie's shoulders, and Carlie cuddled against her. All at once, despite three quilts and a blanket, she was icy cold.

She awoke in the morning with a vague throbbing headache and the memory of the scene hovering distantly like the vestiges of a dream. Mrs. Benson, moving quietly about the kitchen preparing breakfast, looked as if she too had slept but little. Her auburn hair was smoothed in its accustomed coil low on her neck, but above the electric blue of her challis housedress her face looked waxen, and her sensitive mouth was pressed in a thin, straight line. Mr. Benson watched her closely as he stirred his coffee.

"Clarissa, sit down." He spoke so abruptly that everybody jumped. Mrs. Benson looked up, startled, holding out the toasting-fork.

"I'll do that, Mama." Laura slid it deftly out of her mother's hand, and she sat down silently. Mr. Benson took a long swallow of coffee and cleared his throat.

"Laura's right. No point in all this gloom when there's not

[ 48 ]

a thing we can do about it, and no point in your making yourself half-sick like this with worry. You need a change. I'm taking you back home for a visit."

Mrs. Benson opened her mouth to speak, and he put his hand up quickly. "No earthly reason why not. The children are old enough to be responsible, and with old Dan out in the barn, they'll be perfectly safe."

"But the paper . . ."

"That's another thing. I've been thinking for some time it would be wise to run a series of articles based on first-hand observations—cut through the rumor-mongering that's been going on. We can come home through Washington and cover the Inauguration. I worked it all out in my mind last night."

*Last night* . . . Involuntarily Carlie's eyes met Ben's and, just as quickly, Mr. Benson's caught them both. There was more to this than appeared on the surface, Carlie realized, and she realized just as clearly that they were not to speak of it.

Mrs. Benson's fingers touched her throat. "When do you want to leave?" she asked faintly.

"Tomorrow."

"*Tomorrow!*"

"You can manage, Mama," Laura said quickly. "You've your new walking-suit, and your green brocade. Today's wash day, anyhow. If we start right now, we can have things dry enough to iron by suppertime."

"I can stay home from school and help," Carlie offered swiftly.

"You will not," Mr. Benson interjected brusquely. "Nothing extraordinary about your mother's paying a small visit to her kin. You tend to your lessons."

Carlie was startled by his curtness, the more so because, having no great respect for the local teacher, he was usually lenient. She was glad, when they reached the end of the drive, that Ben did not plow ahead as usual, but hung back for her instead.

"You young ones run ahead," he ordered. When Paul and Oliver, delighted with the opportunity, had raced away, Carlie turned quickly.

"What do you suppose happened?"

"Don't know, but something. That must have been Mr. Baldwin last night. Jupiter, I wish I were going!" Ben kicked a clump of snow forcibly with his toe.

"Maybe it's some kind of secret mission!"

"Huh! You sound like some stupid novel. More likely Papa's looking for material for stories."

"Maybe he's going so he can find out what he really thinks," Carlie said slowly.

Ben turned on her a look of utter scorn. "You're as bad as Uncle Henry! Don't you have any faith in Papa at all?"

To her relief, they had reached the corner of Franklin Street, and with the Garrisons just ahead, the subject was dropped.

" 'Lo, Emily, Tom." Carlie was so glad for the distraction they provided that she momentarily forgot their strained relations.

"Oh, Carlie. Hello." Emily looked flustered. "There's Netta Courtins. Excuse me, I have to speak to her a minute." She ran back down the road with evident relief. Tom loitered until the Bensons drew up beside him.

"Hear your parents are going South."

Carlie looked at him in amazement. "How did you know? It's only just been decided!" Too late she felt Ben's elbow jab sharply in her ribs.

"Are they really?" Tom was staring at her, and Carlie's temper snapped.

"Not the way you mean," she said tartly. "Papa's going to get some material for stories that will fix you all. Honestly,

Tom Garrison, you . . . rumor-mongers make me sick!" She stormed into the schoolhouse, feeling hot.

"You idiot!" Ben came up beside her and whispered sharply. "Didn't you know he was just ragging you?"

"I guess folks will know anyway, if Papa and Mama leave tomorrow!"

"Yes, but not like this. Everybody's got it wrong now, and you know it. Girls!" Ben snorted eloquently and stamped away.

Uneasily she realized that Ben indeed was right. The news had traveled rapidly through the school. There was an undercurrent in the air; she was more conscious than ever of the covert whispering during recess; and when, starting home, she inadvertently fell into step beside Netta Courtins, Netta flushed, mumbled something under her breath, and ducked away.

"See what I mean?" Ben murmured grimly from her other side.

"Oh, hush!" Carlie breathed angrily. She picked up a lump of snow and slapped it vehemently between her palms. Ahead of them, a group of boys loitered together on the far side of the road, and as she and Ben passed, the unmistakable tune of "Dixie" emerged in a taunting whistle.

Suddenly it was too much. Carlie's head snapped around and with the unerring aim Ben had taught her, she sent the hard-packed snowball straight at Tom Garrison's mocking face.

"We'll just see who gets tarred and feathered!" Scarcely hearing Tom's howl of pain or Ben's muttered oath, she picked up her hoops and ran down the road.

Endure all things, Papa had said. He didn't know what he was asking!

She burst into the house to find everything in a frenzy. Open trunks stood in the lower hall and Laura was running to and fro with piles of petticoats fresh from the irons. Mrs. Benson was dashing around abstractedly, and the open library door revealed Mr. Benson putting notes and papers into a bulging carpetbag. Carlie rushed in and closed the door behind her.

"Papa, will you take me with you? Papa, please!"

"Why, Carolina, I thought you'd die if you had to go!" Mr. Benson looked up with a smile that vanished when he saw her face. He gestured to a chair. "A bad day, Carlie?"

Carlie nodded. "Papa, you don't know what it's like!"

"Do I not?" Mr. Benson queried quietly, and she leaned forward.

"Papa, I know I promised, but it's so hard! Papa, please, please take me! I won't be any trouble. I'll be ladylike even if it kills me—only please!"

"You're still trying to run away from things, aren't you, Carlie?"

Her father's tone was not angry, but the truth still hurt, and as always, trying to defend herself, she struck back without thinking.

"*I'm* trying to run away? What on earth do you think it is *you're* doing?"

She ran out of the room, slamming the door behind her.

# CHAPTER

# 6

AFTERWARD she would have given anything to have the words unsaid, but it was too late. The frenzy of travel preparations closed about her, sweeping her along.

Everything was in confusion, but as they entered the dining room for dinner, a stillness seemed to fall, and with it a consciousness that this was the last meal for some time that they all would share. The candles in their silver holders glowed on the mahogany, the striped silk hangings at the windows, and on the Sevres garniture on the narrow mantlepiece. Paul and Oliver, without being told, came down with scrubbed hands and faces. Mrs. Benson came in, smoothing the skirts of her rust French print, and Mr. Benson, when he appeared, had changed into his gray broadcloth suit and patterned vest.

"God bless us all, and keep us safe for one another . . ."

Tonight the familiar blessing had new meaning. And as if by common consent, the coming separation was not mentioned until the meal was done. Then, as the candles sputtered, Mr. Benson pushed back his chair.

"Leaving you here alone is putting on you, particularly you three older ones, a great deal of responsibility. Of course, you'll have old Daniel right in the barn, but aside from that you are completely on your own. You know, without my telling you, that most of our friends and relatives would not think this wise." Uncle Henry's name was present in everybody's mind. "It will be up to you to prove them wrong.

"Laura, since you're head of housekeeping, I'll leave this with you." He slid a purse across the table, and Laura took it gravely. "Benjamin, you are, of course, the man of the house while I'm gone. You younger two are to obey the older ones. Particularly you, Paul, since Oliver will follow your example."

Paul's face was solemn in the flickering light and Laura's eyes were wet. Vaguely in the back of Carlie's mind, the thought registered that not once had her father spoken directly to her. She could not blame him. But she had to set things right before he left.

"God bless us all, and keep us safe for one another . . ."

The words lingered in the back of everyone's mind through the breathless excitement of their parents' leaving. Tuesday dawned crisp and clear, with sun turning the world into a glittering fairyland of ice. They stood on the porch, waving and shouting till their throats were hoarse, as the sleigh went down the drive, through the iron gates, past the front of the house and the little pond, and was lost from sight around the curve.

Since it was now mid-morning, Ben voted that they all skip school—a move which brought whoops of approval from the boys. The absence of parental restrictions intoxicated them and they scuffled in the snow all day. Laura, wearing responsibility like a halo, spent the day rattling pots and pans. Ben vanished into the barn and Carlie to the library where she lost herself in books, emerging dazed, dreamy, and headachy when Laura, in a becoming apron, rang the gong at six.

The sight of their parents' empty chairs made them all fall silent until Laura, after a second's hesitation, slid into one of them and Ben the other. Ben, in a voice unexpectedly deep and sober, said the blessing. At the next meal, Laura decided, the two extra side chairs would be gone.

It seemed strange, after dinner, not having Mr. Benson read aloud, not having their mother in her fireside chair rocking and mending. Even the children felt it and they went to bed without protest the first time they were told. Not long afterward, Ben stood and stretched.

"Think I'll go up, too. I'm tired."

Laura began turning out lamps and Ben went to lock the heavy door.

That, more than anything else that day, brought home to them that they were really on their own. They all stood for a moment, and then Laura, before the fireplace, turned and held out both her hands.

"Mama and Papa wouldn't have left us like this if they didn't think we could be responsible." In the firelight, Laura's face, the coquetry gone, was young and earnest. "I don't know how the rest of you feel, but I promise you I'm going to try my very, very best."

"Me, too," said Carlie, staring at the fire.

They got on fairly well, although there were difficulties they did not expect. Paul and Oliver, as a result of those long hours in the snow, came down with bad chest colds. It was hard, after being up with Oliver in the chill hours before dawn, to be in one's seat at school on time, eyes modestly downcast, hair smoothed demurely, pretending not to hear the whispers eddying around.

Staying home from school that day, Carlie realized, had been a bad mistake. In her absence, the tale of her encounter with Tom had spread and with it his version of her parents' trip. Ben worked out his own pent-up feelings in shoveling snow or chopping wood, coming in at dinnertime weary and cross. Laura was so wrapped up in housework that she frequently did not even have time to change her dress for dinner. She spent long hours over the stove. Unfortunately, her experience ran mostly to delicate concoctions. Ben only groaned, but Daniel, after enduring his share of Laura's cooking for a week, spoke out bluntly.

"Messes like that ain't proper vittles for growing children. They need good hearty food less'n they gets sick, and if you don't see they gets it, I'll tellygraf your Ma."

Instead of the sharp retort Carlie fully expected, Laura only sighed. "I guess you're right. I'll try a pot roast tomorrow." She looked hopelessly around the hot untidy kitchen, and her shoulders sagged.

It wasn't fair for all the work to fall on Laura. "I'll do the dishes," Carlie said aloud, looking pointedly at Ben lounging in the door.

Ben straightened hastily. "That's woman's work!"

"You could sit out here and read to us."

It was good to have the familiar ritual re-established. Carlie, up to her elbows in hot soapy water, was conscious of a peace she had sorely needed lately. She had been in a state of restless dissatisfaction ever since her parents' departure, and she knew exactly why, but it was something she didn't want to face. It was easier to concentrate on solving someone else's worries.

Going upstairs later, she found Laura rubbing her back, and she went over to slide an arm around her waist. "Poor Laura! I'll help more after this, I promise."

Laura sighed. "I never realized Mama had so much to do."

Carlie knew. It wasn't the big tasks—rather it was the endless little things. They were silent for a moment, and then Laura tossed her head.

"Oh, well! We can be Cinderellas on Saturday. There's the Washington's Birthday dance at the hotel."

"Do you think we ought to go without Papa and Mama?"

"Oh, pooh! It's plenty chaperoned! The children will be safe enough with Daniel." Laura went to the mirror and began experimenting with her hair.

It seemed strange, on Saturday, to be getting ready for a party without their parents. Carlie took out the gray-blue silk, remembering the last time she had worn it. She stopped, the dress half on, wondering suddenly whether Brad would be at the dance. Then, face scarlet, she jerked it down and hooked the bodice. But she was conscious, as she bundled her hair into a snood and tied a velvet ribbon around her throat, that she was fussing more than she had ever done before.

The night air was clear and cold. Ben let the girls out at the door and then drove around to the carriage shed as they went into the ladies' parlor to lay aside their wraps.

"Ready?" Laura turned from the mirror, her hoopskirt swinging, her face pink with the cold, and her eyes as dark as the night sky. She snapped her fan open and swirled out into the ballroom. "Why, Peter Van Dirk, are you waiting for me? I declare, I didn't think you knew I had arrived!" Head tilted back, she gazed up at him through half-closed lashes.

He does lap it up so, Carlie thought disgustedly. Peter was a tall, lanky young man, completely and utterly devoted to Laura, but unable to respond in kind to her repartee. Laura's high, sweet laughter trilled back as he swung her out onto the floor.

A group of girls was sitting along one wall, and Carlie

started toward them, but as she did so Emily Garrison darted over and took the only empty chair.

Carlie saw Ben standing by the refreshment table and sailed over grimly. "Let's dance," she said without preamble.

"Sure." Ben loved to dance, and they fitted together with the smoothness of long home practice. He looked down at her shrewdly. "What's bothering you?"

"Not a thing," Carlie said hastily. She could tell, from the way his hand tightened at her waist when they passed the boys, that he was spoiling for a fight. If only she could keep him dancing, keep him away from their raucous jibes and keep herself from having to sit in obvious isolation amid a row of empty chairs! Then someone tapped Ben's shoulder, and she looked up into Brad's twinkling eyes.

"What's up—a family squabble?" he asked in amusement. "You look like a thundercloud."

"Oh, no!" Despite herself, Carlie blushed. He nodded his head toward the group of girls.

"What was that nonsense all about?" He looked so grim that she blushed again and searched frantically for a change of subject.

"Who's that red-haired young man Laura's dancing with?" she asked. "I've never seen him."

Brad glanced over. "Dennis Calhoun. There's a bunch of gay dogs from the militia up tonight." His tone was noncommittal.

"He's—all right—isn't he?"

"My, yes, and 'tis himself would tell you so," Brad said satirically. "Your sister's having a whirl, but her poor gentleman friend looks forlorn." He nodded toward Peter, sitting disconsolately among the potted palms.

The fiddling stopped, there was a fanfare from the piano, and Mr. Ramsey issued a call for squares. Brad looked at Carlie quizzically, and she shook her head. "I'll sit awhile," she said quickly, unwilling to risk rebuffs from the other couples. She started for the ladies' parlor, but Brad moved ahead, held out the nearest chair, and drew another up beside it. Almost immediately, Ben wandered up and presently Laura too glided over, her two swains close behind. "I declare, I'm weary!" She sank down gracefully, but her eyes were sparkling.

Laura had never, Carlie thought honestly, looked as pretty as she did tonight. She was playing up to Dennis outrageously, and he was extravagant with gallantries. Even Peter was goaded out of his usual reticence to respond in kind. The whole Garrison contingent was glowering and the Courtins girls looked forlorn.

Their isolation corner, Carlie thought with thoroughly uncharitable satisfaction, had become the gayest in the room. Normally she would never have dared to try Laura's brand of flirting; now, conscious of Emily's eyes upon her, she turned to Brad with a brilliant smile.

Reaching home after the party, she was conscious that she was terribly tired. That sort of play-acting took more out of one than she had expected. She undressed quickly and got into bed, more than a little ashamed of her own conduct. Laura was undressing dreamily before the mirror.

"That Mr. Calhoun certainly is a charmer," she said, pulling down her nightgown and beginning to braid her hair. "Did you see the way he kissed my hand when we left?"

"I saw," Carlie said shortly. Brad, having witnessed this bit of by-play, had lifted an eyebrow and done the same to her. She changed the subject quickly. "You weren't very nice to poor Peter."

"Oh, pooh! I guess he doesn't own me!" Laura turned out the light and slid into bed. "I meant to make Dennis like me. Emily Garrison was positively green, and it served her right after the way that tribe's been treating you and Ben." She sat up, and in the moonlight her face was almost stern. "If they give you any more trouble, you tell me, hear? I can handle Tom Garrison. The next time he tries to flirt with me, he'll wish he hadn't!"

She looked so vehement that Carlie was touched. "I guess we can take care of it," she said softly.

In the darkness, she heard Laura's sudden giggle. "Little sister, judging from your performance tonight, I just guess you can!"

On Monday the sun shone brightly, but the climate in the schoolhouse was, if that were possible, even more frigid than before.

Letters came from Mr. and Mrs. Benson in New York, Baltimore, and Washington. Mr. Benson had been to call on Horace Greeley; they had met a fascinating gentleman on the train named Colonel Stone; Washington was crowded and dirty; they planned to remain in the Capital until after the Inauguration and then head south, returning home by way of Washington in mid-April.

"Seven more weeks," Laura said, putting the letter describing the Inauguration plans back into its envelope. "I wish they were home."

"Me, too," Carlie said somberly, and sighed.

" 'Now is the winter of our discontent . . .' " The reading aloud in the kitchen after dinner had become a habit, and Ben was embarking on *Richard III*. The phrase struck a responsive chord in Carlie's mind. *The winter of our discontent . . .* It was the sum and essence of the current season. The first of March had come, but life was bitter. Carlie was discontented with everyone and everything, but first and foremost with herself.

She was so ashamed of the way she'd flirted with Brad that she hadn't dared to look at him in church last Sunday. At the meeting of the Dorcas League, the girls' sewing circle, on Tuesday, she had snapped at Emily in a way that made the minister's gentle wife look up in surprise. When Joe Pryor had pinned a copperhead badge on Oliver's unsuspecting shoulder yesterday, she had exploded. But these were minor compared to the trouble that lay deep inside.

She had not made up with her father before he left. She had not had the chance. The last words they had exchanged had been the accusation she had flung at him in her defensive anger.

She had not had the chance—or she had not made the chance. Which was it? *You always run away from things*, her father had said. And now it was too late. She could not write an apology, for Mama always read the letters, and she would not have her mother hurt by knowing what she'd said.

She felt discouraged and uneasy, and even church on Sunday did not help—not with Uncle Henry up front, grim and forbidding, and Bess, half a room away, looking as if she'd been crying.

Monday, the fourth of March, was overcast and raw. "Hope the weather's better in Washington," Ben commented, thinking of the inaugural parade. Carlie didn't care. She was sick unto death of everything to do with Washington, politics, and the controversial Mr. Lincoln. All she wanted was to escape to the attic and lose herself in one of Papa's books. But when she reached home from school, Laura was waiting in the hall wearing her good blue poplin dress and her best bonnet.

"Run upstairs fast and change. Mrs. Zabriskie's invited us for tea." Laura's face was glowing, and it came to Carlie how lonely these past weeks must have been for Laura. Drinking tea with an elderly woman had never been Laura's idea of fun. Now, being shut up, day in, day out, with housework, she must be glad just of the chance of getting out. Carlie flashed her a sudden warm smile and rushed upstairs.

"What do you suppose made her ask us?" she demanded, running down again in her Sunday suit.

"Can't imagine. Mrs. Z. sent her hired girl over with a note this morning, very proper. Maybe she feels we've been neglected with Mama gone. Or maybe your new beau's arranged a rendezvous." Laura quirked her brows at Carlie mischievously.

"Laura Benson, you hush," Carlie said shortly, and was glad that the raw wet air provided an excuse for her reddening cheeks. "He probably," she said briskly, "won't even be there!"

But when Mrs. Zabriskie opened the door, a familiar dark head appeared behind her shoulder.

"Miss Carlie, what a delightful pleasure." Brad's words were formal, but his eyes looked devilish. He took Carlie's hand, started to raise it, then put it down again with a virtuous expression. Mrs. Zabriskie looked amused, Laura looked puzzled, and Carlie blushed.

"I have some pies for Laura in the kitchen." Mrs. Zabriskie spoke up tactfully. "And I want to speak to her about the Dorcas League. Bradley, perhaps you will entertain Carlie."

"Delighted," Brad said. Carlie did not look at him, but she felt his eyes upon her, and when she moved toward the parlor fireplace, he followed.

"Pretty clever, wasn't I?" he asked. "I wasn't sure whether it would be proper for me to call when your folks were gone, so I dropped a hint to Mrs. Z., and here we are." He sat down opposite her and grinned companionably. "How are your parents enjoying their trip?"

"Pretty well, I guess. They're in Washington now."

"Did they say whether there have been any assassination attempts?" Brad looked surprised at her blank face. "Seems some Secessionists were planning to shoot the President when he came through Baltimore. The papers were full of it. I thought your father might have heard some first-hand news."

"I don't know," Carlie said vaguely. "And we don't see the papers much, now that he's gone. Anyway, I'm sick of it all." The remark sounded so petty, she wished she hadn't made it, but Brad's face was understanding.

"Is it something to do with those girls at the dance that night? It's none of my business, but I could tell there was something wrong, and it looked big."

"It is big." Carlie looked away and drew a deep breath. "We're being—boycotted, because Mama's Southern."

Brad gave a low whistle. "Since when was this town that pro-Lincoln?"

"That's just it!" Carlie blinked back baffled tears. "The Garrisons are, of course, and my Uncle Henry. But the rest don't really care. They're just following the crowd."

"I guess a lot of people," Brad said quietly, "do stupid things and then are sorry afterward."

"Don't they just!" She blinked again, less successfully, and turned her head away.

"Carlie, don't." Deliberately he came around the chair and faced her. "There's more than that. I know you well enough to know when you're trying to run away."

The blunt truth of the statement hit home, and she swallowed hard. "You're right," she said in a low voice. Without meaning to, she was telling him the whole story of her scene with Papa. "I never knew before how terrible it could be . . . being misjudged. And that's what I did to Papa! There's not a thing I can do about it now, and I just can't bear it!"

There was a silence when she finished, and she wished fervently that she hadn't been so free in her speech, for Brad shook his head as if he were talking to a child. "Carlie, all those important things you want to do . . . Don't you know the biggest thing you can do in life is to learn to live with the things you've brought upon yourself?"

He sounded so much like her father that her chin went up in an automatic reflex.

"It's easy to stand here and preach," she snapped hotly. "You never had to try it!"

She stopped abruptly, but Brad was looking beyond her, toward the fire. "I've never told you about Alison, have I? My sister," he said abruptly, glancing over, and the unaccountable coldness that had pressed Carlie's heart melted. "You remind me of her—both of you so full of life . . . Alison always had to outride, outrun, and outtalk everybody. And whatever I did, she was always tagging after."

Like Ben and me, Carlie thought.

"We used to spend summers at my grandfather's farm in Pennsylvania. The summer that Alison was eight years old, there was a new horse, a real brute. Everyone said no one but a man could ride him, but Alison did it. We used to ride in the woods along the railroad tracks—she always said she wanted to race the train, but I never let her. Then one day a bunch of the fellows was waiting for me, and I got tired of her tagging along and rode on ahead. When the train came along, the horse got scared and bolted, and Alison was thrown. That was six years ago, and she hasn't walked since." Brad was silent a moment. "I've lived with it."

"Brad, I'm sorry," Carlie said softly.

"That isn't why I told you." Brad turned on her directly. "Carlie—I don't know how to say it exactly, except that everybody's got troubles they have to live with. It's what you let them do to you that matters. And somehow, the bigger the things you have to live with, the better the person you become." He paused, searching for words. "I guess what I'm trying to say is that you have to wrestle with your troubles till they bless you."

Someone else had said that, long ago . . . Mama, on New Year's Day. Carlie looked at Brad, too moved to speak. Dimly she heard the sound of voices in the hall as Mrs. Zabriskie and Laura came in with tea. She put out her hand and felt Brad take it between both of his.

"Thank you," she said simply.

# CHAPTER

## 7

$S$PRING CAME SLOWLY. Even at the end of March there was snow on the ground and ice still clotted the pond. The sun was shy, peering half-heartedly around the clouds. As a gradual thaw began, the schoolhouse walls were clammy, and many of the girls came down with colds. It gave Carlie, who did not, a vindictive satisfaction.

Even the solemnity of Lent did not calm her restless mood. Ordinarily the services moved her with their mood of atonement, confession, and prayer. This year the quietness of the church was a surface quiet only.

At home it was much the same. There was a reckless look in Laura's eyes these days. She had been impatient with Peter ever since the dance. Dennis Calhoun had written, asking permission to call. She had had to refuse, of course, because their parents were away, but for several days afterward she had been edgy, and she had taken some of the household money to buy the most expensive silk the general store carried for her Easter dress.

When Laura was in one of these moods, everyone kept out

[ 66 ]

of her way, and Carlie escaped as often as she could into the garret. Reading dissatisfied her now, so she spent long hours writing in her journal and wishing Bess were there.

That was another thing that would be different. Before, the Demarests had always come for Easter dinner. When Oliver inquired innocently one night why they never came any more, Ben had snapped at him so sharply that Oliver's face screwed up and they all felt ashamed.

Easter came early, on the thirty-first of March. There were still faint traces of snow, but the air was warm, ice was melting into rivers, and the unpaved roads had become a sea of mud. Laura's lilac silk and matching mantle had turned out to be a triumph. As soon as she reached home after church, she whipped an apron over her new finery and hustled to the kitchen, a frown of concentration puckering her face. Carlie followed, tying an apron over her own new dress. It was fortunate that she liked simple things, she thought, smoothing the dress's folds, since she and Laura had had so little time to sew. The princess lines, copied from a much more elaborate version in *Godey's*, clung to her body and then spread out over her widest hoops.

She wished suddenly that Brad had been in church to see it, but he had gone home to New York for the weekend. Well, she would invite him to dinner as soon as her parents returned. Three more weeks, she thought with a lifting heart. Papa and Brad would like each other more and more.

She was startled to find her thoughts turning so often in Brad's direction. But her thoughts were unpredictable these days, like April weather. In the late afternoons she would find herself running to the general store for things she'd forgotten to pick up after school—at just the time Brad would be coming in there to collect the mail. It was not deliberate. In fact, it seemed scarcely to happen of her own volition, but it disconcerted her.

[ 67 ]

After he got the Judge's mail from the storekeeper-postmaster, Brad usually walked her home. His fingers would touch her elbow to help her over the ruts in the muddy road, and inside the thin cotton sleeve of her spring dress her arm would tingle. When they reached the corner where Beaufort's footpath meandered down to the little pond, they often lingered, discussing the mail. The Bensons were back in Washington now, and Brad was interested in hearing about their stay in Carolina.

"There's something big building up down there," he remarked, as she slipped the latest letter back into its envelope. Mr. Benson had referred to a small fortress in the Charleston harbor. Though South Carolina had seceded, the island was still a Federal army base, and the Confederates were demanding that it be relinquished.

"It's part of the South, so why *don't* they give it to them? I don't see what difference one little island makes," Carlie said disinterestedly, but Brad shook his head.

"Both sides have gone too far. Unless somebody finds a diplomatic way out, that little island's going to make a *lot* of difference."

Others too were of the same opinion. After church that Sunday, as John Haring distributed his usual billet of news and papers, the rumors flew. The island fortress had been cut off from outside communication; Lincoln had issued an ultimatum; an expedition from New York was sailing south to relieve the beleaguered men.

That last at least was true, Brad reported on Wednesday. There had been a meeting of county leaders at the Zabriskies' house the night before and the action had been discussed.

"The Judge says Carolina's sitting on a powder keg, and he just hopes nobody strikes a match."

"At least then something would happen," Ben said. He had

seen Brad standing with Carlie by the pond and had come down to join them, to Carlie's great annoyance.

"Let's hope it doesn't," Brad said soberly.

"Huh! It's different for you—you're in on things." Ben flashed him a look that was half scornful, half envious. "All we do is just sit here and vegetate." He looked as if he would infinitely prefer the seat on the powder box, and Carlie shuddered.

"It's probably just talk," she offered brightly. "Papa says if anything happens, it'll be a nine-days' wonder."

"Let's hope so," Brad repeated.

Letters from Washington echoed what Brad had said. The situation, Mr. Benson wrote, was delicate. In Baltimore, Secessionist mobs were rioting in the streets. "Everyone is waiting to see what the new President will do."

Ben devoured this political news voraciously, but for the rest of the family the important information was in the final sentence. "Your mother and I will leave Washington by rail on the twentieth, and reach home a few days later."

Laura put the letter down, drew a deep breath, and looked around. "First thing tomorrow we'd better start getting ready. I'd love to have the spring cleaning done before they come."

"Tomorrow's Friday," Carlie offered. "I could stay home from school."

"Don't sacrifice yourself," Laura retorted, twinkling, and Carlie grinned back. It was as if a door had opened, blowing in a breath of warm sweet air.

*Mama and Papa are coming* . . . The words fitted themselves to the lilt of Laura's humming as she washed the curtains, to the *thwack* of Ben's beating the carpets with Paul and Oliver's inept assistance, and they sang in Carlie's ears.

They worked steadily all Friday and Saturday and even,

after a half-guilty conference, on Sunday afternoon. By the time early twilight fell, the lower floor was all in order. The library's carved doors and creamy paneling had been scrubbed. In the parlors, the fresh muslin summer curtains were looped back and a soft breeze drifted in from the open windows. Ben collapsed on the carpet with a groan, and Laura rubbed her back.

"That's enough for one day. I vote we stop and have a cold supper. We deserve a rest."

"I'll get it," Carlie volunteered, noticing the violet circles that had formed under Laura's eyes. She rummaged in the kitchen for gingerbread and sugar cookies and made a pitcher of cold lemonade. When she returned with the tray, Laura was sitting at the piano.

God, that madest earth and heaven, darkness and light;
Who the day for toil hast given, for rest the night . . .

The music was a part of all the Sunday evenings of her life. The Sunday after next, Mama and Papa would be here, and perhaps Brad would come for Sunday-night supper. They would stand around the piano and sing. If she closed her eyes, she could almost hear his deep baritone ringing out.

Ben pulled himself to his feet and lit the opaline lamp on the piano. Paul and Oliver broke off their tussling and made a dive for the sugar cookies, and Ben grinned. Carlie smiled back, feeling contentment spreading through her body. The magic of the music and the twilight dissipated her troubles and discontent as the lamplight banished shadows.

"When Papa gets here . . ." Oliver was saying something earnestly to Paul, and Carlie's thoughts half-consciously took up the thread. *When Papa's here and Mama's here, then everything's all right* . . . The childhood litany lingered comfortingly in everyone's mind.

[ 70 ]

Laura began another hymn, and Ben started to hum in his familiar tuneless tenor. Suddenly he stopped. "Hey, Carlie, here comes your beau."

"You hush," Carlie said automatically.

Footsteps clattered up the veranda steps and Brad suddenly ducked through the window. "Have you heard yet?" he demanded.

Laura spun around on the piano bench. "Heard what?"

Brad's eyes flicked from one to the other as if debating how to tell them. Then he spoke abruptly. "Fort Sumter's been bombarded."

For a second silence hung in the air.

"*War*." Ben spoke the one word in everyone's mind, and Brad nodded soberly.

"I'm afraid so. There's no getting out of it now."

Silence enfolded them again. Then Laura got to her feet. "There's more, isn't there?" she asked tightly.

Brad hesitated, and to Carlie, as he had once before, he seemed to become years older. He answered Laura gently.

"Beauregard's marching on Washington. It's wide open, there are hardly any troops to defend it, and they say the railroads out of the city have been blown up."

Laura's voice was a dry whisper. "Mama . . . Mama and Papa are in Washington!"

Outside the windows, in the peaceful gloaming, birds twittered softly, just as they had before.

Without a word, Laura abruptly dropped down on her knees, and so did Carlie and Paul and Oliver, awed into silence. Brad and Ben bowed their heads. Laura's voice, though shaky, came with a surprising strength: "Our Father in Heaven, we ask Thy help in this troubled hour. Take care of Mama and Papa." Her voice faltered, then steadied. "God bless us, and keep us safe for one another."

The familiar words made their parents seem suddenly near.

Laura straightened and rose, smoothing her skirts with hands that were very calm, though the corner of her mouth was trembling. Oliver pressed against Ben. Carlie swallowed hard and found that she could speak quite naturally.

"Brad, would you like some lemonade?"

"Thanks, I would." Brad's tone was matter-of-fact. He took the pitcher from her shaking fingers and filled the glass himself. Then he looked at Ben. "There's a bonfire over in the center of town."

"Let's go," Ben said tersely.

"I'm coming, too," Carlie said quickly. Ben frowned, and unexpectedly Laura spoke up firmly.

"We'll all go. I'm not staying home alone tonight." She started to close the windows, then stopped abruptly, flung her shawl around her shoulders, and hurried out, leaving doors and windows open. Carlie, following, understood. Keeping a house safe here now seemed so unimportant. She picked her way down the path toward the pond, trying to concentrate on where she was stepping. She felt Brad's hand at her elbow.

"It's all right, Cara. It's going to be all right. Remember that." Brad's arm went around her waist in the darkness, and she leaned against him gratefully. Ben had Paul and Oliver firmly by the hand, and Laura had pulled her shawl tightly around her shoulders as if buffeted by an unseen wind.

When they reached the corner by the general store, a crowd had gathered, pushing toward the pond where a red glow filled the sky. "There's Peter!" Laura gave a little cry and ran toward him, hands outstretched. Ben turned to Brad. "I'll keep the boys and you take care of Carlie."

Ordinarily Carlie would have resented being disposed of in this summary fashion, but tonight she scarcely noticed. She clung to Brad's arm as they pushed through the jostling crowd. Everyone they knew was there, and more—people from as far away as Sicomac and Spikertown, rough-looking

boys from farms back in the Ramapo hills. In the light of the
leaping flames, familiar faces looked strange, and the heat of
the fire mingled mesmerizingly with the noise. Carlie's temples
throbbed.

Joe Pryor dashed up with a roll of cloth which he threw
upon the fire and the flames reached out, illuminating a field
of blue. There was a shocked murmur, then Tom Garrison
seized the mutilated flag just as Ben, with a loud cry, flung
himself at Joe. Someone screamed, and with a start Carlie
realized that it was herself. Instinctively she moved forward,
but Brad's hand held her tightly.

"Keep out of it." His voice, audible to no one but herself,
was stern. "The Judge is there; he'll stop it if it goes too far. It
will do them good to get it off their chests." He propelled her
firmly away from the crowd, back toward the road. She took
a deep breath, and the cool air hurt her lungs.

Down the road a dim light showed from the windows of
the church, and they moved toward it. As they reached the
pathway, organ music reached them.

> O God, our help in ages past,
> Our hopes for years to come,
> Our shelter from the stormy blast . . .

The stormy blast had come. If Carlie had not been aware of
it before, she was now as they went into the church. A great
silence had fallen. In contrast to the usual social greetings, no
one spoke. The stone interior, lit hurriedly with a few candles,
was dim with shadows. At the organ, Mrs. Ryerson played
with her eyes closed, a housecap on her head. People kept
coming in, some still in Sunday silks, some in housedresses,
many of the women, like herself, bare-headed.

Carlie sank into a back pew and closed her eyes. Dimly she
was aware of Brad sitting beside her, of Uncle Henry's eyes

upon them both, but it wasn't real, nothing was real except that Papa and Mama were not here. Where were they to-night? she wondered suddenly. She bowed her head against her hand and prayed as she had never prayed before. Presently someone sank down on her other side, and she was conscious of the scent of Laura's sweet cologne. She moved her hand over on the seat between them and Laura gripped it tightly.

The organ music stopped and Mr. Courtins, one of the elders, stood up and began to read in his deep quiet voice: " 'I will lift up mine eyes unto the hills, from whence cometh my help. My help cometh from the Lord, which made heaven and earth.' "

The words sank deep into Carlie's heart.

There was no formal service, and as the church became too crowded for latecomers to find seats, others rose and left. Presently Carlie felt Brad touch her elbow, and she rose and followed him outside. They did not speak. They walked past the side of the church and then, instead of continuing down the road, he turned her into the footpath through the cemetery. She looked up, startled, and he shook his head.

When she was little, she and Ben had made up stories about the cemetery, and the vague fears they had aroused then rose up now. She picked her way through headstones, ghostly in the moonlight, and was grateful for Brad's hand beneath her elbow. Then, far ahead, a small figure emerged from the shadows, and Bess ran into her arms.

"Carlie, I had to see you. I tried and tried to signal without Pa noticing. I'm so glad you saw." She looked gratefully at Brad, who nodded and moved off tactfully. In the wan moonlight, Bess's face was waxen and her eyes were enormous. "Carlie, your father and Aunt Clarissa, are they all right? Pa's been talking so, and I've been so worried. Then, when we heard tonight . . ."

A tremor shook her and Carlie, feeling the thinness of Bess's small body, felt her own panic suddenly leave.

"They're all right. Everything's going to be all right," she said fiercely. She held Bess tightly, and her voice had a calmness that she had not known herself capable of. "Bess, don't you remember our family prayer? 'God bless us, and keep us safe for one another'? That's what's going to happen, no matter how long it takes, till we're all back together again. That's how it's going to be."

It was more than a prayer. It was a solemn vow.

# CHAPTER

# 8

HYSTERIA was in the air. As Mr. Benson had predicted, now that war had come things had changed. It was no longer a question of states' rights or slavery. In the firing on Sumter, the North had been attacked. The question was simple: Would the North fight back? The answer came resoundingly.

The town was rife with rumors: Washington was under siege, it was close to capitulation, Southern secret agents planned the kidnaping of the President. But it was too soon yet for any real news or letters to have gotten through. Laura moved through the day with tight-lipped concentration, and Carlie was too keyed up to go to school. Ben had disappeared early in the morning without a word.

"I just hope he has the sense to keep out of trouble," Laura said grimly, jerking curtains down from upstairs windows. They continued the homecoming house cleaning with driving intensity, as if it would prove that all would be well. *When the cleaning's finished, Mama and Papa will be home* . . . The thought seemed to hang unspoken in everybody's mind.

Dusk came, and the supper hour, and still Ben had not returned.

"Maybe he's 'listed," Paul suggested, wide-eyed.

"You hush!" Laura banged a platter of cold meat down on the table. The front door opened and she looked up sharply. "Ben? Where have you been?"

"Hackensack." Ben appeared in the doorway, dusty and disheveled, a three-cornered tear in the sleeve of his shirt. "Old Abe's called for seventy-five thousand volunteers. They were recruiting in front of City Hall." He took a long gulp of water and wiped his mouth with the back of his hand. "Tom Garrison shinnied up the flagpole and put one of those new Liberty Caps on top. The Secessionists were wild. None of them had the nerve to go up after it, so they packed the pole with dynamite and *blew* it off!"

"I wish I'd been there." The words escaped Carlie involuntarily, and Ben looked impatient.

"This is man's work. Tom Garrison's enlisted." His voice was envious, and Laura's eyes filled with alarm.

"Ben, don't you dare! Not without asking Papa!"

"Huh! Pa'd let me." He pulled a newspaper from his back pocket and flung it on the table, his eyes exultant. "Look at that!"

They bent over it eagerly. *Union Must Be Preserved* ran the headline in boldface print beneath the familiar *Journal* masthead. The article that followed was long and carefully thought out, pointing out clearly to the stolid Dutch farmers exactly why it was to their own best interests to have the Union reunited. A later section, aimed at the owners of the great fabric mills in Paterson, showed that the war must be ended quickly so that the flow of raw materials from the South would not be interrupted.

"Do you suppose Papa wrote it?"

"Who else could have? Half the fellows said they wouldn't

[ 77 ]

have enlisted if they hadn't seen it! They all thought the war didn't have anything to do with them, but this changed their minds!"

"I hope you notice the practical approach, not the wild-eyed patriotism you'd have written." Laura's voice was tart, but her eyes had a worried look. "I wish we'd heard from Papa."

"Ben?" Paul's solemn voice spoke up suddenly. "Pa is coming home, isn't he?"

"Sure, feller," Ben said gruffly and rumpled Paul's hair.

Laura stood up quickly, her voice briskly cheerful. "We've all got the glooms because we're tired. So much excitement yesterday! We'd better go to bed early and catch up."

They did go to bed early, but they couldn't sleep. The soft April moonlight drifted in the bedroom's open windows . . . the same moonlight that was falling on Washington far to the south.

"I wonder where they are." Laura's voice spoke suddenly in the darkness.

Carlie turned, punching her pillow to a different position beneath her head. "We'll probably have a letter tomorrow. Or a telegram. Maybe they decided to start home early and will just walk in on us. That's probably the reason we haven't heard." She tried to make her voice as positive as it had been last night with Bess, and she must have succeeded, for Laura shifted and grew quiet.

Vaguely, from a distance, a pounding broke through Carlie's uneasy dreams. She opened her eyes to find the room filled with darkness. The knocking continued, more insistently now. Laura sat up.

"What is it?"

"Somebody at the door." Carlie's heart was pounding.

In the hall they encountered Ben. "Maybe it's Ma and Pa!"

"They'd have a key," Laura retorted. She opened the foyer

doors and stepped out on the balcony. "Who's there?" she called.

A figure came back down off the porch to peer up at them. "Joseph Baldwin. I'm sorry to wake you up, but it's important."

Ben was already going down the stairs two at a time. Laura stopped to pull off her nightcap and throw on her blue wrapper, buttoning it as she ran. Carlie flung a dressing-sacque around her shoulders. They converged on Mr. Baldwin just as Ben was lighting a lamp on the library desk.

The editor was a pleasant-faced youngish man with mild brown eyes that now looked stern. "What's the matter?" Ben demanded.

"Somebody tried to burn down the newspaper office. Some of our friends didn't like today's editorial, and they tried to put us out of business. They almost succeeded, too," Mr. Baldwin added grimly.

"Why, the dirty . . ." Ben began hoarsely, and Carlie interrupted.

"Was it very bad?"

"It would have been if we hadn't caught it fast. Fortunately, I only live two blocks away. I just left old Fritz, the typesetter, there on guard. But the main thing—have you had any news yet from your father?"

"We thought maybe you had," Ben said eagerly, and Mr. Baldwin shook his head.

"I wonder if we ought to close down the newspaper now. I've enlisted. I'll be leaving in a week or so, and if your father's not back by then, we'd have to shut down anyway."

Carlie stared at him, and her own shock was mirrored in Ben's face. "You can't just close. Papa's so proud that the paper's never missed an issue."

"We'll have to," Mr. Baldwin said bluntly. "Old Fritz can't put a paper out all by himself."

"We can together," Ben said with vigor. "I'll be down first thing tomorrow."

"Ben, you can't run a paper!"

"Oh, hush up, Laura," Ben said curtly. "I can learn."

Not until after Mr. Baldwin had left and they were going back upstairs did they realize they'd never asked who'd written the editorial.

Tuesday and then Wednesday dragged by with still no word. Ben went off early in the mornings and returned late, weary-eyed and tense. Laura finished the house cleaning and began doing great heaps of laundry. Carlie wandered around, feeling restless and irritable with nothing to do.

She had offered to help Ben, and the offer had been bluntly refused. Nobody, he pointed out with calm logic, had ever heard of a female newspaper reporter.

"I can write better than he can, and he knows it," she thought grimly, pulling weeds out of the tulip bed in front of the house on Thursday afternoon. The sun beat down on her bare head and a lock of hair, damp with the heat, fell across her eyes. She put up a hand to push it back, leaving a streak of dirt across her forehead. Then she looked up and saw Brad coming up the path.

"Hello!" she called joyfully, getting to her feet and shaking her skirts, grateful for the interruption. Brad waved, but did not speak until he had ducked beneath the maple tree that overhung the path and stood beside her. At the expression on his face she felt a tremor of alarm. "Brad, what is it?"

"There's a telegram," he said gently. "The Judge sent me up from Hackensack with it. I don't know what . . ."

Before he could finish, she was already running toward the house. "Laura! *Laura!*"

Laura came running onto the porch, took one look, and dropped into a chair, her face going pale. "You read it," she said faintly.

"Shall I?" Brad asked, as Carlie made no move. He slit the envelope and scanned the contents. "It's all right," he said quickly. "It says, 'Safe. Well. Taking Mama home. All love. Papa.' "

"It's all right," Laura repeated, her voice a whisper. Suddenly she darted up, hugged Carlie, kissed Brad on the cheek, and rushed inside.

"Whew!" Brad looked after her and grinned.

"It's all right, they're coming home! Oh, Brad!" Carlie flung her arms around one of the pillars and hugged it hard.

"Whoa, easy!" Brad smiled. "Sit down and catch your breath before you swoon!"

"I won't, I never do." She dropped down on the steps obediently, not knowing whether to laugh or cry. "They're coming home," she repeated like a litany. "In a few days they'll be here, and we can all let go." She dropped her head down against her knees.

"It hasn't been easy, has it?" Brad patted her shoulders lightly, and she was very conscious of his nearness.

"Everything's so . . . topsy-turvy. Laura's been so frightened, though she hasn't said, and Ben . . . I was so scared he'd run off and enlist, till he had the paper to work on, and now there's no living with him." She blew her breath out hard with relieved anger. "I suggested, just once, that I could help, and you should have heard him! Women don't work on papers!"

Brad looked amused. "Has he ever heard of M. M. Montgomery?" He named a famous political columnist on a New York paper. "I hate to disillusion him, but that's my mother. I told you she wrote some things that would interest you," he said drily, as Carlie stared.

"But I thought . . ."

"That she just wrote trashy novels? That's how she started, to pay Alison's doctor bills. My father's dead, you know."

Brad's voice altered. "She learned to write, doing those novels, and that led to the column. Who knows—her column just may do a lot of good. She's trying hard to make it a voice of reason in the present mess."

"Things aren't good, are they?" Carlie asked slowly, and Brad shook his head.

"Everyone's in a tearing frenzy of patriotism, just like Ben, and they haven't any more idea than he does of what war really is." He looked sober for a moment, then flashed his one-sided grin. "Anyway, your folks are out of it now."

As he started down the path, he turned. "By the way, let's not disillusion Ben. Mother's publishers don't know, either, and if they found out, they'd probably expire."

He had trusted her with a family secret. She hugged the knowledge to her heart through the rest of the day, which passed in a happy daze. Paul and Oliver came home from school. Ben came home from the paper, looked at the telegram, and let out a whoop.

"I knew it would take more than a mob to keep Pa from coming!"

"You won't be so happy when you have to quit the paper and go back to school." Laura was her old tart self again.

"Maybe I just won't have to, since Mr. Baldwin will be gone. And maybe you just won't like having Ma giving the orders, either."

It felt good to be squabbling again.

After dinner, Laura went to the piano. It was pleasant to have music, to have life going on as it had before. The war seemed very far away, almost like a bad dream that hadn't really happened. No one wanted to go to bed that night; they were too filled with happiness. At last Laura rose, looked at Oliver asleep on the sofa and Paul struggling valiantly to keep his eyes open and gave a rueful sigh.

"We'll have to get to bed. Those two have school tomorrow, and we have work." She turned out the lamp and locked the door as Ben picked Oliver up bodily and led the way upstairs. Laura and Carlie dawled through undressing, talking companionably, hearing Ben's noisy racket in the room next door. The cool breeze of the April night stirred the curtains, bringing in a faint clatter of horse's hoofs on the road outside. Someone was riding fast. Then, unexpectedly, there was a knock. Carlie started.

"Maybe it's another telegram!"

"It's the back door, silly. Probably Daniel wanting liniment for his rheumatism. At this hour!" Laura ran downstairs impatiently with Carlie pattering after. Entirely too many things, she thought with a trace of hysteria, were happening lately in the middle of the night. She stood in the shadows of the back hall as Laura lit a candle and opened the back door slightly.

"All right, Daniel, what is it? Why, what . . ." Laura stepped back startled as a tall red-haired figure slid in swiftly, shutting the door tightly behind him. "Dennis Calhoun, what on earth?"

"Hush, Mavourneen. You'll hide a refugee from the wrath of the constabulatory, won't you now?" Laura reached toward the lamp and he stopped her quickly. "No, leave it out!" Far away in the road came the sound of riders, the faint murmur of voices, and a muffled oath. Then the sounds receded and Dennis let his breath out sharply. "It's all right now." He sank down in a chair at the kitchen table, and Laura pulled another out beside it.

"Dennis Calhoun, you tell me what this is all about!"

"A bunch of us fellows were riding South tonight to volunteer." Laura stiffened and Dennis put his hand swiftly over hers. "Ah, don't be like that, Mavourneen. I thought you'd understand! That's the side with romance, the side for gentlemen. And after the war's over, there'll be lots of opportunity for a young fellow in a brand-new country."

Laura flashed Carlie a panicky glance, and Carlie shut the hall door quickly. All they needed at that moment was to have Ben burst in, she thought, watching Laura shrink back as Dennis, still holding her hand, engulfed her in a flood of Irish eloquence.

"So there we were, off to the wars, when lo and behold the marshal got wind of it and decided to arrest us all. Chased us clear to Franklin and was nigh to capturing us when I bethought myself that I knew a golden-haired Southern angel here who'd not want me to be drawn and quartered. So I took the liberty of hiding my horse in your stable and here I am."

"We're not Southern," Carlie said clearly, since Laura seemed unable to speak. "Mama was born there. That's all."

"But I thought . . ." He looked at Laura and flashed his persuasive smile. "No matter. You'll not throw me to the wolves, will you, Mavourneen?"

"The wolves have gone now. It's safe enough." Laura suddenly realized where she was and flushed to the roots of her hair, pulling the neck-ruffle of her nightgown up high against her chin. "Dennis, you'll simply have to leave."

" 'Tis a cruel sendoff to give a gallant soldier!" Eyes twinkling, he swept her a gallant bow, raised her fingers to his lips as he had done at the dance, and as silently as he had come, was gone.

"Well, of all the . . . It's a good thing Ben wasn't here!" Carlie picked up the candle and started for the stairs. "Laura, are you coming?"

But Laura was standing staring at the door with a dreamy half-smile, pressing her left hand, the one he'd kissed, against her lips.

A wave of impatience swept Carlie. "It's a good thing

[ 84 ]

Mama's coming home. You're as bad as he is!" She banged the candlestick down on the table and went up to bed.

Ben, coming home from Hackensack the next night, was full of the story. "The dirty traitors! The marshal caught a few and slapped them in jail to cool off overnight, but most of them got away. Including our fine Mr. Calhoun! Good thing he hasn't been bothering you any more lately," he said darkly. Laura caught her breath, but Ben was too full of his own news to notice.

Others beside Dennis, it seemed, sided with the South. Some of the footloose younger men had dreams of glory; some, like Mr. Pryor, approved secession because they didn't like the idea of the government telling *anyone* what to do; others saw appeasement as the easiest way not to become involved. There was a name for these Northern Confederates now—*Copperheads*. It had an ugly sound.

Ben was all for writing an editorial denouncing them in no uncertain terms, but Mr. Baldwin had so far managed to hold him back. Wait until Mr. Benson returned, he counseled.

They still did not know when their parents would arrive. It was a good thing that they had left Washington when they did, Brad reported on Sunday morning, meeting Carlie on the way to church. The railroad linking Washington with the North had been blown up. And the atmosphere outside the church was turbulent. Tom Garrison's little brother had heaved a stone through a Pryor window, and Mr. Pryor was loudly threatening to horsewhip any Garrison who came within ten feet of his property line. Mr. Courtins, attempting to intercede peacefully, had almost come to blows with Mr. Garrison. It was with a feeling of acute relief that everyone moved into the church when the organ sounded.

The sun, pouring in the bare uncurtained windows, turned the whitewashed walls to gold. The air was full of the scents and sounds of April, but the atmosphere was solemn. The church was crowded. Little Mrs. Garrison looked gray, and Emily had been crying. The minister, rising to preach his sermon, looked stern.

The war had come, he said; it was an incontrovertible fact. It was too late now to pray for an amicable settlement and reconciliation. Therefore, the thing to do was to lay aside personal differences and unite in purpose. He quoted from the Gospel according to Saint Mark: " 'If a house be divided against itself, that house cannot stand.' "

He prayed for strength, endurance, and determination, and for a speedy end to conflict. After the final hymn there was a time for silent prayer, and then the benediction: *"The Lord bless thee, and keep thee, and give thee courage . . ."*

Carlie, who had been thinking of something else, found her thoughts pulled back sharply. It was not the minister's usual benediction, invoking the peace which passeth understanding. Now if ever, it seemed, would have been the time to pray for peace.

*"And give thee courage . . ."* It gave one cause to think.

# CHAPTER

## 9

Monday ushered in an eventful week. All telegraph lines out of Washington had been cut off on Sunday, the reason why no further news had got through. In Bergen County, the hysteria had subsided, after solemn church services everywhere, and had been replaced by a strong sense of purpose. It was no longer common, or even safe, to be undecided. The few well-known Copperheads, like Mr. Pryor, looked truculent or even carried pistols; the others paid lip service to popular sentiment. Bergen County was closing ranks.

A huge citizens' meeting was held in Hackensack on Monday, at which a Committee of Six, headed by the powerful Democratic leader Garry Ackerson, was appointed to provide support for any families who might be in need because husbands and fathers had enlisted. Ben, who had covered the meeting for the paper, came home keyed up and restless. Tom Garrison had been there in uniform, and the sight had been galling. "He's so afraid the war will be over before Papa gives him permission to enlist," Carlie told Brad with a sigh, meeting him when she went for the mail on Tuesday afternoon. She was not in a particularly good mood herself, having tried to cajole Ben into taking her with him on Monday and having been unceremoniously refused.

Brad laughed. "He needn't worry; it's not going to end that fast."

"The enlistments are for only three months."

"The war will hardly be started by then." Brad's eyes, meeting her startled ones, were sober. "A bunch of enthusiastic volunteers doesn't become an army overnight. It'll take three months just to train them. I've been South, Carlie, and I knew some Southern boys at school. They're all a combination of your brother and Tom Garrison, and they won't quit fast. If you could get your thick-headed brother to print some hard facts like that in the paper, it might do some good. We haven't begun to realize yet what a civil war really means."

They were starting to, though. At Dorcas League meeting that afternoon, the tension in the room was a tangible thing. The twice-monthly sessions, at which girls from the church met to sew for missions, were normally sociable times. Today the feuding that had erupted before church on Sunday morning had carried over to the second generation. Emily Garrison was outright rude to the Courtins girls, who'd been her good friends all their lives. Netta Courtins, who was sweet on Tom, was close to tears, and she in turn was cold to her demure little sister Jessie, who, in the inexplicable way that such things happen, worshipped Joe Pryor from afar.

Laura, by virtue of being eldest and prettiest, had always queened the circle; now Emily, in the reflected glory of Tom's enlistment, had usurped that position, and it did not help Laura's temper. She had a spat with Peter, coming home from prayer meeting Wednesday night, because he pointed out sensibly that he could not very well enlist and leave his widowed mother home alone.

"Why does he have to be so . . . *logical!*" she fumed.

"You'd think he'd want to do something to make me proud of him!"

"With your garter on his lance?" Carlie demanded. "This isn't the Middle Ages. This is real."

"I know it is," Laura said. "Every time I think of Dennis Calhoun going off that way, sacrificing everything for a cause he believes in . . . Peter would look just as handsome in a uniform."

"You won't think either one's so glamorous if he comes home with an arm or a leg blown off," Carlie snapped. "You can just thank your lucky stars that nobody's found out about that Dennis business, too."

Laura shrugged. "Oh, pooh! What could happen? I didn't *ask* him here!"

It was a good thing, Carlie thought silently, that Mama would soon be home.

By the weekend, with still no word, they had all grown edgy. In church on Sunday, Bess glanced over, saw that Mr. and Mrs. Benson's seats were still empty, and sank back as though all her strength were gone. The Saturday edition of the *Journal* had carried the notice of Mr. Baldwin's enlistment, and on Sunday afternoon he rode up to Beaufort to say good-by and to turn the keys of the office over to Ben's care. Laura made tea, and they sat on the veranda. The soft breeze was laden with the scent of lilacs, and war seemed very far away.

Mr. Baldwin, too, was surprised that their parents were not yet home. "I'll inquire about them in Washington as soon as we arrive, but by then they'll probably be here." He looked at Ben, solemn with the responsibility of the paper on his shoulders. "Sure do hate having to go off and leave you on your own, but it probably won't be for more than a few days. If you have to work late any night, go round and stay at my mother's. She'll be expecting you."

"I can manage," Ben said soberly.

Ben arose with the birds on Monday and rode off on Midnight before the sun was fairly up. He was wearing his best suit, heedless of the dangers of printers' ink. Carlie, chafing from having nothing to do, went back to school. The day was hot—unseasonable for April—and the long full sleeves of her cotton dress clung to her arms and shoulders. They would have to start working on summer clothes as soon as Mama was home.

Laura, too, looked warm, coming out to meet Carlie when she reached home after school. Her muslin dress was open at the throat and the sleeves were rolled up. Her hair clung in damp curly tendrils about her face. She had spent the day baking.

"Another nut cake, and a chocolate fudge. And I made cookies too, so the boys wouldn't pester for the others." She dropped down in a porch rocker and rubbed the back of her neck.

Ben came home late, looking hot and dusty, and waved toward them as he rode out back to stable Midnight. Laura pulled herself to her feet. "We'd better start dishing up, even if it will be a while before he gets finished fussing with that horse."

To their surprise, he reappeared almost at once. "Dan's taking care of Midnight, praises be. I'll be down as soon as I wash and change." His good suit, Carlie noticed, was a mess.

"How's the paper?"

"All right. Not as big as usual because there weren't too many ads today." Ben tossed it on the table. "Any news?"

Laura shook her head.

They ate quickly, for the house was hot from the baking. Then they went back onto the porch. The twilight was full of the scent of lilacs. "Mama's missing the prettiest part of the garden," Laura murmured.

They were still sitting there when Netta Courtins' little brother came up the path from the pond, bearing a note for Laura. She opened it wonderingly.

" 'Will Miss Benson please come over immediately on a matter of importance. J. Courtins.' What on earth?" Laura looked at the others blankly; then her face went white. "You don't suppose anything's happened?"

Ben shook his head. "They'd have sent for me. You want me to go with you?" he offered.

"Of course not." The color came back to Laura's face. "Aren't we sillies, always expecting trouble!" She buttoned her dress at the wrists and throat, smoothed her hair with her hands, and followed the little Courtins boy back down the path.

Twilight faded to darkness, the little boys went off to bed, the warm air turned cool, and Laura still had not returned. Somewhere deep inside Carlie, a tiny worry stirred.

Ben stood up. "I'm going over. Pa wouldn't like her out alone this time of night."

"Here she comes now," Carlie said in relief as the bushes rustled and Laura ducked under the overhanging maple tree. They both moved toward her. "What is it? Laura, what's the matter?"

"Uncle Henry!" In the darkness, Laura's face was gray and her lips were pressed together in a thin straight line. "The Consistory wanted to investigate the charge that I was walking disorderly!"

Carlie gasped. It was the most serious charge that could be levied against a member. "What on earth?"

"Stupid busybodies!" Laura's eyes were blazing. "Dennis wrote to me, to thank me for . . . everything. Our dear friend Mr. Winters at the store didn't think it proper for me to be receiving mail from the South, so he turned it over to Uncle Henry. And Uncle Henry thinks he's got some sacred responsibility for my character while Papa's gone. He wouldn't come here to talk to me himself, so he got the Consistory to do it for him!"

"I told you! You shouldn't have let Dennis in here that night." Too late Carlie remembered that Ben had not known, and Ben's reaction was all that she had feared.

*"Laura Victoria Benson, you let that dirty traitor . . ."*

"You just hush up!" Carlie said violently. "You want them to hear you clear over at Courtins'? Laura couldn't help it. He wasn't in the house ten minutes, and I was there the whole time."

"It's my politics they're concerned about, not my character," Laura said darkly. "If it had been their precious Tom Garrison, they'd probably hang a medal on me." She tossed her head. "Let's go to bed. I'm sick of it all."

"What did you do?" Carlie thought to ask.

"Oh, wept and almost swooned and said I'd been too terrified to tell, and I'd never, never do such a thing again. Mr. Pryor fell all over himself being understanding." Laura's tone was flippant, but hours later Carlie, waking in the night, turned over and found Laura's pillow wet with tears.

Carlie punched her own pillow, which had suddenly grown hard. Life, she thought uneasily, was rushing them too fast, propelling them into things for which they were not prepared.

She felt that more than ever the next afternoon when Peter Van Dirk, hatless, his customary calm vanished, walked into the house without knocking and demanded to see Laura at once.

"Peter Van Dirk!" Laura, embarrassed at being caught in an old housedress, was being haughty. "You know you shouldn't call when Mama's not home."

[ 92 ]

"Poppycock," Peter said bluntly. "I just found out about that nonsense last night. Laura, are you all right?"

Laura's face suddenly went pale, and Carlie's eyes shot sparks. "I suppose that nosy Netta Courtins was eavesdropping and blabbed to the whole . . ." She stopped incoherently, for Laura shuddered and Peter's arm went around her waist.

"It's all right, honey, I'm here. I won't let them hurt you." He held her closely, his face determined. "We're going to get married right away. They won't dare criticize you if you're Mrs. Van Dirk." Laura's shudders had stopped, and he might have won had he not, being Peter, added the final stroke of logic. "I knew you'd get in trouble if you got mixed up with that Calhoun. He's not your sort."

"Is that so!" Laura's head came up and her eyes were blazing. "At least he's in a uniform! When I do get married, Mr. Peter Righteousness Van Dirk, it won't be to somebody who proposes out of a sense of duty! And it won't be to somebody who's scared to get out and fight!" She stormed up the stairs.

"All right!" Peter yelled up after her flying figure. "I've put up with a lot from you, Laura, because I knew you were still young. But right now, young lady, you ought to be spanked! When you decide to grow up, you can let me know!" He stamped out of the house.

The whole town *had* heard, as small towns do. It also knew about Peter's fight with Laura and how, when Lincoln's call for three-year volunteers was announced on Friday, Peter was the first to rush off and join. His mother had gone to live with a sister in New York State, and the house was closed. The Van Dirk acres would not be farmed this year.

Carlie, passing them coming home from school, felt a little sick. She could not blame Laura, in a way; Peter's blunt proposal was not the sort that a girl like Laura dreamed about.

But the town elders, who regarded Peter as an estimable young man and fallow acres as a sin, were decidedly cold.

Laura scarcely noticed. She was in a strange, snappish mood all week. Maybe she does love Peter, Carlie thought, more than she admits. It was the only explanation she could think of.

She was so busy worrying about Laura that she almost forgot to be concerned over the fact that their parents still had not arrived. When, late Sunday afternoon, Mr. Pryor came to call and had a determinedly jovial manner in place of his usual truculence, they all were startled.

"Mr. Pryor, won't you sit on the veranda? It's cooler there." Laura's faraway mood, combined with her new pallor, gave her a queenly air.

"Thanks, don't mind if I do." Mr. Pryor eased his girth into one of the narrow rockers, ran his finger inside his tight collar, and smiled. "Just wanted to be sure you kiddies were making out all right without your pa."

Carlie saw Paul writhe from the despised appellation, and Ben's face turned dark.

"Very well, thank you, sir, and of course we expect Papa home again any day." Laura's voice was coolly courteous.

"That so, eh? Of course, of course." To their bewilderment, one of Mr. Pryor's eyes closed in a conspiratorial, friendly wink. "Well, if you need anything, let me know, and Josiah Pryor'll see you get it."

"I don't see how you're concerned," Ben began hotly, but Mr. Pryor, far from taking offense, rested a hand familiarly on Ben's shoulder.

"Come, boy, you have to keep up that bluff with some folks, but with friends it's not needed. We all know your pa's staying with the South, and I want you to know you've got lots of friends here to see you through."

Ben was about to explode into speech, and Carlie kicked

him sharply just as Laura rose and inclined her head with a regal nod.

"We appreciate your offer, Mr. Pryor, but I'm sure Father trusts us to manage on our own. I thank you kindly."

Something in Laura's manner brought Mr. Pryor to his feet. It even kept Ben silent until their visitor had lumbered down the drive and out the gate. Then Ben turned, his face black with anger.

"How could you let him get away with saying things like that? Don't you know what he's thinking?"

"Of course I know," Laura retorted. "And so will half the town if you keep on yelling! The Courtins are probably straining their ears right now." She closed her eyes a second and then went on, her voice deliberately calm. "Come inside. I think we'd better talk. Paul and Oliver, you come along, too."

They followed her silently into the library, and she shut the doors tightly before she turned around. "This came last Tuesday." She opened the secret compartment in Mr. Benson's desk and brought out a letter. "I didn't show it to you before because I didn't know how, but now I must."

"It's from Papa. But it's . . . it's from Carolina!" Carlie's voice rose to a squeak. Laura dropped wearily into a chair as Ben pulled the letter from the envelope. Carlie leaned over his shoulder, and they read in bewildered silence.

Ben put the letter down slowly. "I don't understand!"

"It's plain enough," Laura said quietly. "When Papa said he was taking Mama home, he meant *her* home, not here. He meant Carolina."

"Laura Benson, you don't think Mr. Pryor's right about Papa!"

"What else can we think?" Laura picked up the letter and read the paragraph aloud, her voice calm with effort. "Forgive us, and try to understand that we do only what we must. We love Carolina dearly and long to be with her. Our hearts are with her, and we trust that she is doing what is right. I am sorry that we must tell you in this way, but circumstance prevents any other. Benjamin, look after your sisters and try to take my place. Laura, take care of your little brothers. Remember that we love you all dearly, and remember, too, our discussion at dinner about what Paul had said. Papa."

Dimly, beneath the stunned surface of Carlie's mind, came an unhappy thought. *Papa's still angry with me.* There had been no message for her at all.

Ben had turned violently to Paul. "What did you say that night?"

"I don't remember!" Paul's face puckered with effort.

"You've got to remember. It's important!" Ben was shaking Paul by the shoulders, and Laura intervened.

"Don't, Ben! He can't help it." She knelt down in front of the boys, her face serious. "Paul and Oliver, look at me. We're not going to talk about this, do you understand? It's a . . . special secret, between us and Papa. He isn't coming home for a little while yet . . . because of the war, and we're going to forget all about it until he does. Do you understand?"

"Sure, Laura," Paul said awkwardly. He reached out and patted her shoulder. "We've forgotten it already, haven't we, Oliver?"

"Uh huh." Oliver stopped sniffling and looked up hopefully. "Maybe—can we have some chocklit cake?"

"You can have two pieces. Paul, you get it for him." Laura's tone was gay, but after they had gone, she stood for a long moment resting her head against the door.

Ben had picked the letter up again. "It doesn't sound like Papa."

"Oh, yes, it does," Laura said tiredly. "It's exactly the way he talks or writes when he's saying something important. You do it, too. Like a . . . a valedictory." She turned away abruptly.

Ben, studying the words again, drew his breath in sharply. "You know what I think? I think it's in some kind of a code! See what he says, about circumstances preventing any other way? There's some kind of secret message here, if we could just figure it out. That's it!" Ben's face had come alive. "He's doing some kind of secret service work! Jupiter, I wish I were there!"

Across the room, Carlie's eyes met Laura's. And people think I'm romantic, Laura's eyes seemed to be saying.

Perhaps, after all, it's women who are the realists, Carlie thought. Ben's idea was too wild even to be considered. But she knew, too, looking at his eager, excited face, that it was the only basis on which he could accept what had happened.

She couldn't share that feeling . . . and she didn't have to. Whatever Papa was doing, he believed that it was right. She knew, as surely as if she could hear him speak the words, that he must have good reason, and, for her, it was enough.

# CHAPTER

# 10

I<small>T WAS SURPRISING</small> what a difference *knowing* made. Uncertainty was the hardest thing to bear. Now they knew definitely that Papa and Mama would not be coming home, and the knowledge brought a certain quiet calm.

They stopped trying to keep the house in such pristine condition, and the boys again rampaged through the rooms. Laura stopped making festive desserts and returned to simple fare. She began going through *Godey's* for ideas for summer clothes.

"We'd better start on some next week, the weather's grown so hot. These muslins with bunches of cherries on them are pretty, aren't they? Ask Mr. Winters if he has some the next time you're over at town." After the storekeeper had given Dennis' letter to Uncle Henry, Laura had sworn she'd never set foot in the store again.

She skipped rapidly over the pages of exquisite ball dresses in lace and tulle. "It wouldn't be right, making things like that with a war on," she said. She did not add, nor did Carlie, that they would have no chance to wear them if they did. They were not likely to be invited anywhere at all.

The muslins were purchased, and some new corded lawn, as well as cambric for shirts for the boys. Carlie found she enjoyed plotting out the patterns on the ruled pattern-paper and fitting it to the cloth—it was, she discovered, rather like a problem in mathematics. She also, although she hated it, took over the set of shirts for Oliver, for it was obvious that there was too much for Laura to manage single-handed. They sewed on the back porch while the dinner simmered.

After the first few days, Ben didn't have to work so late. The paper was smaller than it had been when Papa was there. Advertising had fallen off—because of the war, Ben said. He was home by six-thirty, dusty and ink-stained in the sturdy work clothes he'd begun to wear, looking more like a farmer than the substitute editor of a county paper. After he washed and changed, he occupied the boys while Laura and Carlie dished up, and after dinner they sat on the side veranda and sewed while the boys played on the lawn and Ben read aloud.

They had not told anyone about Papa's letter, but the knowledge had traveled as such things do. Mr. Winters at the post office, Carlie surmised. And the Courtins had seen Mr. Pryor leave. Two and two had been added together and come out ten. If Franklin had been frosty to the Bensons heretofore, it was frigid now. Carlie endured two days of sitting between Emily and Netta at school, and then she stopped going. She couldn't do it, that's all.

"I can help with the sewing," she offered to Laura as her excuse for staying home. And Laura, though she knew how Carlie despised needlework, did not comment. After a few days, her staying at home was an accepted fact.

It took all the courage that all of them possessed to run the gauntlet of walking into church on Sunday morning. Oddly enough, it was Laura who was the most insistent that they do so.

"We're not going to act as if we're ashamed of Papa," she said forcibly, hooking her lilac silk as if girding on armor and tying on the leghorn bonnet she'd refurbished with velvet pansies and stylish new purple ribbons. She led the way into church with regal dignity, nodding graciously to the Garrisons and Courtins, ignoring the fact that they did not respond.

She had misjudged Laura, Carlie thought humbly, smiling at Mrs. Zabriskie, who had bowed cordially, a compassionate look in her gentle eyes. There was a strong fiber of steel beneath Laura's frivolous exterior, and if it had not shown before, it was because hitherto it had not been needed.

Laura even went to Dorcas meeting on Tuesday, although she came home with her lips pressed tight together and would not tell Carlie what had occurred.

"It makes me sick!" Carlie told Brad violently as he walked her home from the post office the next afternoon.

Brad looked at her. "How come you didn't go?"

Carlie wasn't going into that. "It's a good thing I didn't. I'd probably have slapped that Emily Garrison across the face!"

Those afternoon conversations, Carlie sometimes thought, were the only things that saved her sanity. They loitered, prolonging the short walk until it took a full half-hour. Sometimes they turned instead in the opposite direction, up the Clinton Street hill toward Zabriskie's Pond. They would sit under the willows at the water's edge, and Brad would let her talk until the impatience and frustration had all run out of her.

Even more galling, perhaps, than the cuts of the Garrisons and Courtins were the Pryors' overtures of friendship. Joe had even attempted to walk Carlie home from church on Sunday until Ben had made it pointedly clear his attentions were not wanted. The following Sunday it was Brad who circumvented Joe by the simple expedient of walking Carlie and Laura home himself.

Brad was also an invaluable source of information, because Judge Zabriskie had access to a great deal of national news and was willing to have some of it passed on to Ben at the *Journal*. It gave the paper a considerable edge over the other local ones, most of which depended on printing second-hand the bulletins that had appeared the previous day in the great New York papers. It was Brad who reported when the New Jersey brigade reached Washington and when railroads again linked Washington with the North. A Massachusetts battalion made up of railway men, en route through Baltimore to the capital, had decided to repair the railroads as they marched. It was Brad, too, who told Carlie when, on the twentieth of May, all telegraph offices in the North were raided by Federal agents who confiscated copies of all dispatches sent during the past twelve months.

"That's not for publication," he warned, "so don't tell Ben. The Judge thought you ought to be prepared because they're probably going to investigate everyone who's received cables from the South."

"I'm surprised anyone as prominent as the Judge can afford to worry about us," Carlie said.

Brad stopped and looked at her directly. "Cara, don't."

"Why do you call me that?"

"Because it suits you," Brad said. "Do you mind? Carlie's a child's name. Cara's more grown up. It sounds—gentle."

For some reason his words made her want to cry. "I haven't been very gentle lately," she said in a low voice. "I've been petty and spiteful, the way I was just now, and I don't mean to be. Laura isn't, not even when I snap at her. She makes me ashamed." She looked away toward the wildflower-fringed pond, and the green and gold colors blurred.

After a second Brad's arm went around her lightly, and they started walking again, not speaking. When they reached the foot of the path, Brad took her hands.

"It can't be much longer. Your parents will be here, and then you can let go."

"They aren't coming," Carlie said distinctly. "Not till I don't know when. There's something going on, that we don't understand . . . and we can't explain." The effort of telling had taken all her strength, and she closed her eyes.

"I'd heard something, of course," Brad said finally, "but I wasn't sure."

"Well, now you know." Carlie took a deep breath. "Now you'd better go, too, like everybody else, before you're contaminated!"

"Don't be silly," Brad said simply. He stood looking at her for a moment, as though wanting to say something comforting but not knowing how. Then, lifting both her hands, he pressed them to his lips.

It was the same thing he had done jokingly, that night at the dance, but this was different. She went up the path, her hands pressed tight against her heart.

A Federal agent did come to call, on Saturday morning when Ben was at home. He was a youngish man, with a military bearing and an impressive manner. Carlie, watching him produce a copy of Papa's telegram and an official notebook, was enormously glad that they had been forewarned. She was grateful, too, that Ben chose to remain in the background, standing against the library mantel, arms folded as he watched. Laura, in Papa's big chair, looked slight and ethereal, and the new dress of lilac corded lawn intensified her pallor, making her eyes appear startlingly blue. She answered questions with a quiet dignity that obviously softened the agent's official manner. When he was finished, he put the notebook back in his pocket with a little bow.

"Thank you. I regret having to disturb you in this manner, but I'm sure you will understand if we find it necessary to call again."

"There's no need for my sisters to be bothered," Ben spoke up. "You can find me at the newspaper office every day. A Union paper," he added significantly, and the agent smiled slightly.

"I know. I read your editorial on Tuesday. An excellent piece."

"Thank you," Ben said with dignity. "I try to write what I know my father would."

They saw the agent to the door with courteous formality, but once it was shut behind him, Laura's shoulders sagged. "Thank goodness that's over!"

"No more crises," Carlie said, deliberately cheerful.

Laura shook her head and looked around. "Come back inside. It's time for another talk." She waited until they were seated, looking at her questioningly. Then her mouth twisted slightly.

"How was the roast beef last night?" she asked irrelevantly.

"Fine," Carlie said, startled.

"You're getting to be a good cook, Laura," Ben said approvingly. "It was jim-dandy."

"That's good. Because you won't be getting it again for quite some time." She took a deep breath. "The money's gone."

"Gone?" Carlie repeated blankly, as Ben stared.

"It lasted a month longer than Papa expected it would have to. But I just couldn't stretch it any further. If only I hadn't bought that silk at Easter." Laura sighed. "And Mr. Winters isn't giving credit any more. He said so very definitely on the bill last week. Very sorry, of course, but circumstances of the war make it necessary, et cetera."

"Circumstances of war is right." Carlie snorted. "I'll bet he didn't cut off the Garrisons!"

"Thank goodness summer's coming and we have the garden," Laura said. "We can live off of that and the chickens, if we have to. But Paul and Oliver really need new shoes."

"Let 'em go barefoot the way the other children do," Ben said. "Now, Laura, I know Mama doesn't like it, but this is an emergency. And they've always teased to, anyway."

"I was hoping there was some money coming in down at the paper."

Now it was Ben who drew a deep breath. "I didn't want to have to tell you. It's the advertising that supports the paper, you know, not subscriptions. And it's gone way down. The contracts that expired weren't renewed, and we're not getting any job printing at all. I guess despite all those Union editorials I've been running, folks just plain don't like our smell."

"Ben!"

"No use trying to pretty it up," Ben said bluntly. "We're barely taking in enough to pay old Fritz."

"Merciful heavens," Laura whispered, staring at him out of eyes black with worry. Ben's face was dark. Carlie stood up quickly.

"At least we've got the garden. And the paper will build back up, once folks start reading the articles Ben's writing." She was talking very fast. "We don't need any more clothes. The boys will love going barefoot. We can last till fall, and by then everything's bound to be all right!" Deliberately she reached out both her hands and after a second Laura's responded, and then Ben's, and the family circle tightened.

Carlie was not altogether as certain as she had tried to sound; in fact she was not sure at all. She lay awake that night long after the rest of the household was asleep, staring out of the window as moonlight bathed the room with silver and the poignant fragrance of early summer drifted up to her on the soft night breeze.

The next morning there were circles underneath her eyes, and it was those, and not her new apple-green corded lawn, that Brad commented on as he walked her home from church. The roadside was alive with flowers now, and the woods around the little pond were appliquéd with dogwood's creamy lace, and bees hummed busily.

"They don't know Sunday's supposed to be a day of rest," Carlie said, watching them.

Brad was looking at her. "You don't look as if you've had any rest yourself. What happened to you yesterday?"

"Why should anything have happened?"

"Your eyes have black circles. I can always tell," Brad said calmly.

"Just a . . . minor crisis."

"Financial?"

She looked up, startled.

"I wondered how you were managing," he said when she did not respond. "I also wondered . . . Your house is so big—have you ever thought about taking in boarders? Mother wants to get Alison out of the city for the summer. She asked me if I'd look around for a place for them. I wanted to ask you, but I didn't know how."

"Why . . . I'd have to ask Laura." Carlie couldn't hide her relief, and she knew Brad saw it, for his own eyes crinkled mischievously. "It would be convenient, having a built-in chaperone," he said. "I could see you once in a while without always having to take you for a walk!"

As Carlie had expected, Laura greeted the suggestion with a sigh of relief. "There's the whole third floor standing empty. We could even fix the extra bedroom as a private sitting room."

"You don't think the extra cooking will be too much?"

"It will be worth it," Laura said expressively.

Immediately after dinner, she sat down to write to Mrs. Sturdevant, in her best handwriting, on Mama's finest vellum. The answer came back on Thursday, in a firm, slanting script. Mrs. Sturdevant was delighted with the accommodations offered, and she and her daughter would be arriving on Sunday because Brad would have the weekend off to help them make the trip. She was glad there was room for him to stay with them as well, and she was looking forward to meeting the family who had been such good friends to her son.

It was the other way around, Carlie thought soberly. What a good friend Brad had been to her, and how little she had been able to do for him in return. How little use she seemed able to be to anybody, for that matter. She was in a somber mood, for the mail had also brought a letter from Mr. Baldwin in Washington, telling them what they already knew. The Bensons had left the city shortly after Fort Sumter had surrendered, leaving no forwarding address.

"We'll just have to write in care of Mama's relatives and hope we reach them," Laura said, getting out ink and paper after supper that night. The next day was the last one on which mail would be allowed to travel South. They all wrote, in a sort of continual round robin . . . even Oliver, kneeling on pillows so he could reach the desk, frowning in concentration as Laura helped him trace the letters. When the bulky envelope had been sealed with wax, Ben put it in his jacket pocket.

"I'll post it in Hackensack. No telling what would become of it if we turned it over to Mr. Winters!"

Carlie had added her message with the rest, but afterward she was filled with a vague dissatisfaction. Long after they had gone to bed, when Laura was sleeping soundly, she was still uneasy. She slid out of bed, took the velvet-covered journal, and tiptoed soundlessly out onto the balcony between the pillars of the portico. The fragrance of the summer night assailed her and the moonlight made it bright enough to read. She riffled through the pages, finding there the stormy day when Bess had given it to her, the day secession news had come, the shock and pain of Uncle Henry's edict, the surprise of her parents' trip, the scene in the library with Papa, which still hurt whenever she remembered it. And the awful day the Fort Sumter news had come, when they had not known what had happened to their parents, and then Papa's letter, with no word for her. She sat for a long time looking out at the darkness. Presently she went inside, crept down to the library, and lit the lamp. Sitting down at the desk in her thin muslin nightgown, she took out pen and paper.

"Dearest Papa," she began, and then, the words once started, her pen raced across the paper. It was true, as Bess had told her once, that it was easier for her to write than to speak. It all poured out—the remorse, the regret, the good intentions—leaving her at last feeling at peace. When she was finished, she addressed the envelope and sealed it quickly, before she had a chance to feel self-conscious about it. She tucked the envelope into the pocket of Ben's jacket, beside the other, blew out the lamp, and tiptoed back upstairs.

# CHAPTER

# 11

T HE IMMINENT ARRIVAL of the Sturdevants threw them all into chaos. Laura had everyone up on Friday morning with the dawn. Before Ben left for Hackensack, he must first move furniture. The bedroom things in the room above Mama's were dismantled, and a small striped sofa was carried down from the garret. The rosy glass lamp from Mama's room was added, and a marble table, and a little desk. Carlie found a capacious inkstand Papa once had used. "It should be handy for a writer."

They stood in the doorway surveying the finished room. "It does look nice, doesn't it?" Laura asked uncertainly, her eyes traveling over the bright summer floor matting, the paper with its stylish pattern of ribbons and roses, the fresh white curtains. "I do hope they like it."

They made the beds carefully with Mama's best embroidered sheets. Carlie found a crocheted throw for the little couch in Alison's room, and Laura had vases lined up in the kitchen, ready to be filled with flowers on Sunday afternoon.

"You'd think," Carlie told Brad on Friday afternoon, "that

we were expecting Queen Victoria and the royal family." She said it lightly, for she was growing apprehensive.

Brad chuckled. "Don't worry so much about Mother, Cara. She'll love it here."

"Brad, tell me about them," Carlie said slowly, and Brad looked baffled.

"Heavens, who can describe his own family? Mother's just . . . Mother. I admire her more than anyone I've ever known. She has enormous calm. But when she really gets her dander up, watch out!"

"Do you look like her?"

"We both do, though Alison takes more after my father's people. Alison's tiny, but she's so tremendously alive that you don't realize it, any more than you do the other." Brad was silent, gazing across the amber-brown waters of the pond.

He had never referred to his sister's accident since that one time, and now, seeing the expression in his eyes, Carlie could understand why he was so gentle with her own soul-searchings. She put her hand lightly over his.

"I'm glad they're coming."

"So am I." He turned and grinned and swung her hand in a wide circle. "You'd better get home. With the tizzy Laura's in, she'll probably be sending the militia out to look for you!" He could not, of course, understand why the remark sent Carlie uncontrollably into giggles.

They reached the foot of the path, and Brad, turning to go, looked over his shoulder at the pond now swarming busily with summer life, with dragonflies hovering and soaring, turtles sunning themselves on rocks, and ducks sedately swimming. He turned back to Carlie.

"Just think, after tomorrow we won't have to admire the beauties of nature. We can sit in a parlor with a chaperone like a courting couple!" He said it mockingly, but there was an expression in his eyes that made Carlie blush.

[ 109 ]

What was it going to be like, she wondered suddenly, living in the same house together, having breakfast at the same table together, going up the same flight of stairs at night? Watching his familiar figure striding down the road, Carlie was filled with a confusion she could not—or did not want to—understand.

Sunday was hot, as hot as only June in Jersey could be, the air heavy with the scent of roses. "Let's hope the heat breaks," Laura said devoutly, "or they'll be dead before they get here!" The trip from New York was arduous, involving a flat-boat ferry from lower Broadway and then a hard ride north by carriage or oxcart.

They were so busy worrying about the Sturdevants' arrival that they scarcely noticed the usual snubs at church. They ate a hasty, makeshift lunch at the kitchen table. The boys, ordered to stay inside and not muss their Sunday clothes, were restless. Laura eyed them apprehensively.

"I do hope they'll behave," she murmured. "What with a writer and an invalid, they'll simply have to learn to be more quiet."

Probably they would all have to change their ways, Carlie thought, as Laura went back to the kitchen. She made a last quick tour of the upstairs rooms, cool and fragrant now with flowers in vases, windows open, and shades pulled down. How would they appear to the formidable Mrs. Sturdevant, who wrote both saccharine novels and trenchant political commentaries, who had lived in New York and traveled extensively abroad?

She went downstairs slowly, trying to see the house through strangers' eyes. The Persian carpet glowed in the downstairs hall. In the front parlor, the carved lacework of Mama's prized Belter furniture gleamed darkly. There were flowers everywhere . . . on the marble table, on Laura's square piano. There was rhododendron over the fireplace and in the open niches on each side of the archway, the fuchsia-edged white blossoms nestling against the glossy dark-green leaves like exploding stars. Through the open doorway came the familiar sounds from the pond, the hum of bees, and the warm fresh scent of summer.

Carlie pressed her cheek against the heavy carving of the door, and even the bumps and ridges were familiar. It was a part of her and always would be, and for the first time she could begin to understand how her mother must feel about that other Beaufort. How would she feel, if she were far from here, and these acres were in danger? Her eyes filled suddenly.

"They're coming!" Paul came clattering down the stairs, his voice high with excitement. "We saw 'em from the portico."

"Where's Oliver?"

"Changing his shirt. He's dirty," Paul remarked with satisfaction as Laura dashed in from the kitchen.

"He would be. Oh, dear!" Laura snatched off her apron, dusted Paul off with it, and stuffed it behind the nearest sofa-pillow as Oliver came charging down, his shirt flapping and his stockings sagging cosily around his ankles. Ben emerged from the library, pulling on his jacket. They converged on the veranda just as Brad galloped up ahead of the carriage. He looked tired and dusty, but his eyes, seeing the breathless group, were twinkling.

"Quite a reviewing stand!" He swung down and stuffed Oliver's shirt in for him before turning to open the carriage door.

A cold chill of misgiving swept through Carlie, and she closed her eyes. *Dear Lord*, she thought, *let this all work out!* Then a rich, vibrant voice said, "So this is Carlie!" and she understood why Brad had found his mother difficult to describe.

Queenly was the first impression she gave—that and a tremendous warmth. Mrs. Sturdevant was tall like Brad, with the same deep musical voice, expressive hands, and eyes like black cherries. Her black traveling suit was simple, deceptively so; a less sure hand would have added ornamentation and thus detracted from the richness of the silk.

Laura was moving forward to give the family's official welcome, Ben was helping Brad unload trunks and boxes from the carriage top, and the boys were everywhere at once.

"Carlie, you'd better show Mrs. Sturdevant upstairs." Laura, looking harassed, grabbed Oliver just as he prepared to climb to the carriage top. Mrs. Sturdevant's eyes twinkled.

"It might be strategic, hmm?" She followed Carlie inside, giving a brief comprehensive glance around. Carlie led the way up the two flights of stairs. In the sitting-room, so carefully arranged, Mrs. Sturdevant turned with a warm smile.

"How you must love it here," she said, and Carlie's heart melted.

"It's a copy of my mother's old home."

"I don't wonder she loves it so." Mrs. Sturdevant's words brought back Carlie's earlier thoughts; involuntarily she flinched and Mrs. Sturdevant saw her do so. She took off her bonnet, revealing smooth dark hair, and came over to rest her hands lightly on Carlie's shoulders.

"Brad has told me what you all are doing, to keep things going here. I cannot tell you how much we both admire you."

The expression in her eyes, so like Brad's, made Carlie feel suddenly shy. "I must go help Laura. Dinner will be served as soon as you're refreshed." As she went downstairs, Brad ran up past her at a breakneck pace, carrying his sister. She heard a high enchanted giggle and caught a brief glimpse of cloudy black hair.

In the kitchen, Laura, a pucker of concentration on her face, was dishing things up onto the best rose-patterned china. When the gong rang, Mrs. Sturdevant came down promptly, in a gauzy black gown, its low neck framed with a fichu of creamy lace. Her hair was coiled low on her neck and held in place with a tortoise comb. Brad, too, had changed into immaculate white linen. Alison, Mrs. Sturdevant said, would not be coming down. "She's exhausted, poor chick, though she won't admit it. I'll take a tray up later."

"I'll take it," Carlie offered. Later, when she had cleared the table, she fixed the tray carefully, adding a rose in a slender crystal vase. When she went through the hall, Laura was sitting at the piano. She could hear Brad's deep voice humming as she went up the stairs. Outside Alison's door, she stopped and knocked.

"Come in!" Alison's voice was like silver chimes. In the big bed, the tiny figure, propped up by a mound of pillows, seemed scarcely more than a child's. Out of a little dead-white face, framed by a gypsy cloud of hair, dark eyes glowed.

"Caralie!" She pronounced it with an extra syllable, making it a cross between Brad's endearment and Carlie's usual name, and held out both her hands. "Brad said I'd like you! Mmm, it's too pretty to eat! Oh, don't go, must you? Stay and talk!"

"For a little while." Carlie sat on the edge of the bed, smiling. "How was your trip?"

Alison rolled her eyes. "*Incroyable!* Have you read *Tale of Two Cities* by Mr. Dickens? Now I know how Marie Antoinette must have felt in the tumbril, only she lost her head at the end of her ride of course, poor dear, but we kept ours!" She sank back breathlessly against the pillows and smiled at Carlie.

Now, close up, Carlie could see what Alison's vitality had

obscured before: the way her dark curls clung damply at her temples, and how the thin cambric of her snowy nightgown rose and fell with her fluttering heart. She barely picked at her food, as though the fork were heavy. Carlie stood up quickly.

"I have to go now. I'll come back and visit more tomorrow."

Alison waved her fork gaily. "Promise?"

"Promise!" Carlie held the smile until the door had closed behind her—then, out in the hall, she leaned her head against the wall and closed her eyes. And we think we've got troubles, she thought. Yet Alison seemed to have not a shred, not the faintest iota, of self-pity.

It was surprising how quickly it became natural to have the Sturdevants there, to have Brad sitting next to her on the veranda in the warm June evenings, to have Mrs. Sturdevant coming down to dinner in her lovely trailing gowns, announcing gaily, "I'm going to kill my villain off tonight! What shall I use, poison? Or a dagger?" By Sunday it seemed as if they must have been there for months.

They caused quite a stir going into church on Sunday morning. Mrs. Sturdevant, in her black summer silk, seemed oblivious of the fact that she was the center of attention. Brad's face was Sabbath-day sober, but his eyes were dancing. Up in the Amen Pews, Uncle Henry surveyed them with a chilly stare.

"Which one's your uncle?" Mrs. Sturdevant whispered as they went down the aisle after the final hymn.

"The one with the tan whiskers."

"That one? Brr!" They had reached the entrance, and before Carlie could stop her, Mrs. Sturdevant had crossed the lawn and touched Uncle Henry lightly on the arm.

"Mr. Demarest? May I introduce myself? I'm Margaret Sturdevant. I'm staying with your nieces and nephews now, and I'm sure you'll be relieved to know they have someone older . . .' "

Uncle Henry had swept her a frosty bow. "Madam, I have no relatives in town." He strode off, leaving Mrs. Sturdevant staring after him in disbelief.

"When I put a character like that in a book, people tell me he can't be real!" Her black eyes snapped. "How much of this sort of nonsense is going on?"

Laura smiled mirthlessly. "Come to Dorcas League with me on Tuesday if you'd really like to see it."

"I'd be delighted," she said grimly.

On Tuesday afternoon, Mrs. Sturdevant came downstairs in a black barege gown with bunches of bright red cherries, more cherries on her black bonnet, and a workbag in her hand. She raised her parasol like a lance. "Ready?"

"Ready!" Laura responded with the hectic gaiety that Dorcas meetings always brought her lately.

Carlie, seeing the flush on Laura's pale face, spoke impulsively. "*Why* do you keep on going?"

"Because it doesn't do any good to run away," Laura said quietly.

Carlie looked at her, then said, "Wait for me. I'm coming too." She ran upstairs, flung her clothing on the bed, and pulled on the apple-green corded lawn. She splashed her face with water, smoothed her hair swiftly, tied on her bonnet, and gave herself a hasty survey in the glass. Her eyes were blazing black, and two pink spots burned in her cheeks.

"They'll probably think I use paint. Well, let 'em!" She seized the sewing basket Papa had given her and stormed downstairs.

The meeting was already in progress at the Garrisons' when they arrived. Emily, opening the door for them, looked startled. But even Emily, for all her daring, did not try to snub Mrs. Sturdevant, who was being as regally gracious as any queen. Conversation in the little parlor stopped sharply as they entered.

"Perhaps someone can read aloud while we sew." Emily, conscious of her responsibilities as hostess, spoke quickly. "Here, Netta, here's the latest Adelaide Somerville installment." She thrust a magazine into Netta's hands. Mrs. Sturdevant, intent upon her sewing, had the ghost of a smile about her lips.

When the story reached *To Be Continued*, everyone sat back with a sigh.

"I can't wait to find out how the story ends." Emily was talking past Carlie to Netta Courtins, and Carlie for the life of her could not help intervening.

"Why don't you ask her?" she suggested demurely, nodding her head toward Mrs. Sturdevant. "That's Adelaide Somerville. Or didn't you know?"

"Carlie, really?" It was Jessie Courtins' soft, awed voice, for Emily, to Carlie's satisfaction, was struck dumb.

Carlie nodded. "She's staying with us, you know," she said sweetly, "since Papa and Mama haven't been able to get back home."

Emily's eyes had narrowed. "How nice for you. I guess authors are very understanding. It must be such a comfort . . . especially now. I do think it's terribly brave of Laura to have come today."

"What do you mean?"

"Why, Peter Van Dirk was wounded yesterday." Emily looked up innocently. "Didn't you know? I thought you heard everything from Judge Zabriskie!" Distantly Carlie was aware that Laura's head had snapped up, her face dead white, as Emily rambled on. "I always thought Laura was kind of sweet on Peter, but maybe I was wrong."

"Emily, my dear." Mrs. Sturdevant stood up, holding out

her hand. "You must forgive us if we run. I've been away from my work too long already. Charming party, but I'm sure you'll understand."

She put a meaning little twist to the final word that Carlie would have relished had she not been too busy worrying over Laura. Laura moved like a sleepwalker as Carlie took one of her arms and Mrs. Sturdevant the other. Together they got her out of the house, down the path, and around the bend of the road before she began to shudder. She shook and shook as if she had chills.

"Oh, Laura! Laura, honey!" Carlie put an arm around her tenderly, but Laura swerved around.

*"Don't you talk to me!"* Her eyes were enormous. "You said this would happen, don't you remember? You said he'd come back with an arm or a leg blown off! I don't ever want to speak to you again!" She swept up her skirts and ran down the road, her breath coming in harsh, choking sobs.

"Let her go." Mrs. Sturdevant put a quick hand on Carlie's arm. "She needs to be alone. Now what is this?"

Breathlessly, Carlie told her. Mrs. Sturdevant looked sad. "So often we don't know we love someone until we've hurt them, and of course she feels to blame. Let her be, Carlie. She has to work it out on her own."

Back at the house, they found Laura nowhere in sight. Mrs. Sturdevant followed Carlie into the empty kitchen and tied on an apron calmly. "Mercy sakes, child," she said, over Carlie's protests, "we're not guests! I live here, remember?"

"Yes, but . . ."

"But me no buts, just go set the table!"

Brad and Ben, coming in, said they had heard the news. Ben's face was sober. "Is Laura around?"

"Upstairs. She knows. Emily Garrison," Carlie said succinctly. "I could just kill her!"

"Was it bad, Brad?" Mrs. Sturdevant asked quickly.

"Just a skirmish. Butler's men ran into some Confederates by accident, someplace in Virginia called Big Bethel. Neither side's ready for a real battle yet. But men got killed just the same." Brad's eyes were somber.

Laura did not come down to dinner. Much later, Carlie, going up to bed, slipped into the room quietly and began undressing in the dark.

"It's all right, I'm awake. I'm sorry I snapped at you, Carlie." Laura's voice came quietly through the darkness. "Did the boys hear anything?"

"Not too much. It wasn't an important battle." How ironic, Carlie thought, those words sounded! "Brad says the Judge is making inquiries."

"I made him go," Laura said. "He wouldn't have, if I hadn't made him feel ashamed. Because he hurt my pride!" She paused, and her voice grew quiet. "Peter's always been . . . *here*. I never knew how much it mattered. Then when Emily was talking, I suddenly thought . . . I wondered, what would it be like, if he *wasn't*, any more . . ." Suddenly she turned over and pressed her tear-wet face against Carlie's hand. "Oh, Carlie, I don't want to be grown up if it hurts like this!"

# CHAPTER

# 12

PETER HAD NOT BEEN BADLY hurt. Judge Zabriskie had checked with county leaders, and they had cabled a congressman who had sent back the word. "A leg wound, but not serious," Brad reported. "He'll be back with his regiment in about a week."

"He could have been killed," was Laura's only response.

June unfolded in warm sweetness, but none of them seemed to notice. Mrs. Sturdevant had reached a crisis in her current novel. Ben was spending more and more time at the newspaper office. Laura's housework went more slowly, and cooking in the kitchen became torture as the heat increased. It sometimes seemed to Carlie that she saw Brad even less now than she had before. And of course, in the back of everyone's mind lurked the trouble no one put into words—the fact that no further news had come from the South.

Surprisingly, although it was Papa she was closest to, it was Mama whom Carlie missed most now. Increasingly she was conscious of the feeling that she and Laura were being rushed into womanhood too fast. Carlie, waking in the night to find

Laura weeping, could only murmur, "Ah, Laura!" and pat her shoulder with pity. Mama, she thought, would have known exactly what to say.

"I'm so ashamed," Laura's voice was a bitter whisper.

"Of what, honey?"

"Of everything." Laura turned toward her. "Why doesn't anybody *tell* us?"

"I guess they can't," Carlie said, startled by her own wisdom. "I guess we wouldn't understand . . . not till it happens to us. It's like a secret language."

Love, she reflected, was very strange. It made you protect people—it made you hurt them. It made you do things that caused other things to happen. Their being on their own right now traced back to the fact that Papa could see two sides of the country's struggle because of his love for Mama, who was Southern. Laura's quarrel with Peter went back to the night she'd flirted with Dennis to get even with Emily Garrison for snubbing Carlie. *Cause and effect,* Papa would say. *Cause and effect.*

Carlie looked at Laura and said what she hadn't dared till now. "Why don't you write to Peter?" Laura did not answer, and suddenly helpless pity made Carlie cross. "I guess pride's a luxury we can't afford! I wrote to Papa." She hadn't meant to tell that but the words spilled out. "If you don't write to Peter, I will!"

As she had expected, that roused Laura. "Don't you dare!"

"Then you do it!"

For a moment they stared at each other through the darkness, and then suddenly Laura leaned forward and hugged Carlie hard. "Honey, what would I do without you? You're so strong!"

*Me strong,* Carlie thought incredulously, watching Laura fling a dressing gown around her shoulders and run downstairs. It was nice to know she was good for somebody, she thought drowsily, and settled herself for sleep.

She wondered, afterward, if she had been wise in giving Laura the advice she had, for Laura's face now wore a pitifully hopeful look that was heart-breaking to see. She had had no answer yet to her letter. Carlie went for the mail each day just before supper, for it was cooler at this later hour, and also she could meet Brad coming home. They walked slowly, side by side, not touching, prolonging the short distance because she hated going in to face Laura with empty hands.

"She'll hear," Brad said reassuringly. He knew all about it, having seen that Carlie was troubled and pried the reason for it out of her. "It just takes time."

He held the branch of the maple up for Carlie to duck under as they went up the path, and as they did so a small breeze sprang up from across the pond. Carlie straightened and took a deep breath. "How good it feels. That's what we all need—a fresh breeze to sweep us clean."

As they went in to early supper, the breeze continued, lifting the striped silk hangings at the dining room's open windows. Mrs. Sturdevant came down in one of her low-necked black gowns, her heavy hair lifted off her neck in a velvet net. "I've finished my opus, and I can't tell you how good I feel!" She glanced at Laura with probing eyes, but her voice was gay. "If you can stand it, suppose we go out on the veranda after supper and I'll read the end aloud."

Mrs. Sturdevant, though she approached her work most seriously, regarded the result of her labor with anything but a sober manner. She read dramatically, interpreting the dialogue with great exaggeration.

Alison, lying in the hammock, clapped her hands. "I do think your stories are better than a play!"

Brad glanced across the lawn. "Looks as if we're having company."

"We are?" Laura looked up, startled, as a tall figure hesitated between the gateposts, then started toward them, limping slightly. The color came and went in her face so fast that Carlie thought Laura would faint. *"Peter!"* Half-stumbling, half-sobbing, she was down the steps and running toward him, her full blue skirts billowing out until the bushes around the veranda hid their meeting.

"I think it's time we all retired." Mrs. Sturdevant stood up and blew her nose briskly. Brad picked Alison up and started for the stairs. Over them all a quiet had fallen. Carlie, going into the kitchen, stood for several moments resting her head against Mama's old green apron hanging from the cellar door.

When she went back inside, Peter was established in state in Papa's chair. Laura, sitting on its arm, lifted a radiant face.

"Where's Mrs. Sturdevant? Tell her to come down. Peter can give her some first-hand information for her writing." There was a new proprietary pride in Laura's voice that Carlie had never heard.

Mrs. Sturdevant came down, and so did Brad and Ben. It was a very gay evening, and it continued long past midnight.

"When do you have to start back?" Brad asked Peter as he started for the door at last.

"Sunday morning."

"The day after tomorrow!" Laura's voice caught.

"I wish I could take you with me," Peter said simply.

*"Why can't you?"* The words seemed to come from nowhere, and Carlie was startled to realize it was her own voice speaking. Everyone stared at her, and the expression on Laura's face was one that she would not soon forget. Peter turned to Laura quickly.

"I asked you once before. Mr. Ryerson would marry us tomorrow. Would you, Laura?"

"Why, I . . ." Laura's face was filled with both hope and

fear. She put her hand out beseechingly. "Mrs. Sturdevant . . ."

"Dear, are you sure?" Mrs. Sturdevant searched Laura's
eyes deeply, then she bent forward suddenly and kissed her
gently. "Bless you, child, I don't see why not."

"But how can I? You all, the house . . ."

"We can manage here," Carlie said stoutly. She looked at
Laura, and her own eyes brimmed. "Honey, sit down and
catch your breath! We got Mama ready to leave in a single
day. We can do it again now!"

Never, Carlie thought, could there be such a Saturday
again. They were up so early that the lawn was still silver
with the dew and the birds had not yet begun their morning
songs. Laura's clothes were sorted out: the new pansy-printed
muslin and lilac lawn, last year's blue organdie, petticoats, and
nightgowns that must be swiftly washed and ironed. How
fortunate that Laura had always liked dainty things. They
looked bridelike, even though they were not new.

She was to be married in her Easter lilac silk. Mrs. Sturdevant contributed an exquisite shawl of creamy lace. "Every
bride should have something old. Take it—it would make me
happy." She also loaned a capacious portmanteau, and she and
Carlie packed it while Laura made her own chocolate-fudge
wedding cake. "It's not traditional, but it's Peter's favorite,"
she said firmly, icing it with rich brown swirls.

Peter had gone off to see the minister. Out in the barn,
Daniel was dusting off the rusty black coat that was his Sunday best. Carlie packed the house with flowers. Bridal wreath,
deep-red and blush-pink roses—she piled them into the fire-
places, the arches, the window niches. She worked swiftly,
intent upon her task, trying not to think of the fact that Papa
and Mama were not there.

How different it was, she thought poignantly, from the

kind of wedding Laura had always planned. But even so, it was tender and solemn. There were no guests, only the minister's wife and the Zabriskies, who had come at their own request. Brad had come home early, and so had Ben, to change into white linen suits. Carlie wore her blue-gray silk. Alison lay on the sofa, and Mrs. Sturdevant was at the piano. Paul and Oliver looked awed and solemn. Old Daniel had a flower in his buttonhole, and his one earring gleamed.

Afterward there was chicken salad and cake, and toasts and laughter, and even dancing as Mrs. Sturdevant played on the square piano and twilight fell.

Laura and Peter were to spend the night in Hackensack's Mansion House and start for Washington in the morning. Peter had hired a rig from the livery stable, and Brad and Ben helped load on Laura's bags.

Laura started down the steps, then turned back suddenly. Carlie ran to meet her, and they clung together.

"Honey, I'm leaving you with such a lot." Laura's eyes searched Carlie's face. "I'll see if I can find out anything in Washington and let you know. Take care of things."

"I will, I will. Don't worry." They hugged again, hard, and then Laura stepped up into the carriage and rode off at her husband's side.

Mr. Ryerson's announcement of Laura's marriage, in church the next morning, caused a stir. All over the congregation, heads were craned, breaths let out in audible gasps. Uncle Henry's face was impassive, but Bess sent over a swift, happy glance. The general opinion, Carlie well knew, was that Laura had been luckier than she deserved. When the service was over, Carlie swept out with her head held high.

"So Laura's married! Well, well! Spunky little thing." It was Mr. Pryor, beaming affably. Carlie nodded distantly;

then, as he moved away, she straightened, struck by a sudden thought.

"Mr. Pryor!" When he turned, she went toward him quickly. "You said we could come to you if we wanted anything." They had moved into relative privacy under a chestnut tree and she looked at him directly. "It seems a shame Papa and Mama don't even know that Laura's married."

Did he understand? Yes—he smiled and nodded. "Does seem so. Well, you never know. Mighty strange how word does get around." He saluted and left and she started down the road.

Ben was waiting, glowering darkly. "Why were you talking to him?"

Carlie took a deep breath. "To see if he could get word through to Papa about Laura. The Copperheads have all kinds of ways, they say. It didn't seem right not to let them know."

"Do you think they'd care?" Ben asked grimly. Carlie stared at him.

"*Ben!*"

"*Well, do you?* Don't you think if they did, they'd have got word through to us somehow by now?" Ben looked at her intently. "Maybe we've been wrong about a lot of things."

"Why, Ben." She was shocked, and she searched frantically for the only comfort she could offer. "What about the secret mission? You said it was so clear, don't you remember?" She put her hand on his arm, but he jerked away.

"I don't know any more. I just don't know!"

It seemed strange not having Laura there for Sunday dinner, and the responsibility for preparing that whole meal was much greater than Carlie had dreamed. Fortunately there were plenty of cakes and biscuits still on hand, but after today those, too, would be up to her. She felt suddenly overwhelmed by the enormousness of the task that lay before her. Keeping house all alone for seven people!

By the time dinner was on the table, she was exhausted, and afterward the thought of dishes was more than she could face. But she had to face them. She lifted the kettle from the stove and filled the dishpan. Ben was out on the front porch talking to Brad, and Mrs. Sturdevant was writing letters. Alison was lying down. Carlie sighed. She was no closer to knowing Alison than she had been on the first night she came.

She was scarcely finished cleaning up from dinner when it was time for supper. She sliced tomatoes and cucumbers, heated the leftover biscuits, and opened a jar of jam. After the wedding's excitement everyone was enervated and subdued. Carlie recognized the signs of Ben's being on the verge of an explosion, and though it tried her patience, her heart still ached. Poor Ben, she thought soberly, if he's lost faith in Papa, things are really bad.

When the meal was over and the dishes done, she went upstairs, pulled off her clothes, and, not bothering to wash, threw herself across the bed. She lay there, listening to the birds twittering sleepily in the twilight, feeling the soft breeze blow across her body, and presently, without meaning to, she fell asleep.

When she awoke, the house was dark and silent. She rose, feeling as if she'd been drugged, pulled on her nightgown, and got back into bed. It seemed strange not having Laura there beside her. She tossed and turned, hearing the grandfather's clock in the foyer strike two. After awhile she sat up, lit the lamp, and taking out journal, pen, and ink, she lay across the bed on her stomach and began to write.

"Car-a-lie?" The whisper was so soft that she thought she had imagined it until it came again. She stared up at the register in the ceiling.

"Alison?"

[ 126 ]

"Mmm-hmmm. If you're not sleeping, come on up!"

Alison was sitting up in the big bed, propped by pillows. She was wide-awake and glowing.

"What are you doing awake?" Carlie demanded.

Alison shrugged. "I never sleep. I saw your light and knew you were up, too. Come sit down! What were you doing?"

"Oh . . . writing. I guess we're all still wound up from the wedding."

Alison hugged herself dreamily. "Do you suppose," she chanted, "there might still be some of that delicious cake?"

"I'll get it," Carlie said and groped her way downstairs. Remembering how little dinner Alison had eaten, she added a pitcher of milk and two glasses, and, after foraging, soda biscuits, a chunk of cheese, and pickles. She carried the tray upstairs triumphantly.

"Spoils of war!" she announced, then winced. Why was it everything made one think of war these days!

Alison glanced at her sharply, but her voice was light. "Oh, lovely, lovely! Let's divide!" She switched in dizzying succession from pickles to milk to cake, licking her fingers like a child.

Carlie watched her in amazement. "I never saw you eat so much!"

"Things taste better at night. Everything comes alive more after midnight." Alison put her hand up suddenly. "Listen!" They sat, scarcely breathing, and outside the window came the sounds of the nocturnal world: the splash of the pond, a moth beating its wings outside the window, a faint breeze in the treetops. Alison stretched and sighed. "I love the night. I think in some other incarnation I must have been a cat. A coal-black cat, in Egypt, with emerald eyes." Her mood changed like quicksilver. "But it's not all soft and velvet, is it? You couldn't sleep. Why not?"

"I . . . just wasn't sleepy," Carlie said evasively.

"It's more than that." Alison's voice was gentle, amazingly like Brad's. Her childlike manner had vanished.

Carlie took a deep breath that was almost a shudder. "I guess I'm just . . . worried." She looked at Alison directly. "You know . . . about our parents?"

Alison nodded. "My heart hurts for you," she said simply.

"We haven't heard from them except once, and it seems so long. Sometimes I don't know how to keep on going." Suddenly the tears that had not come earlier spilled forth. Alison's arms went around her, and she could feel the gentleness of Alison's hands as they stroked her hair. After a moment Carlie straightened. "I'm sorry. I didn't mean to do that. It's just that . . . now even Ben's losing faith. I'm not; I believe in Papa, but sometimes it even seems as if that may be wrong."

"Poor Carlie." Alison caught her hand. "I'll make a spell for you, shall I? I can, you know. I'm half a witch. What is it you're supposed to say? Abracadabra?" When Carlie did not laugh, Alison's elfin face softened. "Carlie, don't worry. It's going to be all right." Her eyes looked dreamy, as if she were seeing distant things. "It's going to be all right," she repeated.

In the realistic light of day, the memory of Alison's confidence still lingered comfortingly in Carlie's mind, and she needed that comfort, for otherwise life was grim. June was drawing to a close in waves of heat. Ben was tense and irritable, given to flaring up at the slightest provocation, and she was not as adept at preventing his outbursts as she should have been, for she was very tired. Washing, ironing, cleaning—household responsibilities multiplied before her. And there was the interminable round of three meals a day, prepared in a kitchen that was like the legendary fiery furnace. She was not giving Paul and Oliver enough attention; she alternately ignored and scolded, and they were running wild. She even snapped at Brad when he ventured to suggest a walk around the pond, and he rapidly withdrew.

It seemed the only peaceful moments she had were the nighttime visits to Alison's room, for these had become a ritual. Alison's moods diverted Carlie, and her unspoken sympathy was reassuring. Her wild imagination had seized on Ben's notion of a secret mission, and she invented thrilling explanations that sent Carlie into bursts of laughter. Alison, for all her childlike manner, had a surprising depth and maturity of understanding.

"I suppose," Carlie thought, "it's because she's suffered."

She asked Brad about Alison's condition, and Brad looked sober. "Her back's healed now, except that she has to wear a brace, but the doctors never discovered what caused the paralysis. Mother and I were hoping that getting her out of the city would give her more incentive to come back to the world, but it hasn't seemed to. It isn't good for her to shut herself off so much the way she does. By the way, speaking of getting out, Paul tells me there's a town picnic tomorrow to celebrate the Fourth."

"I . . . hadn't planned to go this year."

"Oh, come on!" Brad scanned her face with penetrating eyes, but his grin was persuasive. "It would do Mother and Alison both good to get out, and Alison won't go unless you do."

His argument was unanswerable, and she capitulated reluctantly. That night, instead of going up to Alison's room, she went down to the kitchen, lit the lamp, and began to work. She fried chicken, made biscuits, and baked two cakes. When she was finished, she carried some of the cake upstairs.

Alison was bursting with excitement. "I've never been to a picnic! Will everyone be there, and will I meet your friends?"

"It's not so much," Carlie said evasively. Mentally she prayed for rain.

On Thursday morning, however, there was not a cloud in sight. Long before three o'clock, carriages, ox carts, and families on foot were turning into the Courtins' drive to go to the big lake behind their farm where the picnic was held. The Benson party went in state, in the four-seater, with Alison and her mother in the back and Daniel seated with dignity up on the box. Their appearance was greeted by stirs and turnings and a remark from the Garrison family about barbarians who still owned slaves.

Ben's lips tightened, and Daniel snorted and spoke audibly about "Po' white trash what can't afford none." Emily Garrison flushed, and Alison, with swift tact, diverted Ben by requesting that he lift her down. They spread the picnic cloth on the shore beneath a willow. The boys promptly disappeared to go wading. Mrs. Sturdevant took out her tatting, and even Alison produced embroidery. Her needlework was exquisite. Ben went off in search of wood, and Brad brought out a book and began to read aloud.

He broke off suddenly. "Isn't that Oliver crying?"

Carlie, laying out the picnic food, looked up sharply. Oliver was stumbling up the bank, soaking wet. Paul, trying to hush him, had an eye that was rapidly swelling and growing black. Carlie and Brad ran toward them.

"What happened?"

"Neddy ducked me," Oliver wailed, and Paul turned warningly.

"Oliver, you hush!"

"I think you'd better tell us," Brad said calmly.

Paul answered reluctantly. "The fellows ducked Oliver, and Neddy Garrison called Pa a name." He turned to Carlie, earnest and solemn. "I had to fight, Carlie, honest. I couldn't let him call Pa a dirty traitor."

Deep within Carlie, anger grew so swiftly that it would have exploded had Brad's hand not come down warningly on hers.

She had tried to run away from facing things, but when this unpleasantness reached the children it was too much.

There comes a time, Papa had said, when you realize you can't run any more—when you've got to turn around and dig in your heels and fight.

For Carlie, the time was now.

# CHAPTER

# 13

CARLIE ROSE the next morning with her mind made up, and the difference was amazing.

She had been awake late the night before, not talking with Alison but lying in her own bed in the darkness, thinking. For the first time, she began to understand what her father had tried to tell her on New Year's Day. There was a difference between fighting *against* things, the way she'd always done, and fighting *for* something—and she had something to fight for, now.

It was all tied up with the family blessing . . . *keep us safe for one another*. She must keep Papa's name honored and keep them all together. Not just together, she thought firmly, but with their spirits high. There could be no more self-pity, doubting, and hiding their heads in the sand.

After she dried the breakfast dishes, she immediately set the table for lunch. She went into the garden and gathered vegetables for dinner before the sun was high, washed them, and put them in kettles ready for the stove. It was astonishing what a help it was just having those two things done ahead.

Later, going to the springhouse for milk and butter, she made another discovery. The little stone house by the brook was heavenly cool. She went back to the house, brought over the little cane-seated kitchen rocker and a straight-backed chair, and surveyed the results with satisfaction. Tomorrow she would have Ben bring a drop-leaf table from the attic. They might even eat lunch here on the hottest days.

Ben brought the table, and Brad, coming out to see, had a further suggestion—dam up the brook and make a real place to swim. The little boys were enchanted. Even Mrs. Sturdevant came, bringing pens and paper; it was, she said, an ideal place to write. Carlie sat in the little rocker to string beans for Sunday dinner and watched Paul and Oliver wading while she worked.

Sunday morning she set the table, fixed the vegetables, and mixed a salad before she left for church. It was wonderful having almost everything ready to serve when she got back home, and, at church, she scarcely noticed the Garrisons and Uncle Henry.

On Sunday evening, when everyone else was in bed, she sat down at Papa's desk and made three lists. One was of unavoidable tasks that must be done. The next was of things she wanted to correct. The third, suggested by a hymn at church, was to count her blessings.

She listed those blessings down the right-hand side of the paper, opposite the list of burdens which she knew so well she scarcely had to write them down. Her blessings were more numerous than she had realized. They were managing to keep the household going. They all were well. Alison seemed to be improving—although she still should be downstairs more. That was on the list of things to do. More blessings: the money coming in from the Sturdevants, Mrs. Sturdevant herself, the fact that she herself was better organized and her cooking was improving. And last, but not least, Brad. Brad.

She finished the list, smiling, and went to the kitchen to start the week's baking. When the bread dough had risen and the pies were in the oven, she pumped water into the tubs and put the clothes to soak for tomorrow's wash. She had discovered that she loved to work when the house was dark and quiet. It became a ritual, ending in Alison's room with fresh-baked cake and milk.

She didn't get much sleep that way, of course, but she made up for it by taking naps in the afternoons. Afterwards she bathed and dressed and walked over to town to meet Brad coming home. It helped her disposition enormously to have that walk to look forward to all day.

She dressed for dinner nowadays. After seeing Alison's exquisite needlework, she had carted an armload of old summer clothes upstairs and asked for suggestions on how to make them over. Alison's hands were deft, cutting necklines low, finishing them with the fashionable new fichus shown in *Godey's*. Carlie felt self-conscious in them at first, but the low necks and tiny sleeves were undeniably cooler, and their festivity lifted her own morale. Soon Ben, too, began putting on a white suit for dinner, and Alison, lying on the dining-room sofa, or even sitting in an easy chair, looked like a beautiful fairy in her delicate lacy wrappers.

In what Carlie regarded as a major triumph, she had succeeded in getting Alison to come downstairs every night for dinner. She had put it on the basis of a personal favor. "You tell stories so well. If you would keep the boys out of my way while I serve and clear, it would be such a help." The boys were fascinated by her tales and rewarded her with obedience and absolute devotion. Following dinner, after Carlie had cleared the table and they had all sat on the porch until the air was cooler, Brad or, increasingly, Ben, carried Alison into the kitchen. Ben had a gentleness with Alison that he never showed in his own family circle. He had repaired the three-legged sofa and brought it down, and she lay there while Carlie did the dishes and Brad or Ben read aloud. Ben brought home a copy of *The Bigelow Papers*, and Alison's enchanted laugh rang out through the gathering night.

Even dishes weren't bad, if you had company while you worked.

Letters came from Laura in Washington. The city was hot, she wrote, and overcrowded. They had found a room in a boarding-house, and she was working with the Women's Sanitary Commission making first-aid supplies. "Why doesn't the Dorcas League start work for Soldiers' Aid?" she asked. Her landlady was openly Southern, and she hoped through her to get some news of Papa and Mama, but had had no luck. A later letter brought further news. Some troops from Peter's company had been ordered to a little town in Virginia, called Manassas.

"There's something building there," Brad commented as Ben folded the letter after reading it aloud on the veranda after supper.

Ben nodded. "Something has to happen soon. Those first three-month enlistments are almost up."

"They'd be fools to try anything. The army's not half ready."

"Are we supposed to just sit back like cowards? Since when have you been a military authority?" Ben's outburst was so hot and unexpected that everyone was startled. Alison's mouth was open with astonishment. Ben pushed back his chair and stamped into the house.

Carlie followed him into the library and closed the door. "Ben, what's the matter?"

Ben was ruffling through papers he'd brought home with him. "Nothing. He just gets me so mad, always knowing everything first."

"It's more than that." She felt suddenly shaky. "Not . . . not Papa?"

"No, they're all right—at least for all we know." His voice held bitterness, and something more.

She went toward him quickly. "Ben, tell me, please. It's worse, not knowing."

"I didn't want to have to." Ben put down the papers. "I got the tax bill today. I knew it would go up, because of having the army to pay for, but not this much." He sat down at the desk and she saw how weary he looked. "I've been out all day trying to sell ads, but I only got three."

"There's the Sturdevants' board money."

"That won't begin to cover it." His face looked strained. "Seems the property's been reappraised. Guess they couldn't bear the thought of Copperheads living in such style! If we can't pay, the place'll be sold for taxes."

"How much?" Carlie asked faintly.

"A hundred dollars."

"Ben!" They stared at each other.

"We'll never get it together, not in a million years."

"We'll manage somehow. Papa may come home, or . . . or we'll think of something. Only don't, don't lose faith!"

"*In what?*" Ben flung at her, his face dark with anguish. "I don't believe in anything any more!" He jerked away from her, staring moodily out of the window, and she knew that there was nothing she could say. She slipped out quietly, closing the door behind her.

In the kitchen she found Brad waiting. Alison had a headache, he said, and wanted to sleep, and his mother had gone upstairs to work on her column. He had water already heating on the stove. He had brought a book of poetry to read from, and he sat on the edge of the table while she scraped and washed and dried the dishes. Some of the poems were tender

[ 136 ]

and it would have seemed romantic, just the two of them, but tonight she scarcely noticed.

When they were finished, she said good night absently and went upstairs, but she did not even try to sleep. She wandered restlessly, her mind going in circles, unable to stop thinking of the money so unexpectedly and urgently needed. Even the thought of having to leave Beaufort made her feel sick inside. She picked up one of Laura's magazines and flipped through it carelessly, wrinkling her nose at the lurid stories. Then, just as she put it down, a notice on the back cover caught her eye. The editors were holding a contest for the best story submitted by a reader, and the prize was fifty dollars.

"Half the tax money." The thought struck her immediately, though she was afraid to put it into words. She could write something as good, or better, than this trash. She scanned the pages again and then, before self-doubt could creep in, reached firmly for pen and paper.

Part of a poem that Brad had read came back, providing her with character and setting. She wrote rapidly, feverishly, until she could keep her eyes open no longer. The next day, Saturday, she shut herself into the library and continued, barely taking time out to prepare the meals. She finished shortly after ten that evening, read it through swiftly, and set to copying it neatly. When she was finished, she folded it into an envelope, sealed and addressed it, and set it aside to mail. She did not intend to let Ben see it and risk his scorn.

It was now past midnight, and she was spent with effort, but she was too keyed up to sleep. Alison had not come down to dinner, for her head still ached, but Carlie tiptoed up to the third floor on the chance that she would be awake. Alison's light was out, but her voice came through the darkness.

"Caralie? I'm awake. Come in."

Her voice was odd, and when Carlie lit the lamp she knew from one glance at Alison's averted face that she'd been crying. She went to her quickly. "Honey, what is it? Are you sick?"

"No. Oh, no." Alison's voice faltered, and Carlie felt her forehead.

"You do have a fever. Tell me what's the matter."

"You'll laugh at me."

"No, I won't. I promise." Carlie sat down on the bed and Alison turned an anguished face toward her.

"Carlie, something's going to happen. I can feel it inside."

Despite her common sense, Carlie felt a chill. "What do you mean—happen? Here, to us?"

"No. No, I don't think so. But it's something big. Like Sumter. I knew about that, too, but I didn't tell anybody because they'd have said I'm crazy." Suddenly Alison started to sob. She gazed at Carlie, her face white and stricken, and Carlie hugged her tightly.

"Honey, don't. You'll make yourself sick. Don't think about it, and try to sleep. I'll put the light out and sit with you until you do."

The next morning in church, she prayed not only for a solution to the tax problem and for Papa and Mama, but for the country and the course of the war as well. She was troubled, more than she would have wanted to admit, by Alison's fancies.

Sunday was a day of burning, oppressive heat. They all felt it; Ben was closeted in the library and Mrs. Sturdevant was lying down. Alison's head still ached and the boys were fractious. Monday brought drenching rain, but no relief, for the air was hot and muggy. But heat or no, Carlie baked, for she was hostess to the Dorcas League on Tuesday. She had issued the invitation at the previous meeting, in the first flush of her new resolutions, and she was glad now that she had, because the meeting would take Alison's mind off her fancies. She got down Mama's best eggshell cups, washed them, and put them ready on the sideboard. She polished the silver tea set. She intended to offer a choice of tea or raspberry punch, and three kinds of cakes—no one was going to find anything to look askance at in Beaufort's hospitality.

Commencing to mix a cake, she discovered that the baking-powder can was empty. She glanced out of the window. The rain was now only a faint mist. She could go to the store and meet Brad coming home. She flung a scarf over her head, picked up her purse, and stepped outside. Picking her way carefully, she held up her skirts and stepped around the puddles in the muddy road.

To her surprise there was a knot of people around the store, not draped idly along the bench on the narrow porch, but standing silently around the bulletin board nailed to a post beside the steps. The board was customarily filled with old notices of auctions and church socials, but there was a new notice now. She could just catch a glimpse.

### Union Defeat in Virginia

She stood on tiptoe, trying to read over the shoulders of the men, when someone touched her arm.

"Come away." It was Brad. He led her back toward the corner, away from the store. "Some of the men have been at the tavern and they're in an ugly mood."

"Brad, what happened?"

"There was a battle, a big one, at Manassas."

"Manassas—that's where Peter is!"

"Don't worry, he's all right, or you'd have heard. But Tom Garrison's been badly hurt. The telegram just came through."

"Oh, Brad."

"What did you want at the store? I'll get it for you." Brad turned back, and she waited at the corner till he rejoined her. They walked in silence, but when they reached the pond, he looked at her directly. "The Garrisons and some of the other hotheads are taking this pretty hard, and it may not be pleasant. You'd better stay out of things for a few days, and for goodness sake make Ben do the same. Don't walk over to town. And maybe you'd better call that tea party off tomorrow."

"I can't. It's not a social meeting. Anyway, we haven't done anything."

Dinner that night was shadowed by the news of the defeat. Mrs. Sturdevant looked grave, and Alison's eyes met Carlie's with tense significance. Ben did not come home. He was undoubtedly, Carlie knew, working on an account of the battle for the paper. He was still not home when she went up to bed and in the morning she saw that his bed had not been slept in; he had probably spent the night at the Baldwin house.

She did not expect Emily to come to Dorcas meeting, but when the girls arrived at four, Emily was with them, her eyes very bright and her lips pressed tight together. Everyone was being very cheerful for her sake. Mrs. Sturdevant came down to act as elder hostess, and Alison on the sofa was so breathlessly interested in everything that between them they kept conversation going. Inevitably, however, the talk finally turned to the war.

Carlie brought out Laura's letter telling about the work of the Sanitary Commission and suggesting that the Dorcas League work for Soldiers' Aid.

"I shouldn't think *you'd* suggest that." Two pink spots burned in Emily's cheeks, and her meaning was so pointed that Carlie bit her tongue.

"I think we all want to help the soldiers," she said gently.

"My, yes!" That was breathless little Jessie Courtins bumbling in, trying to please, but, as usual, doing something very wrong. "Why, just look at Laura! Everybody knows she was sweet on that Southern fellow, but now she's working for the Union just like everybody else."

"She didn't have much choice. I notice he didn't stick around to marry her. Peter was just plain too soft-hearted." Even the other girls gasped at Emily's words. "How do we know which side she's really working for in Washington?"

A door had opened and closed and with a sinking heart Carlie realized Ben had come home. He stopped in the archway, his eyes red-rimmed and his body tense. His voice was very quiet. "Emily, you take that back, or I'll . . ."

"You'll what?" Emily jumped up, her voice coming in a harsh gasp. "Fight? You're too yellow! It doesn't take courage to sit home in a paper office and write brave words!"

There was a deadly silence, and then Alison held her arms out, childlike and innocent. "Oh, Ben, I'm so glad you're home. Will you take me upstairs, please? I'm rather tired." Amid a strained hush, he lifted her gently and carried her out.

With a great effort of will, Carlie was able to make her voice come out quiet and calm. "Shall we all go in to tea?"

The meeting broke up quickly after that. Even the other girls were embarrassed by Emily's outburst. Bless Alison, Carlie thought fervently, for getting Ben out! After the girls left, she went to the kitchen and started dinner. Presently Mrs. Sturdevant came out, too, and began quietly to wash the tea things. She said nothing, but Carlie was grateful for her nearness.

When dinner was ready, Carlie went upstairs and knocked on Ben's door. She tried to make her voice quite natural. "Dinner's on."

"I don't want any."

"But, Ben . . ." She hesitated, then went back downstairs. Ben was not Paul or Oliver, whom she could scold.

Brad had brought Alison back down, and, during the meal,

with Ben not present, the incident was thoroughly discussed. Alison's eyes were very black. "That girl's a witch!"

"No, just confused and unhappy." Mrs. Sturdevant's voice was sad. "So civil war makes enemies of us all."

When Carlie went up to bed, light showed underneath Ben's door. She would have knocked, but Brad touched her arm. "Let him be. There are times when a fellow has to be alone."

And there were times, Carlie thought, when a girl has to have someone else around. After she had written in her journal, she went up to Alison's room, and they talked for hours, lightly, gaily, the subject of the afternoon never mentioned, though it was always there, just beneath the surface.

When she went downstairs at last, her tensions drained away by laughter, light still showed around the crack of Ben's door. She hesitated and then knocked.

"Ben? I know you're awake. Please let me in."

There was no answer. She knocked again, frowning, and then tried the knob. The door swung open on an empty room.

"Ben?" She looked around disbelievingly, then saw the note propped on the pillow. She lifted it with trembling fingers, and the words, terse as only Ben could be, leaped out at her:

*Gone to enlist.*

# CHAPTER

# 14

ARLIE STARED at the message numbly. Oh, no, she thought dully. Not this, not now. It's just too much. Papa will thrash Ben if he goes out and gets himself killed. Then the incongruity of that last thought struck her and she laughed helplessly, clinging to the bedpost, until the giddiness drained out of her and she was able to think more clearly.

She could not blame Ben for running off to war. On the contrary, her first reaction was not anger but swift, sharp envy. It was so terrible having to sit idly by at home!

But we need him here, too, she thought. There was so much that depended on him—the paper, the taxes. Somehow she would have to make him see that, persuade him to return. She would have to do so in a way that did not hurt his pride. And she did not even know where he had gone!

She felt at that moment more completely and utterly helpless than ever before in her life. She rested her head for a brief moment against the bedpost. I've tried, she thought dazedly, but this is something I don't know how to fix. Oh, please, somebody tell me what to do!

*Brad.* She didn't know why she thought of him instinctively, but suddenly she was running up the stairs. She opened his door without knocking and called him in an urgent whisper. In the darkness, she saw him stir and sit up.

"Cara? What is it?"

"Please come out!" She waited, hands locked tightly, until he did, in a hastily donned dressing-gown, carrying a candle. In the frail light, his familiar face was like a strong, solid rock.

"What's the matter?" He took her arm, for she was trembling.

"Ben's gone." She held the note out dumbly, holding onto the banister while he read it.

His response was a low whistle. "I thought this would happen, sooner or later."

"I know. I don't blame him. But we need him so! Brad, what am I going to do?" She drew a deep shaky breath. "I don't even know where he's gone!"

"I do," Brad said grimly. "New York City. One of the politicians is trying to organize a regiment. I heard it from the Judge, and Ben was pumping me about it all last night. I should have guessed!" His arm went around her. "Go to bed, Cara, and don't worry. I'll go after him."

"I'm coming, too."

"No, you're not! A trip to New York at this hour of the night is no joke."

"I don't care! He'd never come back just for you!"

Brad considered, then capitulated. "All right. But hurry! We'll have to catch him before the enlistment office opens in the morning."

He went back to his room and Carlie ran down to hers. She pulled on an old cotton housedress. Its skirt was scant and short, more practical than crinolines. She slid her feet into flat-heeled slippers and stepped out just as Brad came down the stairs.

"Ready? Good." They crept down the back stairs and out to the barn. Brad opened the barn door cautiously and slid in as Carlie crossed her fingers. If only Dan would not awaken! To her relief, there was no sound as Brad silently led out his obedient horse.

"Dan's sleeping like a baby. Can you ride without a saddle?" She nodded, and he lifted her up, then swung himself in front and with Indian stealth guided the horse down the drive. Once on the road he sat back with relief. "Good! The poor chap's going to feel humiliated enough being dragged back, without anyone else having to know. I told Allie, because she's got tact not to let on, but she won't tell Mother unless we're not back by morning. You set? Hang on!" They flew off down the road.

At any other time it would have been exciting. She had rarely been out this late at night, certainly not alone with a young man. The air was cooler now, a faint breeze stirred soundlessly through the towering trees, and the world was still. They passed familiar landmarks—the church, the school, Ramsey's Hotel, all looking strange and ghostly in the darkness. They went down Stagg's Hill, clattered over the wooden bridge and down another hill past the Van Horn house, one of the first in town. Here, as they entered Spikertown, the roadside grew less familiar, and soon all sense of recognition disappeared.

It startled her to find how night magnified all sounds. The crash when a horseshoe struck a stone seemed loud enough to wake the dead, and when an owl shrieked suddenly she shivered violently.

"You all right?" Brad called over his shoulder.

"Yes." She answered in monosyllable, disgusted with her voice for quavering, and tightened her arms around his waist.

She closed her eyes, but the motion made her so nauseated that almost immediately she opened them again. They crossed another narrow bridge. The roads were better here; some were even cobbled. The clouds separated briefly, and the moon shone down upon a sleeping town. High in a church steeple, a clock's hands stood at one. Brad made a sound of dismay and dug his heels into the horse's flanks. Picking up speed, they galloped up another rise and the road grew rutted. Carlie had lost all sense of direction; she locked her hands tightly and concentrated all her effort on just staying on the horse.

They reached a narrow river and Brad reined in so suddenly that she almost lost her balance. He let the horse drink deeply. He swung down, and she let herself slide gratefully into his arms. She had to steady herself against the horse to keep from swaying and was glad Brad could not see. He cupped his hands and scooped up water for her, then drank himself.

"Are we almost there?"

"Not half way."

She almost groaned, but stopped in time. "Hadn't we better go on?" She braced herself as he lifted her up, her body aching now from the cramped position. "Wait a minute." She pulled her skirts up and swung her leg over the horse's back so that she sat astride. How shocked Papa would be, she thought, choking back the giggles. She wrapped her arms around Brad again, and they started out on the road along the river.

Farms, fields, and trees; farms, fields, and trees—there was nothing else for miles. Then paved road began again, and they jolted through a town. Hackensack—she recognized the courthouse dome. A clock struck two. Brad reined in and turned toward her.

"There's a short cut from here. I took it once, so I know the way, and it would save an hour. But it's hard riding."

"Let's take it." She swallowed and willed her voice to sound brisk. "What do you think I am, a helpless female?"

"No, not quite." Brad chuckled.

There was a tone in his voice that made her add, impulsively, "What *do* you think?"

"I'll tell you sometime." Through the darkness she could see a flicker of his wicked grin; then he turned and they moved again, down streets between quiet houses, and onto another road full of stones and holes.

Presently the road grew narrow. High grasses brushed eerily against her feet. Gray clouds, weirdly luminous around their edges, crossed the moon and the world went black as pitch. She rested her face against Brad's shoulder, and it seemed as if nothing else existed. Nothing else, anywhere in space, except herself, and the horse jogging along, and Brad's body, warm and sure, for her to cling to.

Then abruptly the moon pierced the clouds. She gazed out upon endless meadows and a chill of recognition shook her.

The Jersey marshes—not meadows at all, but swamp, stretching for endless miles, west of the Palisades, along the Hudson River. She had read of them. They had formed a natural protection for New Amsterdam's settlers in the early days, for the Indians would not cross them—held back, it was said, by tales of ghosts who roamed at night.

The wild marsh grasses, reaching to her knees, stirred and swayed with the slightest breath. She could hear the squish of water as the horse picked his way precariously on spongy hillocks. Finally the horse stopped dead and would not budge.

"Oh, King. It's all right." Brad stopped. "It's no use. Have you got anything you can take off?"

"Take . . . off?"

"To put over his head. He's afraid because he sees the

water." Brad lifted her down, and she stepped out of her petticoat and handed it to him, grateful for the darkness, for she knew she was blushing. He set her up again and wrapped the cloth around the horse's eyes. Taking the bridle, he led the horse slowly from hillock to hillock. Carlie's heart was pounding. At last they came out onto solid ground and climbed a hill to a high, flat road of hard-packed earth that ran above the river. Brad let his breath out sharply.

"Almost there. The ferry's not too much farther." After a while, faintly, they could make out the great hulking shape of the flatboat's paddle-wheel. But there was no sign of life, and the shanty by the shore was all in darkness.

"It's just our luck! To come all this way for nothing!" Suddenly, uncontrollably, Carlie started to laugh.

"Cara! Stop it!" Brad turned and slapped her face sharply, and she pulled her breath in with a shudder.

"I'm sorry. I don't know what . . ."

"I know, honey." He went down the embankment, and she waited silently as he pounded on the shanty's door. Finally a light flared and a grizzled head thrust out.

"Ferry's closed till mornin'!"

Brad pulled out a roll of bills and there was an exchange of words. Soon the ferryman came out, buttoning a tattered topcoat over his nightshirt. He squinted at Carlie. "Ain't runnin' away, is you? I don't want no trouble."

Brad chuckled. "Just getting my girl home kind of late, that's all." He said something in a low voice, and the ferry-man laughed hoarsely.

Brad came back up. "It's all right. He probably thinks we're eloping, but he'll take us." He led the horse down onto the swaying platform, the ferryman untied the ropes, and the boat pushed off.

Once they were out on the water, Brad lifted Carlie down from the horse. She had not let herself think before of how tired she was and how her body ached; now in the relative stillness, the pain closed in on her and she swayed. Brad's arm went around her and she rested her head against his shoulder. His fingers touched her cheek. "I'm sorry I slapped you."

"You had to." Carlie looked out across the water. "Brad, I don't know how to thank you . . . for coming like this. I'm sorry I acted childishly."

"You didn't." He bent and kissed her mouth. She swayed toward him, speechless. He took her face between his hands and kissed her a second time, more gently.

There was a swoosh and a thud as the ferry nosed into the slip. The ferryman sprang ashore and lashed the ropes, and they went up onto solid ground. Here in the city there were paved roads, and street lamps glowed. Great bulks of warehouses loomed up through the dark. They mounted silently, and Brad turned the horse into one of the narrow streets.

"Where will we look?" Carlie ventured. It was the first either of them had spoken since the ferry, and she was relieved when Brad was matter-of-fact.

"Down Broadway, first, and around City Hall. Then around Union Square. That's where all the rallying went on after Sumter."

They clattered down the streets of the sleeping city, past Printing House Square with the tall buildings, five stories high, of the New York *Times*, the *Tribune*, and the *Sunday Times*. City Hall, its imposing marble front gleaming in the intermittent moonlight; the elegant Astor House, where Papa and Mama had stayed before taking the steamboat South; the raucous wholesale district of Lower Broadway—the scenes flashed like a kaleidoscope before Carlie's weary eyes. But the streets were deserted. They turned and circled Union Square. A policeman stopped them.

"What are you young folks doing out at this hour?"

Carlie suddenly realized how she looked and blushed furiously, but Brad's voice was calm. "I'm Sturdevant, from Washington Square. We're looking for this lady's brother; he's run off to enlist."

"That so? Good for him. Sure looks like he's needed. Haven't seen any young fellow wandering around this neighborhood, though. I'll send him to your place if I run across him."

"Thanks, we'd appreciate it." As the policeman moved off, Brad clucked to the horse. Then suddenly he clapped his hand to his head. "Our house! It's closed, of course, but the furnace room door won't lock. And Ben knows it. I told him all about it. I practically drew him a blueprint! What a great fool I am!"

He jerked the reins sharply, and they dashed down another tree-lined street, turned a corner, and came out onto a broad square that surrounded a grassy park. Street lights shone on gracious tall brick houses. Brad stopped before one and looped the reins swiftly to the hitching post. Narrow steps with a swirling iron railing led up to a black, brass-knockered door, but Brad turned instead to another door beneath them, swung it open, and called inside.

"Ben?" There was no answer. They stepped inside into darkness. Brad's voice was stern.

"Look, Ben, we know you're here. Stop acting like a thoughtless child and be a man!"

To Carlie's unutterable relief, she saw Ben emerge from the blackness. Brad slammed the door quickly and lit a hanging lamp. In the wavering light, Ben's face was taut with anger.

"Just what do you think . . ."

"I think you're *not* thinking," Brad cut in bluntly. "Rushing off like this with no thought of your family! Hasn't Carlie got enough to contend with now?"

"I don't see that it's any of your business!"

"I'm making it my business," Brad said curtly. "If you're

[ 150 ]

idiotic enough to think it's patriotic to leave the whole responsibility for a newspaper and a household in the hands of one young girl . . . Or maybe it's not patriotism you're thinking of, at that. I guess it does take less courage to enlist than it does to stay at home where you're really needed, and get no glory!"

Ben's fist swung back, and instinctively Carlie did the only thing she could think of. She caught her breath, pressed her hand to her breast, and fell over in an uncomfortable, but she hoped convincing, faint.

It worked; both broke off immediately and rushed to her side. Ben's voice was awed and anxious. "Is she all right? Laura's always having the vapors, but Carlie never faints."

"About time you realized she isn't a workhorse," Brad retorted. To Carlie's relief, Ben did not flare back. Brad was rubbing her wrists. How long, she wondered frantically, was a faint supposed to last? Her leg was doubled up uncomfortably, so she let her eyelids flutter.

"It's all right—she's coming round." Brad's arms lifted her up. She felt like an utter fool, but at least the fight had been averted.

"You win," Ben said dully. "I couldn't see where I was doing anybody any good. The paper's gone down so, and Carlie's got everything under control at home. I thought that in the Army I could at least be of some use."

"Why, Ben!" Carlie's eyes opened wide. "You're the man of the house. The boys look up to you, not me. There has to be somebody . . ." Suddenly her eyes filled with tears. "Oh, Ben, I'm so tired of being strong!"

"Ah, come on, Sis." Awkwardly Ben pressed a handkerchief into her hand.

Brad spoke briskly. "We're all dead tired. Come upstairs and have coffee before we start back." He led the way out of the furnace room and up the narrow steps. Ben held Carlie's arm; to her amusement both boys were being enormously protective. Brad unlocked the door and lit a lamp.

"I'll make coffee. Alison's room is at the top of the stairs, Carlie. Why don't you see if you can find something there to wear?"

Upstairs in the little room, all white and silver like a fairy's bower, she looked at herself in the mirror and did not wonder at Brad's suggestion. She looked like a weary, filthy guttersnipe and her dress was torn. Alison's clothes were too small for her, but she washed her face and hands, combed and braided her hair, and made herself as presentable as she could.

When she went downstairs, Brad had coffee waiting in a cream-colored drawing room curtained in red and gold. There was no milk, and the brew was dark and bitter, but it seemed to put strength into them all. Ben pulled out the gold watch Papa had given him at Christmas and turned to Brad. "Hadn't we better start?"

They went into the street, now beginning to fill with a pale gray light, and around a corner into a narrow alley—a Mews, Brad called it—to the carriage house where Ben had stabled Midnight. Brad brought a saddle out for King. When it was fastened, he lifted Carlie up and swung up behind her. They started slowly.

The city was just beginning to stir. In the wholesale district, porters pushed laden handcarts toward the docks and the oysterman blew his raucous horn. The ferry was waiting at the dock and dawn was just beginning to gild the river.

The trip home was uneventful. They went by road instead of through the marshes. As they passed the farms, roosters were crowing. The eastern sky was red and already the air was hot. Carlie pushed her damp hair back from her forehead wearily. It was going to be a scorcher. They passed through Arcola, Paramus, Spikertown, and up Stagg's Hill. Mr. Pryor was just going out to milk his cows. At last they turned into Beaufort's driveway.

"Made it," Brad said succinctly. The house was still silent. They turned the horses into the paddock and went up the back steps. Carlie stumbled.

Brad's hand closed about her arm. "Cara, go to bed. Ben and I will rustle up a picnic breakfast. The boys will love to eat outside and so will Mother." She groped her way up the back stairs and into her room and fell across the bed, too weary to undress.

What a day, she thought. It was hard to think that it was only just beginning. Even grown men, she knew, considered the hard journey to and from the city too much for a single day. She turned over on her back, as the blurred kaleidoscope of that wild ride rushed past, and suddenly she blushed. For the last thought she had, just before she fell asleep, was of the way that Brad had kissed her on the ferry.

# CHAPTER

# 15

WHEN CARLIE AWOKE, the sun was pouring in and a heavy blanket of heat hung over the roof. She bathed with cold water, put on her thinnest dress, and went downstairs. She was shocked when she passed the clock to see that it was nearly two in the afternoon.

The house was quiet and the shades were drawn. There were no signs of life, but in the kitchen she found evidence that lunch had been eaten. Thank goodness for that, she thought, pushing open the back door and stepping outside.

The boys were swimming in the brook, and Alison was lying in the wicker chaise, placidly shelling peas.

"Well, hello!" She looked up and waved her bowl. "Look, Paul picked these for me and I'm fixing them for supper. I peeled potatoes, too. I'm getting quite good, really! Mother's in the springhouse, writing. She was sorry to hear about your headache," she added meaningly.

"That's no lie," Carlie said, dropping down on the grass. Her head was, indeed, beginning to throb. "Have you seen Ben?"

"Off to Hackensack, looking grim as the Black Knight."
Alison shook her head with sadness. Carlie sighed.

It was an odd sort of day, somehow outside of time, so still
with heat that nothing seemed to move. Nothing seemed real.
Problems seemed to have receded off somewhere in the shim-
mering air. But she was conscious, as she moved slowly
through dinner preparations with Alison's unexpected help,
that they still were there.

She set the table down by the brook, beneath the willow
trees. She fixed it carefully, with flowers in a silver basket, and
despite the heat she baked Ben's favorite berry cobbler. She
had a feeling, although she could not put it into words, that
she owed Ben something.

She had, in a very special sense, humiliated him by going
after him—doubly so, in having Brad along. It was not that
she doubted the rightness of what she'd done—Ben himself
had admitted that. But all the same, there was something.
When Ben came home that night, she could see it in his eyes.
He walked heavily as if he carried a great burden on his
shoulders.

The worst part was that she could not apologize, for putting it into words would make it worse. During dinner they
scarcely spoke. She could not quite look at Ben, but he was
lost in his own thoughts anyway. Mrs. Sturdevant glanced at
them shrewdly, and Alison's eyes were full of a questioning
sadness, though her voice was gay. After dinner the boys
clamored for a story.

"Not now, chickens! Maybe afterward, when you're in
bed."

"Aw, Alison!" Oliver was endeavoring to clamber into her
lap when Ben grabbed him by the collar and pulled him
down.

"She said no! Don't you know when you're not wanted?
Go away!"

"Why, Ben!" Carlie, starting to clear the table, stopped and stared at him. Paul, at Alison's signal, was already leading Oliver off.

"I have letters to write," Mrs. Sturdevant said tactfully, and withdrew.

Brad picked up the tray with one hand and with the other touched Carlie's elbow, propelling her toward the house. As they crossed the lawn, she could hear Alison's soft voice saying, "Ben . . . ?" like a questioning caress, but Carlie did not look back. They went into the kitchen, and she set the platters on the table.

"Oh, Brad, I feel so awful. I didn't want to hurt him."

"He knows that, Cara. But you made him feel ashamed. He needs Alison to put him back together."

"It used to be me." Carlie looked up through brimming eyes. "Now . . . I can't get through to him, any more. I know just what Ben meant; I feel so useless."

Brad shook his head. "It isn't that. It's just that you're too close. You know him too well. He needs someone outside, who can see him as a separate person."

Carlie followed Brad's eyes out of the window toward the tableau on the lawn. Ben was sitting on the grass, arms locked around his knees, with Alison looking down at him, her chin propped on her hand.

"Actually," Brad said thoughtfully, "they're good for each other. Mother and I were still treating Alison as a child. It seemed easier for her. But she's not one any more."

No, Carlie thought, remembering the look on Alison's face, she was not. None of them was.

The letter that came from Laura the next day underscored this thought. Ben read it aloud at the dinner table and when he finished they all were silent. Laura had seen the battle and she was deeply shaken.

Everyone in Washington had known a battle was imminent, and many had driven out to watch. "Just like going to a picnic!" Laura wrote. A woman she knew from the Sanitary Commission had been going in a Senator's party and had invited her to come along. They had sat beneath trees on a hilltop and watched through opera-glasses as the two armies drew into position like toy lead soldiers. When the fighting began, it had seemed at first like a fireworks display.

"It didn't seem real," Laura wrote. But it had become real, terribly so. Her pen had scratched and sputtered over the paper in the shocked rush of her words:

"All at once somebody cried out and we could see more enemy troops circling from the rear. After awhile we realized the Federals were retreating. Nobody could believe it. It was very orderly at first, but then a wagon crossing the bridge tipped over and cut off the only road. After that it was chaos."

The spectators had fled back toward Washington. But almost immediately they had been engulfed in the tide of running men—men leaving weapons behind them in their haste; officers shouting hoarsely, trying frantically to rally terror-stricken men; the wounded falling along the road and being left to die. Laura's wagon had overturned, and she and the other women had taken refuge in a farmhouse, helping the housewife carry water and bandages out to the stricken men. She had not got back to Washington till long past dark.

Lamps had burned in the White House windows all that night. Morning had brought the rain. "We dripped heat, rain, and despair," she wrote. "The whole city expected imminent siege. Then McClellan arrived, and we breathed again.

"Peter's all right, thank God. But so many others . . . We went to the hospital yesterday with a load of bandages, to find out if there was anything we could do, and I saw Tom

Garrison. Carlie, they had to amputate his leg, and he can't bear to write home and tell. I wish you'd go to see them. I know it's a lot to ask, but if you'd been there . . . Tell them he's doing well and will soon be home.

"Oh, Ben, you've got the paper to talk through. *Use it!* Try to make people see what I saw there. It's not a game anymore, it's *real!*"

Ben stopped and there was a silence. After a minute, he folded the letter carefully, put it in his jacket pocket, and went outside. Alison's eyes followed him as he crossed the room, and Carlie was shaken by the expression on her face.

Carlie did go to the Garrisons' the next day. She didn't want to; all the while she was putting on her dress and bonnet, she didn't think she could do it, but she did. It was not as bad as she had feared, for Mrs. Sturdevant went with her, and old Mr. Garrison was not at home. Mrs. Garrison was dazed by the news, and Emily, the gaiety shocked out of her, was tight-lipped and silent. Carlie, remembering her in the bright glory of Tom's enlistment, felt sick at heart.

War had become real now; everyone knew it. Horace Greeley took the "On to Richmond!" masthead off the *Tribune*. Mrs. Sturdevant headed her column with a quote from Laura's letter. Ben came home late, looking ineffably weary, dropped a copy of the *Journal* on the table, and went to the kitchen for a long drink of water while the others read in silence.

"*Battle of Bull Run*," he had headed it, taking the name from the river that ran beneath the bottled-up bridge. "Report from our Washington Correspondent." He followed it with excerpts from Laura's letter, not rambling as that had been but skillfully tightened. It was for Ben a remarkable piece of writing. He had done no editorializing—only the stark words themselves forced the reader to his own conclusion.

Carlie, looking up to meet Alison's eyes, breathed a sigh of relief. She did not need to worry about Ben now; he had worked out his own destiny and found where he could serve. Indeed, although she was slightly ashamed of it, she felt a stir of envy.

"Seems like everyone's found something important to do," she said ruefully to Alison one night the following week. "Laura with the Sanitary Commission, Ben with the paper. So what do I do? Pickles!" She stared balefully at the cucumber she was holding and Alison giggled.

Despite the fact that it was past two in the morning, and they were in Alison's bedroom, they were peeling cucumbers. The garden had suddenly flourished and was yielding bushels of vegetables. The fruit trees were laden, and Paul and Oliver had been berrying in the woods. The state of their finances, and their long training, would not let them watch things spoil, so Carlie was perforce learning to do canning.

She had started in all innocence with recipes for preserves that had appeared in *Godey's*. It had seemed simple enough, though it was hot work standing over the simmering range. But the resulting ruby, amethyst, and amber jars had been impressive, glowing on the kitchen shelves in the summer sun. She had progressed to tomato conserve, and then whole to-matoes, and now, by the first of August, she felt as if she never again could look at the vegetable. Peeling the tomatoes was arduous—they slipped and squirmed out of her fingers as if they were alive.

She had turned gratefully to the cucumbers, for they at least were firm. The trouble was that there were so many. Each day produced another three or four baskets full, and the tomatoes, too, kept right on ripening. Carlie worked in the middle of the night and early in the morning.

She would never have got through it had it not been for Alison's help. Alison's fingers flew like lightning, cutting, peeling, dicing, as deft with this as with her needlework. Her gaiety never flagged; despite all she was doing, she was as patient as ever with the boys, and Carlie blessed her fervently for keeping them out from underfoot.

Housework went by the boards, dinners degenerated into picnics, and by Sunday everyone was glad of temporary respite. "Now I know why the Lord ordained a day of rest," Carlie said after church, and Alison chuckled.

Although she had been peeling cucumbers at three that morning, Alison was wide-awake and glowing. The unaccustomed activity had been good for her. She stayed downstairs nearly all day now, being outdoors had given her a healthy flush, and the bones at her throat and wrists did not show quite so sharply. Brad was right about her needing a chance to grow, Carlie thought. But she was too busy to dwell on the thought. She mixed cake ingredients in a yellow bowl, said, "Here, beat," and dumped bowl and spoon unceremoniously into Alison's lap.

She was fussing more than usual with Sunday dinner, to atone for the week's scant rations. Chicken was roasting in the range, filling the air with tantalizing fragrance and an awful heat. Carlie pumped water into a kettle for the potatoes and stopped to splash some on her face and wrists. "I should have done the baking last night. If it hadn't been for those dratted cukes!" she added darkly.

The sight of a civilized meal was greeted by the family with obvious relief. And the cake was a triumph. "I made it! Really!" Alison preened and winked at Carlie.

"No cucumber pie?" Brad inquired wickedly. "No jam? No berries?"

"I never," Carlie said firmly, "want to hear cucumbers mentioned in my presence. Nor tomatoes. Nor berries, either!"

"I hate to tell you," Ben interrupted, "but there's three baskets of each sitting out on the back steps right now. Picked them before church."

"Oh, Ben!"

"They do keep right on coming," Ben remarked complacently. "You girls were the ones who wanted a garden, remember."

"And you know why." Carlie stopped. By unspoken agreement, finances were not mentioned before the warmhearted, perceptive Sturdevants. She looked at Ben and ran her fingers through her hair. "We can't can any more; we've more than we need right now. Throw them out. Or sell them!"

"To whom? The *farmers?*"

"Then take them to Hackensack and try." Ben looked so scandalized that Carlie went on perversely, "Or Paterson! Most of the rich folks there don't fool with gardens. You can take me down on your way to the paper and I'll peddle door to door!"

"Caralie! You wouldn't!" Alison stared at her, wide-eyed.

"Wouldn't I just!" The hot, confining work of the past week had made Carlie reckless, and Ben's disapproving face was the final push. "Anything's better than more canning, and it's perfectly respectable. Tom and Emily used to do it all the time a few summers back. We've used up all the preserving sugar already, and it would be a sin just to let things spoil. And it won't hurt any, anyway," she added meaningly in Ben's direction.

"'Course it won't." To Carlie's surprise, Paul spoke up solemnly. "I can help. We can pull the stuff in my old wagon."

[ 161 ]

"Me, too," Oliver suggested happily.

"You're going to help me make milkweed pillows," Alison reminded him quickly, saving Carlie the necessity of refusing.

The next morning, dragging herself out of bed at five, Carlie regretted her rash impulse, but it was too late now to back down. She put on the old dress she had worn to New York and tied on a sunbonnet—already the rising sun gave indications of fierce heat. She went down the back stairs, half hoping Ben and Paul had overslept, but they were sitting at the kitchen table, eating a bachelor breakfast. Paul, barefoot and in blue-jeans, looked up with a shining face.

"Ben's harnessed up, and I put the wagon and the baskets in back. I put some branches over them, too, to protect them from the sun."

"I still think you're crazy," Ben told Carlie bluntly.

"You won't if we come back with money," she snapped, as she sailed outside.

By the time they reached the heights of Paterson, the day was already hot. Ben stopped at the top of the hill, lifted down the wagon and produce, and surveyed them both. "When you're finished, go over to the park. There are benches there. I'll pick you up as early in the afternoon as I can get away. You sure you want to go through with this?"

"Uh-huh." Paul picked up the wagon's handle and started off stolidly. No one in the Benson family, Carlie thought with amusement, had a monopoly on stubbornness. She followed with dignity, conscious that Ben was watching.

At the first house, the door was slammed in their faces. At the next, they were told to go around back, and after that they fared fairly well. Six tomatoes, three cucumbers, a pint of berries—slowly their stock dwindled, but it was tiring work.

"Two more houses, then let's eat our lunch." Carlie arched her back and rubbed it wearily.

"Hey, mister! Wanta buy a tomato?" Paul flagged a passing butcher's wagon, and the smiling driver bought two for his lunch.

They sold another six and two more cucumbers, and then pulled the wagon up on a corner beneath a tree.

"I wish I never had to look at another of these things!" Carlie bit into a tomato grimly. "What I wouldn't give for a good cold drink."

"There's a fountain in the park."

"We'd have to walk back uphill again." Carlie sighed and stood up. "I guess it will be worth it, though. Come on."

The park was shady and relatively cool with a faint breeze from the river. Paul promptly rolled up his jeans and went in wading. Carlie rubbed her aching feet.

"Come on in!"

"I can't. It wouldn't be proper."

"Who cares?" Paul asked logically. "Nobody will see."

She watched him longingly for another minute, then bent and began to unbutton her shoes. Who would see, indeed! She sat on the bank, swung her feet luxuriously, and splashed some water on her face and neck. When they started up the hill again, her shoes stayed in the wagon.

Might as well look like a complete gypsy! she thought recklessly, conscious that her hair was straggling and there was a large berry stain across her dress. She rolled her sleeves up high above her elbows, looped up her skirt, and started ringing doorbells again.

The sun was beginning to affect the produce now, so she lowered prices, but even so it was slow going.

"Carlie?" Paul looked up at her suddenly. "Do we need money?"

"What makes you think that?"

"Because you and Ben have been snapping," Paul said shrewdly. "*Do* we?"

"It's . . . something about the taxes, but you don't need to worry."

"Huh," Paul said. "I'm not Oliver's age. Tell Ben I've got twenty-six cents I was saving up for Christmas."

"I'll tell him." Carlie wanted to hug him, but she knew he felt too old for that, so instead she gave him a special warm smile. "Only six tomatoes left now, and a box of berries. Two more stops should do it."

"Here comes a wagon—maybe they'll take some." Paul cupped his hands. "Hey, Mis—"

The words died on his lips as Carlie jerked sharply on his arm. The wagon turning the corner looked alarmingly familiar, and in a moment she was looking, numb with shock, into Uncle Henry's scandalized face and Bess's dark, startled eyes.

# CHAPTER

# 16

WHEN CARLIE told Ben about the encounter, after he had picked them up at the park at four and they were jolting home, she tried to turn it into a joke.

"To think you wouldn't let me go to Hackensack for fear of running into folks we know!" She glanced at Ben, got no answer, and sighed. "Oh, well. Uncle Henry can't be any more scandalized than he was already. And at least we made some money. So there's no harm done."

She was trying to be philosophical, but she felt remarkably foolish. Ben had been right. She ought not to have gone, and underneath she had known it all along.

Mule-headed! She jeered at herself in silent disgust. It was all very well to say the Garrisons had often done it, but Emily had had an older brother with her, not a younger, and Emily herself had been twelve years old. There *was* a difference. Carlie had a sudden picture of how she must look, and her face grew hot.

She didn't speak much going home, and to her relief Ben didn't either. Fortunately, however, he seemed to be in a good mood. He lounged back in the seat, guiding Midnight with one hand and whistling. The Sturdevants were on the front porch when they reached home. Ben waved, but kept on going until they reached the back of the house.

"Better skin up the back stairs," he advised.

She did, flushing furiously, her shoes and stockings bundled up in her skirt. Once in the safety of her own room, she shut the door quickly and set about repairing the damages.

After she had washed, put on a fresh dress, and pinned up her hair, she felt a little better, but not very much. The skin on her shoulders was tight with sunburn that showed plainly above her low-necked gown, and her nose was red. When she reached the kitchen, she dusted some cornstarch on it before starting to assemble supper.

Fortunately it was too hot for anything but a cold meal, and to her intense relief no one asked about her day. They were poring over the paper Ben had nonchalantly dropped on the table. There were three good-sized ads on the front page. As soon as the meal was over, Carlie caught Ben in the pantry.

"Ben! What happened?"

"It was Laura's letter." Ben's voice was light with relief. "You know we sold more copies that day than we had in weeks. I bumped into Mr. Hale from the furniture store on my way to open up this morning, and he said what a fine piece it had been. He was quite impressed with our having a Washington correspondent. I don't know how it came so quick, but I said yes, it was a shame that we wouldn't be able to keep on with one unless advertising picked up some. Seemed almost like a civic duty to keep the news before the people at a time like this. I didn't give him a chance to say a word, just nodded and kept on walking. It gave me an idea, so later I just ambled by a couple of other stores and happened to mention that the first ads in would get the best positions, right next to the exclusive Washington news. Sure enough, within an hour all three took the bait. I sat right down and wrote Laura to keep the news coming fast. I'll go after a few more fish tomorrow."

Their glances met with shared relief and Carlie drew a deep joyful breath. "Now we won't have to worry so about the taxes!"

"Oh, yes, we will. This will hardly make a dent, we're so behind on bills right now. But at least the tide's been turned. Maybe if people advertise with us again, I can get an extension on the tax deadline."

Outside the kitchen windows, the sky had suddenly grown dark. Now a cool breeze lifted the curtains and thunder crackled. Ben looked out and grinned. "About time we had a change in the weather."

Carlie stretched her arms high behind her head and breathed deeply of the fresh rainy air. I'd like to go out and stand in it, she thought. Or turn cartwheels, maybe. "Ben," she said aloud suddenly, "I'm so happy."

The storm gave everyone new energy. They sat on the front porch, enjoying the breeze and watching the lightning flashes. Ben pointed out faces and buildings in the weird cloud formations, and Alison was enthralled.

There was rain the next day, also, not a thunderstorm now, but a steady downpour that lasted all day and cooled the air. It also finished off the tomatoes, to Carlie's secret joy. She took advantage of the weather to do her baking, and it actually felt good to have the oven going. The dampness had penetrated the walls.

The kitchen, with the range glowing and the lamps lit, was a cheerful place. Alison, ensconced on the old sofa, was peeling apples and doling them out impartially to Oliver and Paul. Carlie was humming a new Army song. It was supposed to be very sad, but she gave it a decided lilt. Alison looked up and smiled.

[ 167 ]

"You sound happy!"

"I am." Carlie broke off in the middle of her cake to swoop down on her with an impulsive floury hug. "Oh, Alison, I think things are finally working out."

Alison hugged her back. "Oh, I do hope so."

There was an odd note in her voice, and Carlie sat back and scanned the wan face closely. "Honey? Something wrong?"

"It's the rain." Alison gazed out the window and shuddered slightly. "It makes me see things."

"What kind of things?"

"Oh, ghosts and goblins, and a pink and purple dragon with a long, long tail!" Alison's elfin smile flashed suddenly, and Oliver giggled.

"I could spank you!" Carlie gave Alison's shoulders a little shake and went back to her baking. But as she stirred the batter, she glanced over at Alison once or twice with a small pucker of worry. Something was troubling Alison—there was an unaccustomed wistfulness about her. But after awhile, seeing Alison's face sparkle as she told Oliver about the purple dragon, Carlie decided it must have been her own imagination.

She did not walk over to town that afternoon, for rain was coming down in torrents, but Brad brought the mail home with him when he came. There was another fat letter from Laura, which Ben read aloud at dinner. Washington was settling down now to the grim business of war. Fresh regiments arrived daily, not three-month volunteers now, but men who had signed up for the duration of the war. McClellan was the man of the hour.

For God and our country we are marching along;
McClellan's our leader, he's gallant and strong . .

The troops were singing it lustily as they marched and counter-marched each day among the sands of the Potomac bottom.

It was not likely, Laura wrote, that there would be a new offensive until spring. McClellan was concentrating on whipping the new troops into a smooth-running machine. Everyone was concerned over the appalling number of casualties there had been at Bull Run—over twenty-eight hundred. Laura was working with the Sanitary Commission nearly every day.

"Peter thinks I should go back home, but I hate to leave when there is so much here that needs to be done."

She had seen Joseph Baldwin once, briefly, and Tom Garrison frequently. "I try to visit him whenever I can. He should soon be able to travel home, as he is recovering well, but he's so bitter."

There was another surprising bit of news. "I told you that my landlady is Southern. Somehow or other she got hold of an old Charleston paper, and Mama and Papa had put an announcement of our wedding in it! How on earth do you suppose they knew?"

The Copperhead grapevine . . . Carlie looked at Ben, and Ben had the grace to flush. "They must have put the notice in, hoping we'd see it somehow and know they were all right," he said, putting the letter carefully away to take with him to the newspaper office.

The rain was still coming down in torrents when they did the dishes. Carlie had lit the stove to heat the water, and she left it on, for a damp draft came in across Alison's couch. The teakettle was humming cheerfully.

> I see the lights of the village
> Gleam through the rain and the mist . . .

Brad was reading Longfellow aloud. Alison stretched and sighed. "Rainy nights are the best of all. They always seem as if you should use them for something special."

Ben grinned down at her. "Like what?"

"Mmmm, like telling fortunes. Or reading *Macbeth*. I know!" Alison pulled herself up, holding tight to the back of the sofa in her eagerness. "Making taffy! I read about it, in a book, but I never have! Is it very hard?"

Ben was already getting out the big preserving kettle. If she had suggested it, Carlie thought with amusement, he would have scorned it as women's work, but its being Alison's idea made a difference. They cooked up a sizeable batch and waited for it to cool. Brad had gone for *Macbeth*, and Alison was reading the sleepwalking scene, dramatically, with gestures. Ben, reading over her shoulder, took up the Porter's part. He had just reached the "Knock, knock!" when a real knock sounded at the back door. Involuntarily everyone jumped.

"Spooks!" Alison breathed in a throaty whisper. The knocking came again, more urgently. Ben threw the door open, and a small, rainsoaked figure almost fell inside.

Carlie ran forward. "Bess! What on earth?"

"Carlie! Oh, Ben, shut the door. I came through the woods so nobody'd see me." Out of breath, Bess doubled up, as Carlie put an arm around her quickly. Ben had already closed the door tightly.

"Bess, what's the matter?" he demanded.

"It's Pa . . . I just had to tell you, even if he finds out. Yesterday . . ." Bess swallowed and pushed the wet hair out of her eyes as Carlie looked at Ben.

Brad stood up. "Look, is this family stuff? We'll clear out."

"It's all right. We'll go inside. Ben, come light the fire." Carlie led Bess into the library quickly as Ben followed. "Bess, what happened? I know Uncle Henry was shocked. It was a crazy thing for me to do, and I could kick myself. I don't blame him if he's disgusted."

"It's not you." Bess put a small hand out quickly. "It's . . .

[ 170 ]

Uncle Richard. Pa says if he's left you here so destitute that you have to go out like beggars, something ought to be done legally. He's petitioning the court to appoint him as your guardian. He wants to put a tenant farmer here and have you all live with us. Oh, Carlie, I'd love that, but I know how you all feel about your home."

Carlie stared at Bess, and Ben looked at Carlie. "You *should* kick yourself," he said grimly. "There goes the extension on the taxes. It would be proof positive that we can't manage on our own."

"What are we going to do?" Bess gazed at them both with troubled eyes. "I'm so sorry. It's not that Pa wants to hurt you."

"Just that he has to manage everything," Ben finished. "Don't worry, Bess. We'll think of something."

"Maybe Brad could talk to Judge Zabriskie . . ."

"I'll talk to the Judge myself." Ben looked at Carlie sternly. "And don't you go telling Brad about this, understand?"

"All right," Carlie said humbly. She looked at Bess's small desolate figure and made her voice deliberately calm. "Come, let's have some tea."

In the kitchen they found that Brad, at Alison's instructions, had already filled the pot, and cups stood waiting on the table. Bess gulped half a cup of tea and then stood up quickly. "I have to go!"

"Stay and pull taffy!" Alison waved her spoon.

"Oh, no! I shouldn't have come at all." Bess looked frightened and ducked out quickly.

The taffy-pulling fell flat, despite Alison's gay chatter. Brad was carefully casual, and Carlie and Ben made an effort to fall into his mood. Not until they were turning out the lights for the night did anyone allude to Bess's visit, and then only indirectly. Alison stretched her folded hands out before her, gazed at the rain-wet windowpane, and repeated the last lines of the poem Brad had been reading:

And the cares, that infest the day,
Shall fold their tents, like the Arabs,
And as silently steal away.

Her glance traveled from Carlie to Ben and her face lit suddenly with her tender smile.

Ben did go to see Judge Zabriskie the next day and came home looking somewhat optimistic. "The Judge said just what I thought about the taxes. Uncle Henry has a pretty good case. But there's just one hope. Remember the Committee of Six?"

"The one that was formed to look after soldiers' dependents?"

Ben nodded. "The Judge says that if Pa went south originally for newspaper reporting and was caught there against his will, they could stretch a point. The trouble is, there'd have to be some kind of proof that Pa was pro-Union. I remembered that article in the *Journal*, the one that helped enlistments, and went all through the files for evidence Pa had written it, but there wasn't a thing."

"We'll find something!" Carlie looked at Ben with a surge of joy. "Taking help from the Committee of Six wouldn't be like charity. It would take care of the taxes *and* Uncle Henry!"

"Even Uncle Henry would be better than having Beaufort sold."

"I know. And I could put up with him, if we had to, if he were doing it out of kindness. But it wouldn't be for that reason; it would be because he thought Papa had failed us. And I couldn't bear that. Oh, Ben, we'll find something, we've just got to!"

They searched in every spare moment during the rest of the week, which was drowned with rain. Ben tore the newspaper office apart.

"I even went back through stories Pa wrote when he first bought the paper, but I couldn't find a thing. Pa was always so careful to be so blamed impartial!"

It was hard to search when they did not know what they were seeking, and hard, too, to do so without the Sturdevants knowing what was going on. Certainly all of them suspected something was wrong. Mrs. Sturdevant's manner invited confidences and Brad was particularly gentle, but none of them, to Carlie's relief, pressed the matter. After a day or so, they tactfully kept to themselves. Alison was alternately remote and filled with a questioning sadness that would have worried Carlie had she not already had so much on her mind.

Saturday it poured all day, providing an ideal excuse for indoor work. They had the house to themselves because Mrs. Sturdevant was writing, Brad was doing extra work at Judge Zabriskie's, and Alison was in her room. Even Paul and Oliver, who were regular ferrets, joined in.

"Bring us anything you find that has Pa's writing on it," Ben instructed.

He himself took the section of the garret where old papers were stored, and Carlie took the library, after locking the door and pulling down the shades. She pulled all the books from the shelves, looking for notations in the margins—a habit Papa was addicted to—and emptied the big desk completely.

In the bottom drawer, she discovered a large blank-book, half-filled with Papa's writing. She felt like a guilty child going through it, but she had to, so she curled up in the big chair and started at the beginning. Mostly it was remarks on the weather, crops, visitors—nothing remotely political. She came to an entry dated January first.

"A stormy session with my Carlie this afternoon. She sobs and says I do not understand her, when the trouble is that I do—too well. Poor child, she will have a hard time until she learns to twist her troubles round. Part of me sees that, and another part shares her blind impulse to run and hide. There is a stormy time coming for us all, and it is not just children who are going to have to learn the lesson she does now."

The page blurred before Carlie's eyes and she turned it quickly. There were only a few more entries after that. She closed the cover with a hopeless sigh. Nothing, nothing at all.

She put the book back, tidied the room, and went upstairs to the attic. The boys had long since given up the search and were playing pirates with Papa's old boots and a rusty sword. Ben, still rummaging in the far corner, looked up questioningly. "Any luck?"

She shook her head and sat down on a pile of books as he went through the last papers. He dropped them back into the box and pushed it away. "No luck at all." Ben ran his fingers wearily through his hair. "We should have known we were just fooling ourselves!"

"Ben, don't."

"Oh, Carlie, face it! I thought I had, but I guess I was still hoping. Well, now we know." Ben sounded matter-of-fact and very tired, and it shook her more than bitterness would have done. There was something so final about it, and for the first time she began to question her own faith—not to doubt it, exactly, but to wonder whether she was living in a dream. She felt discouraged and sick at heart.

She longed to talk to Brad but could not, not only because she'd promised Ben but because she could not bear to have Brad doubt her parents, too. She wanted Brad's sympathy, but not his pity. She went down to the kitchen, and despite the fact that she had baked the day before, she got out flour and the yellow bowl and mixed another batch of bread. There was something about kneading and stirring that quieted her heart.

It was past midnight before the loaves were ready for the oven. While it baked, she made a cup of tea and sat down on Alison's sofa. Alone in the empty kitchen, her thoughts flashed back over the words in Papa's journal. She could not remember now what the lesson was that he had said she had to learn. But since that time, she mused, she had learned so many. And perhaps the hardest one lay yet ahead—to accept the fact that Papa believed in a cause in which she did not.

She sighed, took the crusty loaves from the oven, and cut two generous slices. She carried them upstairs, hoping that Alison was still awake.

"Caralie." Alison, lying back on the pillows, held both hands out to her and drew her down. "You should not work so late. You look so tired."

"You're awake, too."

Alison's eyes lowered. "It's nothing. But you—I worry about you, Caralie. You should not be so sad." Now it was Carlie who looked away, and she felt Alison's thin hand cover hers tightly. "Caralie, I told you once that you need not be troubled."

"But I can't help wondering . . ."

"That's just it," Alison said gently. "You wonder, but if there were reason to worry, you would *know*. Believe me, Caralie."

"I wish I could." Impulsively Carlie bent and kissed her. "You do me good, honey. Now go to sleep."

Alison's eyes followed her as she crossed the room. Carlie went downstairs through the silent house, feeling as if the weight of all of it were on her shoulders.

CHAPTER

17

T HE RAIN had stopped by morning, but the sky was
gray and the air was misty. They rode to church, for the
roads were a sea of mud. The church's stone walls were
clammy.

Mrs. Sturdevant slipped decorously into the uncompromis-
ing wooden pew and bowed her head.

Carlie bowed her head, too, but she did not pray. She could
not seem to concentrate her thoughts. Reverend Ryerson em-
barked on another sermon on the Bull Run defeat, pointing
out lengthily that there must have been a purpose behind it.
Carlie wondered if the Garrisons found any comfort in the
thought.

She herself found none in the service, and it troubled her.
She stared out of the window at the wan gray landscape and
felt filled with a vague depression. There was no reassurance
anywhere these days. Except from Alison. Carlie smiled in-
wardly, remembering her earnest words. Despite her common
sense, Carlie found a kind of comfort in Alison's faith.

She felt Uncle Henry's eyes boring into her and dragged

her own away from the window. Unconsciously her mind turned over yesterday's search, re-examining each thing. Hoping against hope, as Ben would say. Alison's "feelings" were making her unrealistic, Carlie realized.

". . . has to be some great reason, even for seemingly senseless things." The minister's words cut through suddenly, sounding oddly familiar, and she straightened. "Even in the face of great sacrifice and suffering, we are called upon not to be discouraged, to endure all things, remembering the words of the Apostle Paul, how now we merely 'see through a glass darkly.' "

Carlie's head jerked up. In the back of her mind pieces fell into place and the truth burst forth like a blaze of light.

She did not know that she had gasped aloud until she felt Ben turn to look at her sharply. She flashed him a wide smile.

Fortunately the minister had reached the end of the sermon and the organ swelled with the final hymn. As soon as the benediction was pronounced, she rushed down the aisle, heedless of staring eyes.

"Carlie, what on earth?" Brad and Ben caught up with her outside the door and Brad caught her hand. "You lit up like a firecracker!"

"I can't tell you. I'm afraid to tell you, not till I look! Please, let's go home!"

Hope flared in Ben's eyes. "You don't mean . . ."

"I think so. I'm not sure. Oh, Ben, hurry!"

Ben yanked the boys unceremoniously into the carriage and cracked the whip. They flew down the jolting road, scattering mud. When they reached their front steps, Carlie jumped down breathlessly and rushed into the library.

Alison, lying on the sofa, stared wide-eyed as Carlie yanked the drawer from the desk, spilling things recklessly as she felt for the secret panel, her fingers clumsy with haste. Then she had the letter out, it was open on the desk before her, and she was bending over it, as the words swam before her eyes. For the first time in her life she felt as if she might really faint.

"Cara?" Brad's arm was around her, and she leaned against it for a moment and opened her eyes.

"It's all right." She thought she was shouting, but to her surprise her voice emerged a mere whisper. Then she flung her head back and looked into Ben's tense, half-fearful face, and her breath came back. "It's all right! I thought I understood, in church, and I was right. Ben, it was Paul the Apostle Papa meant! Don't you remember, that night at dinner when we wondered why things that seemed to be wrong had to happen? And Papa quoted Thirteenth Corinthians."

Ben drew his breath in sharply. " '. . . see through a glass darkly.' He was trying to tell us there were reasons we couldn't know till later, that we had to take on faith! Why didn't we remember?"

"Because we thought he meant *our* Paul. People were meant to think that, if they read the letter. You said there was some kind of secret code, and there was—our names!" Carlie's own breath was coming so quickly that it hurt her. "*I'm* the Carolina! I almost guessed it yesterday, when I read the journal. They long to be where I am, *here!* In the North! Their hearts are with *us!* Oh, Ben!"

She was laughing and crying all at once, and Brad was shaking her by the shoulders, and then she was in his arms and he was rocking her, holding her tight. Then he was kissing her, and that brought her round quickly.

"Oh! I'm all right. Everything's all right. We won't have to lose Beaufort after all!"

"Lose Beaufort!" Brad straightened and stared. "I knew something was wrong. What's been going on?"

"A combination of taxes and Uncle Henry, but it's all right now!" Ben gave a whoop of relief. "The Committee of Six will fall all over us now. And wait till we tell the high and mighty Garrisons and our saintly uncle!"

An odd look crossed his face, and he stopped abruptly, just as Carlie caught her breath. "We can't use it, can we?" she said slowly. "If Papa couldn't come right out and tell us, there had to be a reason."

"It has to be because folks mustn't know."

Brad looked at Ben. "Let me get this straight. You mean you'll keep quiet, even if it means losing your home?"

"We have to," Ben said simply. "We can't jeopardize whatever Pa's doing." He looked at Carlie for confirmation and she nodded. "I guess you think we're kind of crazy, but it's just the way we are."

"I think you're wonderful," Alison said softly. There were tears in her eyes. "And it won't be so hard after this, will it, now that you know?"

Ben nodded. "And no matter what happens—well, we'll know we tried. Besides, it may still work out." He took a deep breath. "I got five more ads today, three of them on contracts. People are beginning to respect the paper again. They like the Washington news. If Laura will just keep the letters coming!"

"You might write to Mr. Baldwin, too," Carlie suggested.

"I think I will." Ben ran his fingers through his hair. "I just wish I knew more about writing. There's a knack to war stories."

"Why don't you ask my mother?" Brad suggested, and Ben looked embarrassed.

"I appreciate it, old man, but I don't think it's quite . . ."

Brad looked at Carlie and grinned. "Shall we tell him? That's M. M. Montgomery you're talking about, my boy."

Ben's jaw dropped. "Holy Jehosophat!" he breathed, and took the stairs to Mrs. Sturdevant's study three at a time.

After that Ben's stories did improve, and so did the paper's circulation. So, too, did their own morale. The petty snubs were easier to bear, somehow. And that was fortunate.

*Harper's Weekly*, on August seventeenth, ran a lurid etching, purportedly from life, showing rebel soldiers bayoneting helpless Federal wounded after the Bull Run battle. Both the Garrisons and Uncle Henry subscribed to the weekly, and the postmaster's own copy received considerable circulation at the store. The climate in church the next day was as frigid as February, a condition that Reverend Ryerson's sermon did nothing to alleviate. Outside afterwards, Mr. Garrison and Mr. Pryor almost came to blows, and Emily made an audible aside to Netta Courtins that made Ben grit his teeth.

Toward the end of the week Tom Garrison came home. He came on the train to Newark and Mr. Garrison met him there with the big farm wagon. It was in the nature of a triumphal procession—or would have been, had Tom permitted it. Brad, who had managed to be downtown at the time, reported it that night.

"Everybody was out in the front yards and most of the flags were flying. Mr. Winters and your uncle and the pastor were on the porch of the store, along with a whole flock of others. They had a flag they were going to present, and Reverend Ryerson was just getting into one of his patriotic speeches when Tom reached out and jerked the reins and off they flew, leaving everyone standing there."

Ben had not been present, but the next day he swallowed his temper and went to interview Tom for the paper. He came home, tight-lipped and angry.

"You know, in spite of everything, I felt just sick over what happened to Tom. But he's killing it, the way he feels so sorry for himself!"

"Did you get your interview?" Carlie asked.

"Huh! The little he said, I couldn't print!"

Ben made a good story out of it anyway, although he ad-

[ 180 ]

mitted to Carlie privately that it had taken all of his self-control.

Sunday again was gray and muggy—the whole of August had been drowned in rain—but despite that fact the church was crowded. The hymns were martial ones, and Reverend Ryerson preached on the "Soldiers of God." Everyone was hoping to see Tom, but the Garrison pew was empty except for Emily, who came late, left early, and spoke to no one. The Dorcas League was meeting at Garrisons' that Tuesday, and there was some talk of changing it. But Emily had been adamant about having the meeting, Netta Courtins reported, walking over with Carlie that afternoon.

The Courtins girls were talking to Carlie again now, though whether because of Ben's Union editorials or because they were lonely without Emily to chum with, Carlie was not sure. No one saw much of Emily these days.

"That's why I was so surprised she wanted us today." Netta looked perplexed.

"Maybe she thought it would force Tom to see people."

The meeting was held in the big country kitchen, which the Garrisons used for everyday living—the parlor, Netta whispered, had been converted into a bedroom for Tom, and its door was tightly shut. They were making havelocks, a sort of Arablike head-covering supposed to be ideal for soldiers in southern climes. Though needles flew rapidly, conversation was forced. Emily was looking too drawn and tense. There was a feeling of general relief when the meeting broke up for refreshments. As Carlie was about to leave, Mrs. Garrison plucked at her arm.

She was a little woman, overshadowed by the rest of her family, and her voice was almost apologetic. "Carlie, dear—would you stop and speak to Tommy? He told us how kind Laura was to him in the hospital, and I thought—you were such friends once . . ."

Carlie started to say no, but Mrs. Garrison looked so piti-fully hopeful that she changed it to an awkward, "I'll try." When she reached the closed door, she hesitated. Then she knocked firmly and opened it as Mrs. Garrison hovered nearby nervously.

Tom was in an invalid's chair, staring out the window, and at the sight of his pinned-up trouser leg, Carlie's heart lurched for a second. He had not heard her knock, but as she entered the floor creaked and he spun the chair around sharply. She was shocked at the expression on his face.

"What do you want?"

The pent-up venom in his voice made Carlie stammer. "Why . . . To say hello, to see you . . ."

"So now you have. Get out! I'm not a sideshow!"

Instinctively she snapped back at him, as she would have done to Ben. "You're supposed to be so brave! You haven't even got the courage to show yourself!"

She was stunned at her own words, and Tom's face had contorted. For a second she thought that he would strike her. But he could not, of course, and the realization of this hit them both at once, making her unable to hide her look of pity. Without a word, he jerked the chair around again to face the window.

"Oh, Tom. Tom, I'm sorry . . ." Her words came in a whisper. She put her hand out, then let it drop.

"Here's your bonnet." Emily was standing in the doorway, her eyes cold. She thrust the bonnet out, and Carlie took it and escaped.

She was ashamed and embarrassed by what she'd done, and it was no comfort that when she told the tale at home nobody blamed her.

"He had it coming," Ben said tersely, and Brad agreed.

"He's been in a shock. This may be just the jolt he needs to bring him out."

Brad was right in his prediction. Tom came down to the store the next day—slowly, hobbling on his crutches. He sat there on the gossip bench for two hours before going home. He was not social, but at least he was there.

"The Garrisons are overjoyed," Brad reported that night. "They were just about out of their minds with worry. Tom wouldn't take any interest in the farm or anything—just sat and stared. Now at least he's decided to live."

Tom appeared with his family at church on Sunday just as the first hymn was beginning. Throughout the sanctuary, people stared. If only they wouldn't do that, Carlie thought, and Mrs. Sturdevant's eyes darkened with compassion. Reverend Ryerson shuffled his notes hastily and switched from the posted hymns to the martial ones of the week before. He switched his sermon, also. Everything went smoothly until just before the closing hymn when, as he occasionally did, he called upon the elders for testimony and closing remarks.

Mr. Pryor, with remarkably poor taste, invoked a lengthy prayer for the "speedy end of this misguided conflict," with a lugubrious reference to the poor lad recently returned. He was no sooner back in the Amen Pew than Uncle Henry was on his feet with a ringing prayer for God's blessing on the Union army and a thanksgiving for this brave boy's glorious sacrifice in the cause of right. All over the congregation, there were shocked gasps. Everyone realized what the two men were doing, but it was several seconds before they knew what else was happening. Tom was standing, bracing himself with a crutch, and he was laughing. His laugh rang through the nave and the galleries and up to the belfry tower.

"Prayers!" he jeered. "Prayers and preachers! What we needed was men and guns! But you didn't send them. You stayed at home and *talked*. Cowards!" His eyes raked the crowd, fixing on Ben, who whitened, and on Joe Pryor, who turned an angry red. "Cowards or worse! Why don't you pray for the destruction of the serpents in our midst?"

Amid a great silence, he slowly made his way down the aisle. He had reached the door before Mrs. Ryerson came to herself and brought her hands down hard upon the organ. The congregation plunged into the closing hymn.

Tom's outburst would be the talk of the town for weeks— that was obvious from the stunned faces of everyone. Today, however, no one stopped to talk. Even Mr. Pryor vanished, dragging Joe. There was a thin white line around Ben's lips. When they reached home, he strode into the library, said tersely, "Don't wait dinner," and shut the door. Carlie looked at Brad.

"You don't think he'll try to enlist again?"

Brad shook his head. "No, but I wouldn't much blame him. Hero or no hero, Tom should be horsewhipped."

Alison, lying on the kitchen sofa, shook her head somberly. "I pity him. It hurts to hate like that."

Ben did not emerge until late in the afternoon. Looking exhausted, he came out on the side porch, where they all were sitting, and dropped a sheaf of papers on the wicker table. "See what you think of that," he said to Mrs. Sturdevant, threw himself into a hammock, and closed his eyes.

Mrs. Sturdevant read it through, first quickly and then more slowly. When she looked up, there was an odd expression on her face. "What made you think of this?" she asked.

Ben looked puzzled. "I don't know. Just seemed it had to be said."

Alison reached out her hand for the papers, and Carlie read over her shoulder. As she read, she felt something akin to awe. What Ben had written was an answer to Tom, not an angry answer, but a quiet and thoughtful one, which had a depth of perception that amazed her. What amazed her even more was that Ben had been able to see both sides. "Perhaps we should remember that God is not the God of the North alone," he had written. "Perhaps what we should be praying for is a better understanding. Perhaps we forget that we are at war not *against* something, but *for* something. There is a difference."

It was a piece that Papa might have written, a point of view that Ben would not have understood a short while before. How much he had changed, she reflected. How much they all had! It frightened her a little.

# CHAPTER

# 18

B EN RAN the editorial in the paper. He did not speak of it again, but Carlie could tell from his manner that there had been comments, and after a few days she questioned him directly.

Ben shrugged. "I knew there would be talk, but that didn't matter."

Carlie knew what he meant. What other people thought no longer bothered them, not when something really important was at stake. The change had come about so gradually that she had hardly been aware that it was taking place. Outside things didn't trouble them any more.

She had wondered about the editorial mainly because she was worried about paying the taxes. But Ben's right, she thought. This is something that had to be said even if a few people do cancel ads. We'll manage somehow.

They would manage, because they had to. It was as simple as that. She did not quite know where this new faith came from. I guess some of Alison's faith rubbed off, she thought. In a strange sort of way, as Carlie's faith had grown, Alison's seemed to have diminished. She was restless and moody, although she covered it quickly whenever she realized anyone was watching her. But more than once her gaiety slipped, and Carlie could glimpse the somberness underneath.

Perhaps it's just the weather, she thought hopefully.

September was making up for the rainy August with a burst of unseasonable heat. It was not good for Alison; her skin had an unhealthy pallor, except for the two red spots in her cheeks. The hot still air made everyone feel tired. Carlie was grateful for it, though, in one respect. It postponed the necessity of buying new shoes for Paul and Oliver. Until cool weather came, they could still go barefoot.

They were all going to need new clothes this fall, but she was putting off doing anything about it until the tax question was resolved.

She did not like to mention the taxes to Ben for she knew that he was doing all he could. But the end of September, at which time they would be due, was rapidly approaching. Finally, one night before dinner, she waylaid him in the hall.

"Have you thought of anything yet?" she asked anxiously. "I saved five dollars out of last month's housekeeping account and there's the egg money."

Ben shook his head and smiled. "You keep it. I paid the taxes today."

"Ben! How?"

"Sold the gold watch and the first edition Pa gave me for Christmas." His tone was casual, but Carlie knew what a sacrifice it had been. Those things had been, for Ben, a symbol that Papa considered him a responsible adult.

She was careful to match her casualness to his. "Who bought them?"

"Brad."

"Oh, Ben!"

Ben looked at her. "He wanted them, and they were worth

the money. And I was glad to take it, because I thought for a while I'd have to part with Midnight, and I didn't know how I'd get to the newspaper office every day without him. Things sure do go in circles!"

"They're coming out wonderfully now!" In impulsive relief, Carlie flung her arms around him, and he backed off, looking sheepish and embarrassed.

"We're not out of the woods yet! We're going to need coal, and feed for Midnight, and shoes for the boys." Ben chuckled. "Have to tell Alison to get out her crystal ball."

"Ben? What's the matter with her lately?"

Ben shrugged. "Search me. Girls! By the way, a package came for you." He produced a bulky manila envelope with a New York postmark.

"Ace Publishing Company?" Carlie stared at it wonderingly. Then comprehension came. The story she had written, just before Ben had run away—so much had happened since that she had forgotten it entirely. Face flushing, she tucked it hastily into a desk drawer until she could open it alone.

Ben was looking at her curiously, but fortunately dinnertime distracted his attention and later he had apparently forgotten. Indeed, she almost forgot it herself. Alison tired early and was put to bed, but the others lingered on the porch. Brad had borrowed a new book from Judge Zabriskie to read aloud. Afterward there were clothes to be put to soak for tomorrow's washing, and rooms to be tidied, and the breakfast table to be set. It was not until she was upstairs, undressing, that Carlie remembered.

She pulled on a wrapper and slippers and went downstairs, lit the library lamp, and took out the bulky package. The manuscript, as she had guessed, had been returned with a mere printed note. Despite the fact that she had forgotten its existence, she felt a stir of disappointment. She settled into Papa's big chair, pulled out the manuscript, and began to read.

It was almost like reading something she had never seen, and she was startled and chagrined. "Oh, well," she told herself wryly. "I didn't expect it to be very good. None of the ones in that magazine is." But one thought troubled her more than she wanted to admit. The other stories *had* been printed; hers had not. And she had always thought that she could write.

"Carlie?" She looked up, startled to see Mrs. Sturdevant standing in the doorway. "I came down to get Alison a drink and saw the light. Is anything wrong?"

"No, I'm just . . . working late." Carlie jumped up and the papers spilled to the floor. She ducked for them hastily as Mrs. Sturdevant knelt beside her.

"Here you are, my dear." There was an odd expression on Mrs. Sturdevant's face as she held out the papers, and when Carlie looked at them she realized why—the printed rejection slip was face up on top. Mrs. Sturdevant smiled without comment and went to the door.

"Mrs. Sturdevant . . ." She had not known she was going to speak until she did so. Mrs. Sturdevant turned questioningly, and Carlie held the manuscript out straight before her. "Will you read this, please?"

"Of course, my dear." Mrs. Sturdevant looked at her keenly. "But let's go upstairs. It's cosier there." She led the way up to her sitting room. Carlie settled down on the little striped sofa, her hands locked tightly, while Mrs. Sturdevant, in the high-backed chair, read the story.

When she had finished it, she looked up at Carlie with penetrating eyes. "What do *you* think?"

The directness of the query caught Carlie off-guard, and she considered. "I'm disappointed," she said at last.

"In what? That it was rejected?"

"No, in myself."

"Ah." Mrs. Sturdevant's eyes warmed. "Then this has

served its purpose. You *can* write, Carlie; even this shows it. But you must never again commit the sin of working without respect."

"But it was only a . . ." Carlie stopped and blushed.

". . . trashy romance?" Mrs. Sturdevant's brows quirked mischievously. "That's not the point. A worker must always take pride in his craft." Her face grew serious. "Your success or failure is judged, not by the limitations of the medium you work for, but by how well you create within those limitations. The trick is to make the limitations work for you." Her warm smile flashed. "Sometime, Carlie, I would like to see what you can really do. Now I must get my chick her glass of water."

"I'll get it." Carlie ran downstairs. When she came back up, she paused at the second floor. On a sudden impulse, she snatched her journal from her bedside table, carried it upstairs, and thrust it into Mrs. Sturdevant's hands. "Here." She turned away quickly, before she could reconsider and take it back. She knocked on Alison's door and slipped inside.

"I brought your glass of water. Alison? Honey, what's the matter?" Even in the darkness she could tell that Alison was crying. She sat down beside her quickly and stroked her black curls, the only thing visible, for Alison was huddled into the pillows like a broken-hearted child. "Is something going to happen again?"

"Don't make fun of me!" Alison's voice lashed out, angry and bitter. Then she turned over and sighed, pressing her face penitently against Carlie's hand. "Ah, I'm sorry. I don't know what's the matter with me."

Carlie bent and hugged her. "I wasn't laughing at you, silly! And don't you ever wonder again why you get those 'feelings'! I'd never have found out about Papa if you hadn't made me go on having faith. And, Alison, knowing's made such a difference! Particularly to Ben."

"Ben . . ." Alison's whisper was barely audible, but it brought illumination suddenly to Carlie's mind.

Ah, Alison, she thought with tender pity. Brad had been right in saying it would have been easier for Alison if they could have kept her still a child. But life, Carlie reflected, didn't pay much attention to things like that. It was like the game the boys played—*Coming, ready or not . . .*

Carlie wished suddenly that Laura were here. Laura could cope with this better than she. Her own heart ached for Alison, but she was not old or wise enough to know what to do. Or perhaps, she corrected, her trouble was that she understood too well.

She was particularly conscious of this just now, for autumn was beginning, and October always filled her with a nameless yearning. She wrote pages about it in her journal, together with the character sketches she was now attempting. She was taking her writing very seriously since Mrs. Sturdevant had returned the journal, for she valued Mrs. Sturdevant's quiet remark, "I think you can write, Carlie."

"I'm going to really work at it this winter," she resolved. She had already decided that she would not go back to school when it resumed at the end of October. It was quite customary for girls to study alone at home once they were fifteen, and she would have more than enough to keep her busy.

She had already started on the family's winter clothes. Ben had squeezed out enough money for shoes for the boys, but the rest was up to her. She was grateful for the experience she had had helping Laura sew last spring. Fortunately there were very few style changes this fall; there was little fashion news at all, for everyone was preoccupied with the war. She had retrimmed her last year's bonnet with new bright blue ribbons, and Alison was helping her remodel her old Sunday dress with fashionable black velvet quilling.

The sewing machine hummed most of the day, and in the evenings she took the hand sewing up to Alison's room. She took her journal up sometimes, too, to read aloud—the gay parts only, for she was trying to lift Alison's spirits. Alison had withdrawn abruptly from the evening read-aloud sessions in the kitchen, and both Brad and Ben were growing impatient with her moods.

"I don't know what's got into her," Brad said ruefully. "She was coming along so well for a while, and then boom! She's as nervous as a witch. She's never been like this before."

"I guess she's just growing up," Carlie said slowly. Unconsciously she sighed. She felt Brad's hand tighten over hers, and she changed the subject quickly.

She was finding it increasingly difficult these days to cope with her relationship with Brad. It was not good, she acknowledged with deep honesty, to be living in the same house with someone about whom she felt like this. That morning on the ferry had brought a change, and both of them knew it. They weren't as natural with each other any more. There would be long pauses in their conversation, and then both of them would speak at once. She wished fervently that her mother were here. Or Laura—she was beginning to feel closer to Laura now than she ever had before.

She was almost grateful for the distraction of fall house cleaning, and actually it was not as difficult as she had feared, for she had learned to keep the house clean day by day. The summer curtains were taken down and the lace ones hung. The windows were washed, with Paul and Oliver's grudging help. School had still not started, for the teacher had unexpectedly enlisted and a replacement had not yet been found. The boys were, of course, overjoyed.

"Papa would have a conniption," Carlie said ruefully to Mrs. Sturdevant one afternoon in late October, watching the boys tearing into the house through the back door, their tanned faces dusty from helping Daniel in the barn.

Mrs. Sturdevant laughed. "Cheer up, they're happy savages. And healthy, and perhaps they're learning more than they would in school."

That was true. They were both growing more self-reliant, particularly Paul. And even Oliver had taken on more chores. Carlie handed them each a sugar cookie and sent them upstairs to wash. "And use the back stairs! I just waxed the front ones. I want to have the cleaning all done by Sunday!"

It felt good to have the house back in its accustomed winter order, to have the doors shut and the fires lit in the evenings. There was a security, a continuity, about it. Carlie needed that. She had a feeling, when she was sitting in Mama's chair behind the silver tea service, with Brad lounging at her feet and Ben bending over Alison on the sofa, that some things were changing far too fast.

She was glad to have the house cleaning finished by the weekend. The spell of glorious Indian Summer weather broke, Sunday was raw and chill, and rain poured down. Ben went to the cellar and started the furnace before going out to harness Midnight to the carriage so they could ride to church. So that Mrs. Sturdevant could hear the choir sing her favorite cantata, Carlie was staying with Alison, who had one of her sick headaches.

After the others had gone she went through the quiet rooms in their winter dress. The rain made slow lonely music against the windows. It reminded her of a poem Brad once had read:

> A feeling of sadness and longing,
>     That is not akin to pain,
> And resembles sorrow only
>     As the mist resembles the rain . . .

[ 193 ]

She glanced at Alison, lying on the parlor sofa with her eyes closed.

Carlie had begun to keep a soup-kettle always on the stove, and it was steaming a delicious invitation when the others burst in after church. She knew at once that something had happened. Even Alison's eyes opened.

Brad, hanging up his wet overcoat in the hall, grinned at Carlie. "You picked a good Sunday to miss."

"What happened?"

"Tom Garrison, of course." Ben's voice was trying to pass it off as a joke, but his eyes did not. "You know that editorial I wrote on Monday about the defeat at Ball's Bluff, saying we should avoid getting maneuvered into battle till we're better prepared? Tom thought it was Copperhead propaganda. He wanted to take a poke at me then and there."

"What did you do?"

"What could I do?" Ben shrugged, but his lips were tight. "I couldn't fight him, and I told him so."

"How could you!" The words burst from Alison so harshly that everyone was startled. She had pulled herself bolt upright on the sofa, her eyes black and enormous. "Did you have to *remind* him that he's a cripple? Don't you know he still feels like a whole person inside? Do you think anyone ever *realizes* that they're not?"

"Ah, my poor child." Mrs. Sturdevant made a pitying gesture toward her, but Alison turned away.

"I'm not a poor child! Take me upstairs, please!" It was Brad, not Ben, to whom she held out her arms, and he scooped her up quickly. Mrs. Sturdevant's lips pressed tight together, and she closed her eyes for a long moment.

Now we all know, Carlie thought. "Dinner's ready," she said briskly.

She was grateful for Paul's new grown-up thoughtfulness, for during dinner he kept conversation going, egging Oliver into excited chatter about the coming Hallowe'en. They needed that distraction, Carlie realized, snatching glances at the others as the meal progressed. Ben's face was remote, and there was a look in Brad's eyes that she had seldom seen.

Afterward she fixed a tray and carried it upstairs, but Alison's door was closed, and when she knocked Alison called out violently, "Go away!"

Alison's voice was so tight that Carlie knew any show of sympathy would be a mistake. She made her voice quite calm. "Your tray's out here. If you decide you want it, just holler." She put it on a chair and went back downstairs.

Brad was leaning against the library mantel, staring at the fire. He looked up when she entered, flashing the ghost of a crooked grin.

"Brad?" She put her hands up and ran her fingers along the lapels of his jacket. "Remember what you told me once, about having to learn to live with things?"

"But *Alison* shouldn't have to. It wasn't her fault—it was mine." Brad's face was somber.

"Alison's not a china doll, Brad; she's human. She has to learn to—accept things the way they are, just as I did, and Ben. Don't you remember what you said to me? 'It's what you let your troubles do to you that matters.' And I think if you try to protect somebody from facing up to them, you're even cheating them a little." She did not know where this wisdom came from, except that it was a gift Brad had given her and the time had come when she must give it back to him. She gazed up at him earnestly, and then she was in his arms and they were clinging together and Brad's face was against her hair.

It was with something curiously like relief that she heard a knock at the door. "I'll get it." She broke away, conscious that she was trembling, and went out to the hall. She paused a moment to compose herself and smooth her hair. She opened the door and stared unbelievingly.

"Hello, honey, one more mouth to feed! Peter's regiment's been transferred so he sent me home." From beneath an unfamiliar bonnet, Laura's face, a little tireder and thinner now, was smiling at Carlie. In another moment, heedless of Laura's wet cloak, Carlie was hugging her hard.

"Oh, Laura, I'm so glad you're home!"

# CHAPTER

# 19

HERE WAS SO MUCH MORE that Carlie longed to say to
Laura, but there was no chance now. Almost immediately everyone was crowding around, kissing her, helping
to carry in her bags. Ben went out to pay the livery driver who
had brought Laura from Hackensack. Brad and Mrs. Sturdevant were eager for Washington news, and Laura wanted to
hear about everything in Franklin.

They told her about discovering the true meaning of Papa's
letter, and Laura's reaction was to burst into tears. Presently
she looked up, lifting a radiant face.

"I'm sorry. I've been needing to do that for a long time.
Oh, I hate being away from Peter, but it's so good to be
home!"

She said it again that night, when at last she and Carlie were
alone together getting ready for bed. Laura shut the door and
took a lingering look around the familiar room. "You don't
know how good it feels!"

"It's wonderful to have you back," Carlie said softly, feeling suddenly shy.

"Washington was exciting, but it's not like home. If only Peter were here, everything would be perfect." Laura threw a blue dressing gown around her shoulders, sat down on the bed, and leaned forward intently. "All right, now tell me what's really been going on."

Carlie settled on the foot of the bed, and they talked far into the night. She told Laura about the taxes and Uncle Henry's guardianship proceedings, and Laura's lips tightened.

"I thought something like that might happen. That's one of the reasons Peter decided I should come home. There are other women to do war work in Washington. I'll be needed more here, particularly when the Sturdevants leave."

"When . . . *what?*"

Laura looked at her. "They only came for the summer, you know. It's nearly winter, now."

It had not occurred to Carlie that the Sturdevants might leave. The thought brought a pang. Yet perhaps, indeed, it might be for the best . . . for herself, as well as Alison.

She told Laura about the relationship that had sprung up between Alison and Ben, carefully avoiding any reference to herself and Brad. Laura's comment was terse.

"Alison's been wrapped in cotton-wool too long. Of course it hurts for her to find out all of a sudden that she's human, too." Laura glanced at Carlie shrewdly. "It wasn't easy for us either, was it?"

Carlie wasn't going into that. "For Alison, it's—different. Ben's such a . . . what is it Papa calls him? . . . 'a restless dreamer.' He needs to wander free. And it's just struck Alison that she can't do that, too."

"You couldn't have protected her from it, Carlie. Being hurt's a part of being alive. She'll come through it. Alison's strong in the ways that count."

That she was, Carlie thought. And she was not the only one. The next afternoon, after the rain had stopped, Laura put on her most sober-looking suit and bonnet and went out without a word. When she returned, just at dinnertime, she was smiling, but her smile was grim.

"Heaven and the Township Committee be praised, we can stop worrying about the coal bill. I have a job."

"You *what?*" Carlie stared at her.

"I'm the new schoolmarm. Guess it was getting so late in the season that they couldn't afford to be choosy."

"It's a wonder they'd hire you, considering you're Pa's daughter," Ben said dourly.

"Oh, they mentioned that, but I pointed out that I was also the wife of a wounded soldier. But what really swayed them was the fact that they could get me for ten dollars less than they paid last year. Most of their patriotism's in their pockets." Laura took off her bonnet and followed Carlie out to the kitchen, looking tired. "Can I help? I'm sorry I didn't get home in time to cook."

"You sit down and be a lady," Carlie said. Laura had acquired a fragile look that worried her; there were violet shadows around her eyes and her face seemed too finely chiseled. She loaded Laura's plate with meat, potatoes, and gravy and watched her closely while she ate.

Dinner, spiced with Laura's announcement, was gay. To the Sturdevants, Laura passed her new venture off lightly. "I've grown used to having something to do, working in Washington. And besides, it's really sinful for the children not to be able to go to school. I seem to be the only person around to fill the position. It's practically a duty."

Mrs. Sturdevant nodded warmly. "I think educating our young ones is one of woman's chief concerns, and it's always good to have interests outside one's own home circle. It will be a good thing all around."

Carlie, seeing Mrs. Sturdevant's wise eyes, suspected that she had guessed there was a deeper reason. But the subject of finances was not touched on till later, when the family was alone together. Laura dropped down into the kitchen rocker and drew a deep breath.

"I feel so much better, knowing it's settled. I was so afraid I wouldn't find something I could do!"

"Some of those kids are a real handful. Neddy Garrison's been running wild since Tom's been home." Ben looked at Laura closely. "You're not used to coping with stuff like that."

"Nonsense," Laura said strongly. "I can learn. After the way you sold your gold watch, and your work on the paper—and the way Carlie's been doing all the housework, when she hates it so . . ."

"Not so much, now," Carlie said hastily. "I almost like it, now that I have a system. It's almost scientific."

Ben hooted, but Laura's eyes warmed. She held out both hands suddenly, the way she used to do. "It's funny, isn't it?" she said softly. "We all do—pull together. And a year ago, who would have thought we could?"

"We had to," Ben said simply.

Laura nodded. "I guess life's like that game we used to play, remember? *Coming, ready or not . . .*"

It was the same thought Carlie had had, and she looked up, startled. Their eyes met and Laura flashed her old gay smile. "It's like the time I wore my first hoop and went out to show Daniel. Only I couldn't get through the door! I was so mad! And Daniel looked at me and said, 'You didn't know how 'cause you didn't *need* to know how before, only now you does.' I learned!" She stood up, giving her full skirts an impish swing.

They *had* learned to pull together. It awed Carlie almost, when she considered how far apart they had all seemed a year ago.

The next afternoon Mrs. Garrison and Emily came to call,

to thank Laura for her kindness to Tom. It was an awkward visit, despite their best efforts, for Emily was tense and silent, and even Laura's graciousness could not make Mrs. Garrison seem at ease. It was as if Tom's bitterness had infected them both.

Ben had been right in saying that Neddy Garrison was becoming a problem. He was as fearless and daring as Emily had been, and he had always worshiped Tom. Now Tom ignored him, and Neddy seemed to be trying frantically to recapture his esteem by acts of mischief.

There was no doubt whatever in Carlie's mind about the identity of the culprit when, the morning after Hallowe'en, she discovered a copperhead snake sketched crudely on the front door in bright red paint.

Paul's fist doubled up. "Wait till I get hold of him in school next week!"

"Just you don't," Ben advised tersely, getting a bucket of white paint to erase the stigma before leaving for work. Afterward, he spoke to Laura. "There's quite a situation building up. You sure you want to go through with teaching, Laurie?"

"Certain sure." Laura looked pale but firm. "They need a teacher and I need a job. That hundred dollars the school board's paying will help a lot. Not to mention the four dollars extra for doing the sweeping and starting the fire."

"You're not planning to do that, too?"

Laura tossed her head. "Why not? We can use the money as well as anybody else."

Ben didn't answer, but on Monday morning, when school was to begin, he got up even earlier than usual and left the house at six. When Laura reached the schoolhouse at eight she found the stove already stoked and giving forth a cheerful warmth. When she told Carlie about it, after she reached home late that afternoon, her eyes filled with tears.

"Without even telling me he was going to do it, either! I can't imagine why."

Carlie could. Coal buckets were heavy, and in her plain snuff-colored gown with its prim white collar and cuffs, Laura looked almost as fragile as Alison. Now she sank back on the old kitchen sofa and put up her feet. "Give me a minute to catch my breath and I'll help with supper."

"You will not." Carlie poured a cup of tea and handed it to Laura. "Stay put and talk to me. You've done enough today."

"Not so much." Laura stirred her tea slowly. "Not next to you and Ben. I guess you don't realize, maybe, how much you *have* done. But to me, coming back after being away—it shows." Her glance traveled around the big kitchen with its bubbling soup-kettle, its polished copper, the glowing lamp on the center table. "It's *home*, again. It wasn't for a while, last spring. It makes me feel ashamed, to have gone off and left you with so much to do."

"Oh, honey!" Carlie dropped the soup ladle and went to sit beside her. "You belonged with Peter. It was good for you. And it was good for me, too." She flushed slightly under Laura's warm comprehending eyes. "Even if things did get—involved."

"You're learning, honey," Laura said softly. Then she flashed a rueful smile. "I hope I learn to cope as well with my *young* men."

Teaching school was not easy for Laura. Carlie knew this instinctively, but she knew and respected the way Laura kept the darker side of the picture to herself. The tales she told at the dinner table were always gay, sending everyone, particularly Alison, into gales of laughter. Alison was eating downstairs again regularly now. Laura had hinted that it was unfair for Carlie to have to carry trays upstairs, and tender-hearted Alison had been immediately remorseful. She looked rather apprehensive these days, and it was Brad, not Ben, who carried her back and forth, but she *was* downstairs.

Laura had helped in other ways as well. By her very presence the evening kitchen gatherings were no longer an uneasy thing of two couples. It was better for them all. Carlie was startled to find that even Brad looked relieved, for it had not occurred to her that he, too, had found the situation strained.

Laura's return meant music around the piano again, too, and singing. She was never too tired to play the piano, even when there were little white lines around her mouth, as there were when there was no mail from Peter or when she'd had a bad day at school.

There *were* bad days, although Carlie would never have learned of them from Laura's own behavior. It was Paul to whom she turned for information. Paul, tall, thin, and unbelievably grown-up this winter, had constituted himself Laura's protector. And she needed one, from the way Paul spoke.

A regular underground campaign of innuendos, maliciousness, and petty goadings had broken out in school, just as it had against Carlie last year. The leader was Ned Garrison, of course. The other children, Paul said, had nothing against Laura, but with the thoughtless cruelty of children, they had gone along with Ned. There was added spice in the fact that their target was the teacher.

It had begun mildly, with veiled insolence, books left at home, slates dropped during class—all things that could seem accidental to Laura, if not to Paul. But by the middle of November, it was obviously a planned campaign. Laura came home every afternoon looking so frail and exhausted that everyone else felt grim. Alison's eyes blazed with indignation, Mrs. Sturdevant looked compassionate, and when Carlie went to Dorcas League, the atmosphere fairly crackled.

"I don't know which is worse," she told Ben violently,

"Emily's antagonism or everyone else's pity. Now they feel sorry for me because I'm Papa's daughter! One of these days I'm going to burst out with the truth. Particularly if that Garrison brat doesn't let up on Laura. I wish she'd quit."

"She won't, and you won't," Ben said bluntly. "We don't do things like that!"

Carlie knew it, too, but it didn't help. The certain knowledge they had now—that they were being misjudged—was some comfort, but not very much. Not when Laura came home with her lips pressed tight together and violet shadows around her eyes, when she tried to hide behind a handkerchief the racking cough she'd developed. The schoolhouse was poorly heated, and the teacher's desk was farthest from the stove.

It was going to be a cold winter. The first snow came early. It did not last long, but it was followed by several days of driving rain and sleet and great gusts of wind that shivered the windowpanes. Ben ordered coal for the furnace, and they all began spending their evenings in the kitchen, around the table, which Ben had pulled up close beside the range.

"I must see about getting Alison some warmer clothes," Mrs. Sturdevant murmured absently, glancing up from her manuscript. "She hasn't anything warm enough for these country winters."

Country winters! Joy surged up in Carlie. "You mean you're staying on?"

All three Sturdevants looked at her in surprise. "But of course we're staying!" Alison said in astonishment. Brad said nothing, but his eyes met Carlie's with a look that made her wonder suddenly whether she should be glad or apprehensive.

Later, when they were going up to bed, Mrs. Sturdevant stopped her in the upper hall. "You will still keep us, won't you? I'm afraid we just assumed that nothing need be said."

"Of course. I'm so glad." Carlie put her hands out impulsively. "It's just that I thought—I wondered . . ." She stopped and blushed.

"Whether it would be wise?" Mrs. Sturdevant looked at her directly. "Alison's come alive here, and even if it hurts her somewhat, I don't think I'd wish it any other way. She could never go back to being a little girl again, so why try to make her? It was time for things to change." She was speaking of Alison, but she was looking at Carlie with a smile. And Carlie, smiling back, felt her own heart eased.

It was fortunate that she had this one happiness to cheer her, for November grew progressively cold and grim. Laura came home on Friday looking extremely tired and worried.

"I had to switch Ned Garrison today."

"Oh, Laura!" Carlie stared at her. "Why?"

"He had that slingshot with him." Laura dropped down wearily into the kitchen rocker. "He was shooting at squirrels at recess, and afterward he brought it in to shoot paper wads at the younger children. When I told him to bring it to the desk, he just said, 'Make me.' I had to do it."

"I wish you hadn't," Carlie said soberly.

It was not that the switching itself was very bad. It was the customary schoolhouse punishment and the light birch rod, struck across the open palm, administered only a sting. But the humiliation for a small boy was indescribable, and when that boy was Ned Garrison, there were bound to be repercussions.

They were not long in coming. Monday was rainy and chilly, and when Laura came home, she went straight upstairs without even stopping to take off her bonnet and cloak. "I'm going to skip dinner. I have a headache," she called over the banister, and Carlie looked up, frowning. Laura's voice was hoarse from the cold she'd contracted, but there was a quiver in it as well. As soon as she was out of sight, Carlie turned to Paul.

"What happened?" she demanded grimly.

"There was a live copperhead in her desk drawer this morning."

"*Paul!*"

"It's all right," Paul said hastily. "It was half-asleep from hibernating, and Laura slammed the drawer shut quick and acted as if nothing'd happened. I guess Ben will have to get rid of it tomorrow. I thrashed Ned good at recess."

"Oh, Paul, that won't help any."

"It helped *me*," Paul said bluntly.

There was a Dorcas meeting the next day; there always *was* one, Carlie thought mirthlessly, right after every crisis. It was at the Garrisons, too, as luck would have it. Carlie did not quite trust herself with Emily just now; she would have given anything to stay home, but she did not. She put on the brown princess walking dress that she had made over from one of Mama's, copying a picture in the latest *Godey's*. It had long, tight sleeves and a lace collar and cuffs, and it made her look at least eighteen; it was also, she knew with vindictive satisfaction, more becoming than anything Emily had ever owned.

The meeting was not a happy one. The atmosphere at the Garrisons' house was no longer conducive to good times. Emily looked so thin and drawn that Carlie's enmity dissolved into sudden pity. It could not be easy for Emily, living in a house of hate.

Emily's eyes were lackluster, but they sparked when Laura came in late from school, looking wan but lovely in her last year's dark blue dress. Carlie was conscious of a current passing through the room. Obviously the news of Ned's punishment had spread.

Netta Courtins flashed Laura a sympathetic look, and pretty, bumbling Jessie rushed into speech with her usual indiscretion.

"Has anyone read Mr. Greeley's piece about the blockade along the Carolina coast? You know, folks said it couldn't be done, but it's really working. Our boys have captured one or two ports already and sent everything up in flames." Jessie suddenly stopped, looked at Laura, and turned very pink. "Oh, dear!"

Emily glanced at Laura through her lowered lashes. "I do hope they haven't burned your home. It's near there, isn't it?"

"Our home is here." Laura's voice was quiet, and Carlie choked back an angry speech.

"Honestly!" she exploded to the others after they were back at home. "One minute I feel sorry for them, and the next I'd like to shake them all!"

"I do feel sorry for them," Alison said somberly, and Laura nodded.

"Tom Garrison's doing more harm now, cooped up in that room of his, than he ever did before."

"*Because* he's cooped up," Alison said wisely.

"That's just it. I wonder . . ." Laura broke off, looking thoughtful.

The next afternoon, when Carlie went out to the spring-house, she was surprised to see Daniel, dressed in his best rusty black, marching solemnly down the drive.

"Where are you going?"

"To call on Mister Tom. Your sister thought he might take kindly to some walking lessons from an old hand." Daniel slapped his own wooden leg and his earring gleamed.

"I'm surprised you'd waste your time," Carlie said spitefully, and Daniel regarded her calmly.

"It ain't his fault he's ornery. He just ain't learned yet how to wrestle with his angel."

"How to . . . *what?*"

"Ain't they taught you nothing?" Daniel looked scandalized.

"When Jacob was a-sleepin', the Lawd sent an angel that wrestled with him the whole night. But Jacob grabbed ahold of the angel and wouldn't let it go until it blessed him." His old eyes were wise and knowing. " 'Pears like now angels don't fly so free, the Lawd sends tribulations instead, and it's up to us to twist them till they bless us."

It was an echo of some other words she had heard, long ago, and it stirred some chord deep within her. She locked the thought away in her heart to consider at some future time. Right now there was too much else to occupy her mind.

Tomorrow was Thanksgiving, and she was determined that it should be happy. She was making pies, both pumpkin and mince, as Mama always had. Ben had bought a goose from Mr. Courtins, and Daniel had plucked and cleaned it.

Carlie was a little worried about that goose, for she had never cooked one, but it turned out wonderfully. Thanksgiving was wonderful, too, even though they were all conscious of their parents' absence. But the Sturdevants made a special effort to keep things gay, and the weather, too, was lovely, unexpectedly warm and golden.

After three o'clock dinner, Carlie and Brad went for a walk in the woods, up behind the Courtins' farm. They did not speak much; they did not have to. All the awkwardness that had been between them lately seemed to have vanished. As the afternoon waned, the air grew cooler and Carlie pulled her worsted shawl tight about her. Brad reached around her shoulders to straighten it and did not take away his arm. And Carlie's heart, instead of growing turbulent, was full of quiet peace.

In the evening there was music and singing and pumpkin pie and coffee before the fire. Alison lay on the sofa with Ben sitting beside her, and Brad read aloud.

Later, getting ready for bed, Laura smiled dreamily. "It *was* a good day, wasn't it? If only Mama and Papa and Peter had been here, it would have been perfect." Her eyes grew dark. "I wonder where they are."

"I don't know, but I hope they're happy. I hope they know that we are." Carlie gave Laura's slight shoulders a tender squeeze. " 'Night, honey." She slid into bed, sank back into the softness of the pillows, and closed her eyes.

It was hours later, although it only seemed like seconds, that she heard Alison's piercing scream.

# CHAPTER

# 20

W HEN ALISON'S SHRILL CRY came, Carlie sat bolt upright in bed. Then she was up and running to the hall, but fast as she was, Ben was even swifter. He had already reached the third floor, and a second later he came bolting down, his face ghostly white in the darkness.

"The roof's on fire! Wake the boys and get them out of the back door fast! The *back* door!" Without waiting for her cry of horror, he clattered past her down the stairs. Brad rushed by, carrying Alison, who was sobbing against his shoulder. Carlie stared numbly.

"It's just the roof. The fire department will have it out in no time!" Mrs. Sturdevant's voice cut through Carlie's shock, and she turned swiftly.

"We don't have a fire department! Just the neighbors. The whole house will go!" Awareness came sharply. "We've got to get out!"

Already she could hear a crackling noise upstairs, and from the boys' room came the sound of Oliver crying and Paul's voice, hoarse with apprehension, trying to reassure him.

"I'll get the boys." Laura appeared in the dimness of the foyer, clutching her blue wrapper around her. "Carlie, Mama's best furniture, and Papa's books and etchings . . ." They exchanged a glance of immediate comprehension. At a time like this, with assets so low, everything of value must be saved.

The third floor, where the antiques were so lovingly arranged, was most in danger. Carlie rushed upstairs, her nightgown billowing out behind her. Mrs. Sturdevant's voice, sharp with fear, called after her, but she paid no heed. Already smoke was billowing from the sitting room. Even as she entered, flames licked down from a corner of the ceiling. Her eyes smarted and smoke gagged her, but she dragged the little sofa out to the hall and grimly plunged back in.

As from a distance, she heard a hollow clanging from outside. Ben was ringing the great bell that hung by the barn. It was the custom of the countryside to summon help in this way, but this was the first time since war had divided neighbors that an emergency had come, and she wondered whether anyone would respond.

"I won't think about it! I mustn't!" Blinking and choking, she tugged at the curtains. If they caught fire, the whole room would go up in flames.

"You little fool!" Brad's voice struck her from the doorway, and then he was jerking her roughly away.

"I have to . . ." She could not see him clearly for smoke was blinding her, but suddenly he knocked her to the floor and blackness closed in upon her. She choked and struggled. Then the darkness fell away, and she was in the upper hall, where the air was clearer, with Alison's comforter wrapped around her.

"Your gown caught fire. It's out now." Brad's face was white. "What are you trying to do? The furniture doesn't matter!"

"It does! We can't afford . . ." Carlie stopped abruptly, but Brad's eyes had filled with comprehension.

"I'll save what I can. But you've got to promise me you'll stay out on the lawn with Alison and Mother. Understand?"

"I promise." She was so relieved to have someone telling her what to do that she did not question his peremptory tone.

"Then get out quickly." He fairly pushed her down the stairs. She could hear him dragging furniture as she ran.

Pain shot up her leg; it must have been burned when her gown caught fire, but she did not stop to look. The second floor was still in darkness, but in the lower hall a candle flickered grotesquely. From the back the bell was still tolling. Forgetful of what Ben had said, she ran instinctively to the front door and turned the handle.

"*Stop that!*" Before she could pull the door open, Ben was there, wrenching her away, his eyes blazing. "If a draft goes up the stairs, we're really done for!" His voice was hoarse.

"Oh, Ben, I'm sorry!" She caught her breath. Ben dragged her with him through the kitchen and out of the back door. A wan orange moon illuminated the night sky. He pulled her around to the side of the house and then released her.

"Go round to Alison and stay there! I've enough to worry about!" Ben plunged down the path toward the pond, where she could make out Daniel's stooped figure scooping up buckets of water. How pitiful, how utterly useless those buckets seemed!

The night chill cut through her flannel nightgown, and the fresh air hurt her lungs. She stumbled around to the front of the house and across the lawn where Mrs. Sturdevant was sitting on the cold ground, cradling Alison in her lap. Laura was holding Paul and Oliver tightly by the hands.

High along the line of the roof, flames flared wildly against the sky, and at the sight Carlie involuntarily cried out. Alison caught her hand, and Mrs. Sturdevant's voice came quietly.

"It's all right, help's coming." Already figures were running down from the Courtins' farm, and a wagon careened to a stop beside the pond. Two tall figures went down toward the water, and another, more slender one in a worsted wrapper came running up the path. Carlie stared.

"*Emily?*"

"Carlie? Thank heaven you're all safe!" Emily dropped down on the ground beside them, and even in the darkness Carlie knew that she'd been crying. Her hand was pressed against her waist and her voice was shaking. "Carlie, we didn't know—you've got to believe that."

"Know what? *Emily!*"

"It was Ned!" Emily made a swift savage gesture toward the blazing roof. "With that slingshot and a live coal. I don't know how! It must have hit some dry leaves or something. When he heard the bell, he woke Tom up and told him. He thought Tom would be *pleased!*"

Alison made a soft sound of comprehending pity, and Emily shuddered. "I'm so ashamed," she said. "About . . . everything. I thought I was being patriotic. I didn't realize what it was doing to us."

Carlie couldn't speak, but her hand closed over Emily's tightly and Emily flashed her a grateful look.

"It will be all right now," Alison said gently.

Emily shook her head. "These wooden houses! Why don't we have a fire department!" She jerked abruptly to her feet. "There must be something we can do!"

Paul stood up. "Maybe I can help. I won't get into trouble." Laura considered for a moment and then nodded, and he ran down toward the pond.

Carlie stood quickly, too, and winced.

"Carlie, you're hurt!" Emily knelt beside her, as Mrs. Sturdevant leaned forward.

"It's all right!" Her leg didn't matter, nothing mattered

except that the house be saved. Carlie ran down toward the pond, scarcely conscious of the cold or of the ice and stones cutting into her bare feet.

"Wait, Carlie!" Emily caught up with her and wrapped her own woolen shawl around Carlie's shoulders. A moment later Mrs. Sturdevant, too, came down the path.

The men had formed a bucket brigade. In the faint light Carlie could make out familiar faces: the Pryors, Mr. Courtins, Mr. Garrison. To her astonishment, she even recognized Uncle Henry's light beard. The neighbors *had* rallied round! She flashed a sideways glance at Emily and saw her own expression mirrored on Emily's face.

They fitted themselves into the line of workers. Scoop, pass, throw. Scoop, pass, throw. Ben and Mr. Courtins had long arms, but even so the water could not be flung high enough. Even as they worked, flames crept down hungrily toward the second story. Tears blurred Carlie's eyes.

Tom Garrison, balancing doggedly on his wooden leg, straightened and rubbed his arm across his face. "Not good enough! Takes too long." His eyes caught Paul. "Can you climb? Get the longest rope you can find and loop it over that branch in the maple tree. We can hoist buckets up there for you to throw."

Ben was already running toward the barn. He reappeared with a great coil of rope, and Paul, his face tense and solemn, began to shinny up the tree. Carlie's throat tightened. The tree was so tall, and Paul in his nightshirt seemed so small. A shout went up as he reached the branch, and a moment later the rope came hurtling down.

Carlie swayed, and Emily turned to her. "Let's go sit down. They don't need us now."

Carlie was grateful for Emily's arm around her as they went up the hill. Someone had brought blankets and dragged the little wicker couch from the porch for Alison. She reached out both hands to Carlie and Emily as they sank down beside her.

"It's all right now. Brad got most of the furniture down and he's helping Ben. See, the fire's not spreading any more!"

The rooftop still blazed sullenly, but flames no longer reached down toward the lower floors. Ben, dashing up to them for a second, confirmed this. "The rest of the house is safe, thanks to Tom! It's just the top floor and the attic, and there's nothing of real value left there."

"Ben!" Carlie gasped. "Papa's letter—the Carolina one! And his journal! I put them in the tin chest in the attic for safekeeping!"

Ben's face whitened. "I just hope it's not too late. No telling when we may need . . ." The rest of his words were lost to them as he raced across the lawn. As he neared the house, flames flared again against the sky.

"Ben, don't! It's too dangerous!" Alison's voice was shrill. "Carlie, don't let him! Ben!"

Carlie stared at her. "*Alison!* You're *standing!*"

Alison's face turned toward her blankly. Then she swayed and toppled as Carlie rushed forward. Emily had already caught Alison in her arms.

"I'll take care of her. You go get Ben!"

Carlie dashed off blindly. The flames were bright again now, and the smoke so thick. Her heart was pounding. She groped her way around to the back and only barely realized that Ben was already coming down the steps.

"It's all right, I got them." Ben grabbed her arm sharply. "Carlie, wake up! I said it was all right."

"That's nice," Carlie answered faintly. "Ben, Alison . . ." All at once Brad was there with his arms around her, and she leaned against him gladly, not knowing exactly why she was crying except that she was too tired to stop.

"All right, Cara. It's all right. It's almost out now." Brad was leading her gently across the lawn. They reached the others, and she sank wearily down onto the cold ground. Emily was cradling Alison's limp figure in her arms. Mrs. Sturdevant was rubbing one of Alison's hands and Ben the other. The flames had almost completely died, although smoke still billowed, and men now began to straighten up and rub their backs. Brad wrapped one of the blankets around Carlie's shoulders.

Everything *was* all right, she thought drowsily, seeing the tender look on Emily's face as she bent over Alison and the way Tom and Joe, down by the lake, were working side by side. What was it Daniel had said the other day? Something about tribulations being blessings in disguise. It was too bad that it had taken a crisis like this to turn new enemies back into the old friends they had once been.

Deep beneath her consciousness lay the knowledge that some things were most definitely not all right, but she was too tired to face them yet. Just now nothing mattered except that they all were safe, that Beaufort still stood, and that perhaps one day Alison might walk. She leaned back in Brad's arms and closed her eyes as their neighbors, their friends, began drifting over from the pond. She could hear Laura admonishing Oliver not to run off and Mrs. Sturdevant praising Paul.

Mr. Courtins was talking to Ben. "The fire's all out now, but I'd advise you not to stay here tonight, just to be on the safe side. You can stay with us if you don't mind being crowded."

"They'll stay with me, of course." That was Uncle Henry's voice, quiet and positive, with a note in it that Carlie could not name. She opened her eyes quickly just as Tom moved forward.

"I told Ma we'd bring you back with us. She'll have everything fixed, and we brought the wagon so we could drive you all." Tom's tone was decisive, but his eyes, meeting Ben's, were not, and Emily added a breathless "Please!"

Carlie looked at Ben, and Laura said softly, "Why, thank you, Tom. That's right nice of you. We'd be proud to." That was one of Mama's Southern expressions, but nobody noticed or minded. Almost before Carlie knew what was happening, the boys were guiding them down the path to the big old wagon. She could hear Paul's questioning voice and Laura's low tone as she answered. Ben lifted Alison into the wagon and turned to Brad.

"I'm going through the house once more with Daniel. I'll be over later." Mr. Garrison touched the stolid horses with his whip, and the wagon jolted off, its lanterns swinging. Carlie looked back for a last glimpse of the ravaged house, and her eyes met Uncle Henry's. There was a look in his eyes that she did not understand. Or, rather, that she could hardly believe was truly there.

Lights shone from every window of the Garrisons' house and the strong fragrance of coffee greeted them at the door. Mrs. Garrison peered anxiously as they entered, then her face cleared and she bustled around the kitchen with more energy than she had ever shown before. Emily flew about, settling Alison on the sofa, bandaging Carlie's leg. Ned hung in the background, looking pale and scared. Tom turned to him.

"Boy! Pillows and blankets for the ladies, and more wood on the fire!"

Ned vanished as if grateful for the order. Laura glanced at Paul and, after a moment, looking solemn and determined, Paul rose and followed. Emily was handing out coffee, and Carlie sipped it slowly, feeling a deep contentment spreading through her. Things were working out. Nothing needed to be said, and nothing was, not until Ben had come and was telling of his inspection tour.

"The roof's gone, and a part of one wall in the front room,

but the house is safe." Ben turned to Tom and thrust his hand out abruptly, and after a minute Tom gripped it firmly.

"Ben, I don't know what to say . . ." It was uncomfortable to see Tom at a loss for words. "I've been a fool. I didn't know how big a fool till I saw what I'd done to Ned. That woke me up, believe me."

"Forget it." Ben clapped his shoulder. "A fellow has to do what he thinks is right."

"And let others do what *they* think right. That's what I forgot."

Brad interrupted the awkward moment by saying with a grin, "Hate to break up the tea party, but the girls look about ready to keel over. This has been an eventful Thanksgiving."

"It *was* Thanksgiving, wasn't it?" Carlie's eyes opened wide. Suddenly, out of sheer exhaustion, she started to laugh. "We have a lot to be thankful for, at that. Alison's standing . . ." She broke off abruptly, for Alison's face had gone chalk-white.

*"What did you say?"*

"Alison! Didn't you know? You did, as good as anyone, when Ben . . ." Carlie stopped again, for Alison's eyes blazed with hope as she threw back the blankets. Instinctively Carlie moved forward.

"Alison, don't!" Ben's face paled, but Mrs. Sturdevant stopped him with a look. What courage she has! Carlie thought numbly. Not a muscle of Mrs. Sturdevant's face betrayed her own anxiety as Alison slowly, with grim determination, swung her feet to the floor, pulled herself upright, and balanced for a second before falling forward into Ben's outstretched arms.

"Next time it will be longer!" Alison's voice was breathlessly triumphant.

The excitement of Alison's achievement carried over until they were all crowded into makeshift beds, but then, for

Carlie, reality returned. Squeezed in beside Alison and Laura, who were both sleeping soundly, she lay awake and stared at the ceiling, thinking with the clarity that deep exhaustion brings.

*Everything's all right* . . . the intangibles were, perhaps, but there were certain tangible things that definitely were not. They were going to need a new roof, and there was no money. They had scraped the bottom to pay the taxes—all but selling Midnight, and they must not do that for then Ben would have no way to get to work. Laura would not receive her teaching wages until the term was over. With winter upon them, they could not live in the house unless the roof was fixed—and where could they go?

They could not take a mortgage, for the house was in Papa's name. Besides which, she thought ruefully, no one they knew was likely to lend them money—or have enough money to lend, even if they were willing.

Except Uncle Henry . . . The thought came out of nowhere, and she could almost hear Papa's wry voice saying, "The practical Dutch! I'll wager Henry still has the first cent he ever earned!"

A month ago, or even a day, she would not have had the thought, but there had been something in Uncle Henry's face tonight that made her realize he might help them, after all. She realized something else, too, just as clearly.

Ben had a stubborn pride that would prevent his asking help from Uncle Henry; he also had a tactless tongue, and if he should go to his uncle, it was all too likely that he would only antagonize him more. Laura had always irritated Uncle Henry. There remained only herself.

Her heart pounded wildly, and for a second the old urge to run from difficulties rose within her, but she locked her hands together and willed herself to be calm. If she had learned one thing this past year, she thought humbly, it was the meaning of courage. It had taken courage for Papa to do what he was doing—for Ben to give up going off to war—for Laura to teach school. It had taken courage for Tom to admit tonight that he was wrong and for Ben to forgive him. She could not be less brave than they.

The story that Daniel had told her about Jacob wrestling with the angel came back to mind, and she realized all at once what it had made her think of—the words in Papa's journal that she hadn't understood. And something Mama had said, too, long ago: "You fight with life so, Carlie. And you haven't yet learned how to make it bless you."

That was the lesson Papa had meant she had to learn. Use your obstacles; make them work for you rather than against you.

So much of her old rebellion had been directed against things she could not change, against the natural laws that said a woman must be soft and subtle. The laws needn't be a prison, she now realized, but an asset that she could learn to use . . . as Alison had done. Certainly Alison had had obstacles to overcome. Yet, Carlie thought suddenly, how often that very helplessness of hers had extricated them all from awkward situations. And Alison's own suffering had given her a rare understanding that had enabled her to reach out to Ben and give him peace of heart.

Perhaps, indeed, troubles and difficult situations were angels in disguise, and it was up to you to make them bless you. A sudden picture of Uncle Henry in wings and halo made her giggle, but she was serious, too.

Perhaps everyone has to face up to this, sooner or later, she thought. Perhaps even Papa did, when he decided to go South. As Papa said, it's the turning point—and this time I'm not going to run away.

She closed her eyes, and slept.

[ 220 ]

# CHAPTER

## 21

WHEN CARLIE awoke the next morning, Ben had already left. He had been torn two ways, Brad reported, between the urge to start setting things to rights at Beaufort and the necessity of getting the paper out.

"The paper won. But he wouldn't go until Dan and I convinced him we'd personally go through the whole house from attic to cellar to look for sparks."

Judge Zabriskie had given Brad the day off, and in mid-morning the Judge himself came over to the Garrisons' to see how they were all getting along.

"If there's anything you children need, you let me know."

"Thank you, sir. I think we can manage." Laura's voice was composed, but her brow was puckered with worry, and after the Judge had left she sighed. "I wish I knew how."

"We will. We have so far," Carlie said stoutly.

The rest of the morning passed in a fog, for they were all exhausted. Emily was making soup for lunch. Mrs. Sturdevant was busy jotting down notes; the fire had given her an idea for another novel.

"Might as well get some good out of it," she said wryly.

Brad, Tom, and Daniel had gone off to inspect the damage, but they returned in time for lunch.

"Most of the house is all right, except for smoke damage. But it's a good thing I got Mother's manuscript out! Between fire and water, everything on the third floor is ruined, including all our clothes!"

Alison waved her hand gaily. "We can make new ones! I'll start this afternoon!" She had been in a state of feverish excitement all day, and her face was glowing.

For Alison at least, Carlie thought, the fire had been a blessing. Then she glanced at Laura, looking pale and tired, and her momentary happiness vanished. She slid an arm around Laura's thin waist, but she did not mention her plan for approaching Uncle Henry. She did not have the heart to raise Laura's hopes for nothing. In the light of day and her own misgivings, the idea seemed fantastic, and her spirit quailed.

"But I've got to do it," she told herself grimly. There could be no running away now.

"I'll get your dress goods this afternoon, Alison," she said aloud. "I'm going into town."

She was glad that this errand provided an excuse, and, as soon as lunch was over, she slipped away. She pulled Emily's wool shawl tightly over a borrowed dress and slipped Papa's precious letter in the pocket. She would, if necessary, but only as a last resort, show it to Uncle Henry.

After yesterday's beautiful weather, the air had turned icy and the sky was gray. When she reached Beaufort with its torn and blackened roof, her heart twisted, but there was no time for sentiment now. She went up the stairs, looking neither left nor right, turned into her own room, and jerked open the wardrobe doors. The bedroom itself was gray with soot, but fortunately none had penetrated the wardrobe's massive walnut walls. She surveyed her clothing grimly.

Nothing too childish, or Uncle Henry would consider her a chit of a girl; nothing too feminine, or he would think her flighty. She planned her appearance deliberately, as she was learning to plan her stories, according to her audience's taste and not her own. It reminded her of that night in the New York cellar when she had employed feminine frailty to head off the fight that had been developing between Brad and Ben.

"I should have understood then what Papa meant about turning disadvantages into assets," she said to herself. She only hoped she would have as much success today.

She washed with cold water, brushed and braided her hair into a simple knot, and put on the brown dress that was modestly high of neck and long of sleeve. Glancing in the mirror, she noted dispassionately the hollow smudges that showed in her cheeks and temples. She looked plain as an old shoe and infinitely weary, which perhaps was just as well. If appeals to Uncle Henry's logic proved useless, perhaps his sense of duty might help her out. She put on her plainest bonnet and her warmest cloak and started out.

The walk to Uncle Henry's farm was long, but it seemed to Carlie that she reached there far too soon. Her heart was hammering as she went up the narrow path. She hesitated a moment, then knocked deliberately. She heard light footsteps, the door was thrown open, and Bess stared out at her.

"Carlie! Why . . ." Bess's happiness faded suddenly into apprehensive fear.

"Bess, is your father home?"

"He's just going out." Bess made no move to ask Carlie in, but over her shoulder Carlie saw Uncle Henry appear in the hall, hatted and gloved. She stepped in firmly.

"May I speak to you a moment, sir?"

Somehow, after the way he had disavowed her family, she could not bring herself to call him uncle, and for a minute she was afraid he would ask her to leave. Instead, he turned to Bess.

"Elizabeth, go to your room."

Bess, with one frightened look, obeyed, and the two were left facing each other. Uncle Henry looked at Carlie. "Well?"

Where do I start? Carlie wondered frantically. She breathed a swift silent prayer, then the gracious words that Mama might have spoken came almost without any effort on her part.

"I wanted to thank you . . . for helping us last night." It was the right thing to say, and she breathed easier.

"Is that all?"

"No, sir." She took a deep breath and looked clearly into his frosty eyes. "We need a new roof. And we have no money."

"And you think I should give it to you, hey?"

"Not give, sir. Lend. A business arrangement."

"In spite of the fact that your father has proved himself a traitor? Why should I?"

All the businesslike and logical reasons she had rehearsed on the way over flitted through her head and were discarded. "Because," she said simply, "Papa said once that you were a just man."

"And you always think the way your papa does?" Uncle Henry was frowning at her.

"No, sir." She took another deep breath and added daringly, "I've learned this year of the harm that comes when folks accept other people's thoughts. Laura and Ben and I are Union. You know that. I don't believe you'd think it—right for us to lose our home, because you disagree with Papa."

Uncle Henry looked at her oddly, and it came to her that he was testing her somehow, as Papa once had done. "And that's why you think I'll give you the money? Because I'm just?"

"Partly." She looked at him directly, and all at once, inside her heart, the pieces fell into place. "And because I think you're also kind . . . Otherwise you would not have come to us last night."

They looked at each other and, for a second, time seemed to stop. Then, to her amazement, her uncle thrust out his hand.

"Shake, girl!" She felt her fingers crushed between his massive ones. "You're a good judge of character, and I like plain speaking. I like children who stick up for their parents, too. Was just going over to tell you when you walked in." He met her blank stare with a frosty twinkle. "Fact. I realized last night I was being a stubborn and thoroughly uncharitable old fool not to admit it. Don't stand there like a ninny, girl! Sit down!"

He waved a peremptory hand toward the ladderback chair, and Carlie sat down without a word. Uncle Henry *approved* of them. She realized this despite his gruff words and realized, too, that for the first time in her life she was beginning to understand her uncle.

She had spent so much time, last winter, thinking people did not understand her. But perhaps she had been looking at it backward; perhaps *she* was the one who had not understood—herself or others.

She had been so hurt and disillusioned when the townspeople had judged the Bensons by surface appearances, but she herself had been just as guilty. Because Uncle Henry was not a dreamer like herself, she had characterized him as harsh and unfeeling. She had been wrong. She sat in a daze as his blunt words penetrated her consciousness, but the bluntness didn't sting any more.

". . . must admit I wouldn't have given ten cents for the lot of you a year ago. Laura was a flibbertigibbet, that brother of yours was an impractical dreamer, and you were just as bad. I never held with encouraging those kinds of notions. Parents have a moral obligation to teach their children feet-on-the-ground good sense, so they'll have something to fall back on when times are hard."

Carlie opened her mouth to speak, but he waved her to silence. "That's why I was so disgusted with your Pa's tooting off like that. Wasn't till summer that I realized you must have had pretty good grounding, after all, to pull to like you did. I liked the way you held your heads up, too, to show you weren't ashamed. Wish I thought my girl could do as well, but she hasn't got spirit enough to say boo to a goose."

"Yes, she has," Carlie said softly, remembering the way Bess had come to them that rainy night.

"Maybe so." Uncle Henry scowled, and she smiled back at him in complete accord. Uncle Henry's ferocity was no more real than Daniel's . . . and what a pity, she thought suddenly, that Bess had never learned as much!

". . . realized then you young folks were all right." Uncle Henry was going on in that pontifical manner of his. "Wasn't easy for Laura to teach school or for Ben to put a muzzle on his temper and buckle down. I had to admire your independence. And it isn't fair for you young ones to suffer on account of your Pa's misguided notions."

Carlie straightened, and he scowled again. "Trouble is, Carlie, I'm a stubborn old Dutchman, and they always hate to admit they're wrong. But I'm doing it now. You young ones have a strong streak of Dutch, too, and I should have recognized it instead of thinking it pure mule-headedness. It's what puts starch in our spines and keeps us going when everyone else gives us up. A man's got to respect that when he sees it."

His face softened almost into a smile. "You can have your loan, Carlie. Businesslike. Straight six percent. But there'll be no rush about repaying, and you needn't worry about collateral. It's a character loan. Your Pa put good character into you, and I'm glad to know that, for though we weren't alike, I always respected him. That's why it hurt so to find out I'd been mistaken about him."

The brightness in Uncle Henry's eyes faded a little, and he looked away. Carlie rose. As she did, her heavy skirts brushed against her body; she felt a twinge of pain in her burned leg and heard a rustle of paper. All at once she knew exactly what it was that she should do. She took Papa's letter from her pocket and held it out.

She closed her eyes and stood quietly as her uncle read. No need for her to explain; Uncle Henry was keen-witted and he also knew his Scriptures. After he had finished, he looked at her oddly over the top of the letter.

"How long have you had this?"

"Since last May."

"You know that if you'd showed it to me, I'd have helped you straightaway?"

"We were afraid you'd think it necessary to make it public—to clear the family name."

"And now you did show it to me, when you no longer had to." Uncle Henry looked at her shrewdly. "Why?"

"Because I'd misjudged, too. I should have known you wouldn't jeopardize whatever Papa's doing." She hesitated, then thrust her hand out. "But I'm so glad you decided to help us, even before you knew."

"I'm glad too, Carlie." His hand closed firmly over hers. "Now you run along and tell that brother of yours he needn't worry about the roof."

Carlie caught her breath. "Uncle Henry? Would you do something else? Go see Ben yourself. But don't tell him I'd already talked to you."

Uncle Henry raised an eyebrow. "A managing female, hey?"

"Oh, no. I hope not. It's just that there's no need for him to know. And it might hurt his pride."

That was the secret strength of women—to know, to anticipate another's feelings—and to use that insight for their world's good comfort. She could not yet do it as well as Alison, perhaps, but that would come. She had already, she thought humbly, learned a lot.

Uncle Henry cleared his throat. "You're a lot like your Aunt Elizabeth at times," he said gruffly. And Carlie, deeply moved, looked at him with brimming eyes and knew that that was the highest accolade he could give.

Uncle Henry did come that night, bringing Bess, who looked dazed and bewildered. While she and Carlie had a joyous, tearful reunion in the Garrison kitchen, he took Ben into the front parlor alone and closed the door. When Ben emerged, there was a look on his face that made Alison's eyes grow luminous. She held out both her hands.

"Ben! Is it all right?"

"Everything's all right!" Heedless of an audience of Bensons and Sturdevants, Garrisons and Demarests, he bent and kissed her. Uncle Henry cleared his throat, and Carlie's eyes filled with tears. She looked away quickly, very conscious of Brad beside her and of feelings inside herself that she did not want to inspect and analyze—not just yet.

The work on the new roof began the next day, and it was not as expensive as they had feared, for all the neighbors were pitching in. Others beside Uncle Henry, it seemed, had come to respect the Benson children over the past hard months. And though Carlie's heart ached at the knowledge that Papa was still misjudged, she was conscious that she—all of them—had won something very precious.

The fire had indeed been a blessing in disguise. Or perhaps as Daniel said, miracles no longer took place in so spectacular a fashion. Perhaps the real blessing had come slowly, over the whole past year, as she and Ben and Laura—yes, and Paul and Oliver, too—had wrestled with life and come through with their heads held high.

And the changes in them had caused other changes, too. Bess had grown in courage. Emily had learned compassion, and Tom and Uncle Henry tolerance.

Alison's blessing, of course, had been the greatest of all. That, at least, had been an outside miracle, Carlie thought, but Brad disagreed.

"It had to start inside herself. Remember, the doctors never could find out what was wrong. And Alison always had to outrun and outdo everyone else. It's almost as if—I don't know, exactly—as if she was afraid to try to walk because she might fail. Until that night when she was afraid for Ben."

Carlie's eyes filled and she looked away. It was the Sunday of the week after the fire. Although the work was not yet completely finished, they had moved back into Beaufort. Outside the windows, snow was falling, but with the curtains drawn and a fire in the grate, the library was cosy, and she was very conscious of being alone with Brad. With that unspoken thought transference they so often had, he looked up and smiled.

"Do you realize this is the first time in a long while that we've really talked?"

There was an expression in his eyes that disconcerted her, and she tried to answer lightly. "I just haven't needed a father confessor lately. I'm not a little girl any more!"

"No, you're not." His tone was caressing, and she jumped up hastily and began to poke the fire. After a moment he came up behind her. His hand touched her waist, and involuntarily she trembled. "Cara, what are you afraid of?"

"Nothing. I don't know what you mean."

"Yes, you do. You always know," Brad said quietly, but he

did not press her. He went to the window, held aside the curtain, and stood looking out at the twilight and the falling snow. "Winter's really here. Looks as if we'll have a real old-fashioned Christmas."

In fact, winter had come with a vengeance. By morning the earth was heavily blanketed with snow and wind howled round the chimney, but the roof was airtight, thanks to their neighbors' help. And inside the house life had settled again into routine.

Laura's run-down condition, aggravated by exposure to the chill night air, had culminated in a bad lingering cold. By Monday morning, she was feverish and almost voiceless, and Carlie had to teach school in her place. Fortunately there was no longer any discipline problem, now that Ned Garrison was chastened and guilt-stricken, but even so it was not an easy time. To complicate things further, Ned brought a note from Emily for Laura. The Garrisons would be unable to entertain the Dorcas League on Tuesday as planned. Could the meeting be held at Beaufort instead?

Carlie, when Laura read the message, almost groaned. "Emily knows we're not half straight here yet. It's too much to ask!"

"After all the Garrisons did for us?" Laura remonstrated. "We can manage. You'll have most of the day to get ready. I'll be able to teach, myself, tomorrow."

"You will not," Carlie said automatically. Laura looked so wan that she was worried. After the dishes were done that night, Carlie baked two cakes, and she got up an hour earlier Tuesday morning to give the parlors a quick going-over before she left for school. The air was gray and raw and already a thin veil of snow was falling. Perhaps not many of the girls would come, she thought hopefully and then felt ashamed. The Dorcas League had really been accomplishing a good

[ 230 ]

deal lately for Soldiers' Aid, and now that Emily's bitterness would no longer cast a shadow, they might do even better.

She had hoped to leave the schoolhouse promptly at four, but sweeping and banking the fire delayed her. When she reached home, she was surprised that none of the girls had yet arrived. Alison was lying on the sofa before the fire, and Laura, who had dragged herself downstairs, was thumbing listlessly through a magazine. The door knocker sounded as Carlie hung up her cloak, and she went to answer, hoping again that not too many would come, for Laura looked so terribly tired. She threw the door open and stepped back, startled.

The porch was crowded, not only with the girls but with mothers, fathers, and brothers as well. She recognized Tom Garrison, Mr. Courtins, even Mr. Garrison and Mr. Pryor, glaring at each other, but on the same porch, nonetheless. And they were laden with bundles—sacks of flour and sugar, jars of preserves, cardboard boxes, and packages wrapped in tissue.

"Surprise!" Emily's voice was gay, but her eyes were warm and understanding. And Carlie, looking into them as the crowd swarmed past, felt her own eyes fill.

A donation party . . . It was a country custom, given for the minister's family, for newcomers or couples just starting housekeeping—or after a catastrophe, such as sickness or a fire. Not charity in the patronizing sense, it was the highest mark of esteem a town could give.

Behind her, in the crowded parlor, Alison clapped her hands. "I knew! I knew all along! Emily asked me what you needed most!" But what Alison had not known was that there would be gifts for herself as well—silks and hand-woven woolens for new dresses, a fleecy shawl crocheted by Mrs. Garrison, a cane painstakingly polished and carved by Tom.

"Thought we could sort of egg each other on," he murmured gruffly.

Alison was speechless and Mrs. Sturdevant nearly so. "I never heard of such a thing," she murmured.

"I have, but I never thought it would happen to us . . ." Carlie looked at Laura, too moved for words, and saw her own thoughts mirrored in Laura's shining eyes: We belong again . . . If they had still had doubts, after the fire, now they were gone forever.

A year ago, bewildered and unhappy, she had wondered where her place in life could be. She need wonder no more. And the belonging was doubly precious because they'd earned it on their own. Never again, she thought, would she have to be afraid . . . or want to run away.

She looked at Emily with suddenly brimming eyes. "You shouldn't have—you didn't need to . . ."

"Yes, we did." Emily's own blue eyes were very bright. There was nothing Carlie could say, and she didn't try. She put her head down on Emily's friendly shoulder and cried.

# CHAPTER

## 22

CHRISTMAS was coming. Carlie was very conscious of it as December moved along. It was the first time she had not looked forward to the holiday, and the thought made her rather sad.

There had been, of course, no news of their parents at all, but a few days after the donation party Ben came home with a mixed expression on his face. "The Federals have taken Beaufort. I read it today in one of the city papers."

"Ben!" Carlie stared at him and hope surged irrationally in her heart. "Maybe then Mama and Papa *can* get home!" She looked from his guarded face to Mrs. Sturdevant's pitying one, and her jubilation died. "Of course they couldn't. And Papa won't leave, anyway, till his work is done. But it could mean we might hear from them, at least."

"It could mean Mama's home's been burned, too," Ben said soberly. "From what I hear, our Union invaders haven't been too nice."

The sudden picture of their own Beaufort on fire rose in Carlie's mind, together with a sharp sense of closeness to her mother. She glanced at Laura and saw that Laura's eyes had filled with tears.

"It may be for the good," Alison said gently. "So much good has been happening to us lately, hasn't it?"

"We should be grateful for that, instead of behaving like spoiled children about the bad." Laura's voice was bright, but she turned her face away.

Laura's tears came more easily than ever lately, a sure sign that she was none too strong yet. Her cold had gone, but the cough lingered, and she was still very thin. She was worried about Peter, too, Carlie knew. Laura had been blindly hoping that he would get home for Christmas, but he could not. He wrote that there was talk in the air of a new offensive in the early spring. There was no likelihood of his getting leave until after that.

Laura's face whitened when she read his letter, but her voice was brisk. "Oh, well! There are other wives who'll be disappointed, too. And Christmas in wartime can't help being different."

She packed a large box and sent it off to Peter. Carlie contributed cookies and fudge, trying to show her silent sympathy. She longed to find something more concrete that she could do, but could think of nothing save to sew more diligently for Soldiers' Aid and to try harder than ever to keep their home bright and cheerful.

She and Ben and Laura had decided to forego Christmas presents among themselves. They had meant, of course, to make the usual Christmas celebration for the little boys, but she was touched when Paul came to her privately to say that he and Oliver had had the same idea.

"It wouldn't seem right, would it, with a war on, and Ma and Pa not here?" Paul's face was lean and solemn.

So Christmas would be quiet, with only church and a special dinner. Carlie fully expected to be sad, despite her sternest vows, and she was deeply moved to discover that this simpler

Christmas was more meaningful to her than any other she had ever known.

On Christmas Eve it snowed. As Carlie left for Dorcas meeting in the afternoon, soft white flakes began to swirl down through the gray sky, and they continued through dinner. The wind, sweeping across the frozen fields, piled great white drifts against the long windows. But inside there were greens on the mantel above a crackling fire, and candles glowed. Laura played the beautiful old carols, Brad sang, and Alison read aloud the Christmas story according to Saint Luke.

Late, very late, when Carlie went upstairs, she paused in the quiet darkness of the upper hall. She could hear the soft rustle of Laura moving about downstairs, turning out lights, and the sound of Ben's voice as he talked to Alison. Outside the French doors, the snow had just stopped falling, and the world was still.

She was conscious of Brad coming up behind her, and they stood in silence, looking out at the virginal whiteness of the night. A silver curve of moon was shining.

"It's shining on Carolina, too," Brad said quietly. She turned, and he bent and kissed her gently. "I hope you have a very happy new year, Cara."

Christmas meant hot cakes and sausages for breakfast, and a sleigh ride to church for all save Alison and Ben, who remained with her. Afterward there was dinner in the late afternoon—a goose, and one of Uncle Henry's hams, and both plum pudding and pumpkin pie. There were no beribboned packages on the table, but to Carlie, looking across the table into Bess's gentle eyes, it seemed as if invisible gifts were all around.

Saturday was a chill, sleeting day, and Carlie spent most of it in the kitchen, baking, glad for the cozy warmth and the kettle's singing. In the late afternoon Mrs. Sturdevant came downstairs, bonneted and cloaked. Carlie looked at her in surprise.

"You're not going out?"

"I'm stuck on my crucial chapter. Have to drive the cobwebs away!" Mrs. Sturdevant nodded brightly and went out into the storm. When she returned, she brought a letter from Peter that made Laura bloom. Laura was about to read the army news aloud, but Mrs. Sturdevant, surprisingly, was already on her way upstairs.

When she came down to dinner, it was obvious that something was in the wind, for she was wearing a festive dress of heavy black faille and she had an air of suppressed excitement. Alison's eyes were like shooting stars, and Brad's face was quizzical. What the dickens? Carlie wondered. But she would not ask, and dessert was over before Mrs. Sturdevant rose to look at her with an odd mixture of pride and apology.

"Carlie, I have invaded your privacy hopelessly, but I hope you will forgive me. I was so impressed by that piece in your journal about receiving the news of Fort Sumter that I took the liberty of sending a copy to my friend Sarah Hale. I received her answer this afternoon. *Godey's* wants to use it."

She held out a thin envelope, smiling, and Alison clapped her hands. "Carlie, *say* something!"

Carlie could only stand there dumbly, and when she made no move, Brad reached for the envelope. A slip of paper fluttered out.

Laura stooped for it, and her face went pale. "Honey, it's a check—for fifteen dollars!"

It would pay for shoes for them all, and more besides—coal for the furnace, a warmer cloak for Laura. Carlie stared speechlessly across the table into Mrs. Sturdevant's understanding eyes.

Everyone was crowding round, giving hugs and congratulations that seemed to pass over her in a rosy daze. "What did you write?"

"I don't know! I don't remember!" But Carlie would not show the journal to anyone except Alison—and that much later, when they were alone. She sat back with her eyes closed, while Alison read the passages aloud. When she was finished, there was a silence.

Only one small lamp was lit and Carlie was grateful, for her face was flushing. She felt self-conscious, for so much of it had been her own emotional reactions to the way the news had come to them at twilight, their fears for their parents, Joe's burning of the flag, the quiet service at the church . . . It all scarcely seemed important enough to warrant the notice of the great Mrs. Hale.

"Because it was real," Alison said gently. She repeated the family prayer that Carlie had quoted at the end. " 'Bless us, and keep us safe . . .' You *have* been blessed, Carlie."

"I know," Carlie said humbly. "I've been thinking that all week."

Alison waved her hand. "Not the other things. They're outside. You have a gift inside yourself. You can use words to make other people feel."

Carlie was turning over the pages of the journal and her eyes fell on the first entry, a year ago: "I want to be someone, and do something . . . it seems that if I don't find a way to use all I have within me, I'll die, a little." She had found a way that she had never dreamed. If only Mama and Papa were home!

She thought of this again the next morning in church. The news has somehow spread, as such things do, and everyone was offering congratulations. It made her aware, again, of how good it was to be accepted, but she was conscious also of the unspoken sympathy beneath the warm praise, and though it amused her, it also hurt a little. She could not be truly happy until Papa's name was cleared.

Tom, speaking to her after church, touched on this unwittingly. "Won't seem like New Year's without the Open House."

It was a thought Carlie herself had been trying not to face, and as she looked up she intercepted a look of pity in Emily's eyes. Carlie's chin went up. "But of course we're having Open House! We always do! You're coming, aren't you?"

She swept down the path to the sleigh, conscious of Laura's open-mouthed amazement. Ben ran after her. "Are you out of your mind? All that work! And only three days away!"

"We have to!" Carlie turned to him earnestly. "I won't have them feeling sorry for us on account of Papa. Don't you remember what Uncle Henry said about holding our heads up high?"

Ben looked at her and grinned. "All right, all right! Just tell me what to do!"

They all worked, even the Sturdevants and Laura, for fortunately that week there was no school. The floors were waxed, and the rugs rolled up for dancing. Laura made batches of candies, and Carlie baked. She brought up the fruitcakes she had made last fall. Judge Zabriskie told Brad how to make the punch. The boys went into the woods for greens, and Alison's nimble fingers wove garlands that swooped along the stairs. The crystal glistened and the silver gleamed. Carlie, going up to bed on New Year's Eve, could not remember when she'd been so tired, but she was filled with an infinite satisfaction.

She scarcely realized, the next morning, that it was her birthday, but when she went downstairs the breakfast table was laden with ribbon-tied gifts, and for a moment she thought she would burst into tears. They were not as lavish as in the past, but they were filled with love.

[ 238 ]

There was a note in Ben's. "Midnight's yours for the day if you want to ride." Her mind swept back to last year's wild ride.

"Go ahead," Laura said, watching her. "Everything's done. You're entitled to get away."

She did slip out, after an early lunch, but to her joy, before Daniel had Midnight saddled, she saw Brad approaching.

"Thought I'd go with you, if you didn't mind."

She did not have to answer. They turned their horses into the woods behind the Courtins' farm and rode through a silent world of black and silver. This New Year's weather, like the last, was bitter. Carlie stole a sideways glance at Brad and then looked away.

They reached a rise from which they could look down on the whole valley, and Brad reined in. "Wait a moment. I have a present for you."

"But you already gave me one—the book of poems."

"That was different. I asked Mother to send to New York for this for Christmas, but it's only just come." He took a square box from his pocket, and Carlie stared in mingled awe and dismay at a thin gold ring. "It was my grandmother's. I want you to have it now."

"Brad, I can't . . . I'm too young . . ."

"It's a keepsake ring," Brad corrected her gently. "I'd like you to wear it until—well, until I come back."

"Until you *what?*"

"My year with the Judge is up now, Cara. I'm going to enlist." He spoke quickly, cutting through her rising panic. "Mother understands. She'll be going back to New York in the spring, anyway. Now that there's a chance of Alison walking again, she should be close to her doctors. And you read what Peter wrote about a new offensive. They'll need more men. I'm anxious to go. But only if you're waiting for me." He picked up her hand and slid the ring onto her finger.

Carlie looked at the tiny clasped gold hands through brimming eyes. "Brad, I don't know . . ."

"Then wear it till you do." He looked at her for a moment and then, as if understanding her need, rode off and left her there alone.

The wind whistled through the pines and the sky had darkened. In a few minutes there would be sleet, but she scarcely noticed. She thought of Brad going off to war—of what war was, as Laura had seen it, and Peter, and Tom. She thought of Brad coming home as Tom had done, and the picture rose so clearly that she had to cover her eyes. But she could not blot out one fact.

She loved him. It was as if she had always known it. If she had not discovered it before, it was because she had not wanted to. What was it she had cried aloud a year ago? I don't want to grow up!

She twisted the little ring around her finger, remembering what she had said to Laura once, that love was a secret language. It demanded much. It could cause hurt, but it could cause wonders, too. The strength she had found within herself this year had stemmed from her love of Papa and from Brad's faith in her. Love could also work miracles, she reflected, thinking of Alison.

She had been so worried about Ben and Alison, but she wasn't any more. Ben would go off to war someday; Alison would have to accept that, as Laura had with Peter, as Carlie must with Brad. Alison would go to New York. Perhaps she would walk. Afterward—who knew? They both were young. But even if they never met again, their coming together had been a rare and lovely thing. It had made Ben more gentle, more mature. It had turned Alison into a woman. As Brad, Carlie thought humbly, has done with me.

Suddenly she had been outdoors long enough. Suddenly she was urging Midnight forward, hurrying down the twisting path and toward the barn. She turned the horse over to Daniel's ministrations and ran inside, up the back stairs, to put on the blue-gray gown.

When she came downstairs, candlelight was glowing and Brad had lit the fires. The green garlands gave forth a poignant fragrance. Alison was lying on the sofa in one of her soft white gowns, with Ben sitting beside her, and Laura was running her fingers over the piano keys.

Soon the knocker began to sound. The house re-echoed with the sounds of New Year's, with glasses clinking, and music, and laughter. Carlie turned to Brad with a brimming heart.

The knocker sounded again. "I'll get it," she said quickly, glad to move away, for the look in Brad's eyes had made her breathless. She threw the door open and stared, and now her breath did stop entirely.

"*Papa* . . ." To her utter shame, darkness closed in, and for the first time in her life she really fainted. When she opened her eyes, Brad was rubbing her hands, but she scarcely noticed, for she was looking into her mother's face.

"Mama . . . How did you . . ." She could say no more, for she was being held tight in her mother's familiar arms.

"Beaufort was captured three weeks ago. The general knew about Papa, and he gave us a pass through the lines. We wanted to surprise you." Mrs. Benson held Carlie off. "My poor baby! You look so tired and thin!"

"I've grown up," Carlie said giddily. "Laura's married, you know. And wait till you see Paul . . ." But now they were all crowding around, and Laura was crying, and Uncle Henry was shaking Papa's hand. The talk, the excited greetings, swirled around her, but she scarcely heard. She knew, however, that the news of Papa's mission was out. He was vindicated at last.

Mrs. Sturdevant, warmly regal in black silk, was presented

. . . and Alison . . . and Brad. Carlie felt her mother's eyes on the little ring, and she flushed, but she did not explain. There would be time, lots of time, later when they were alone.

Mama was crying with Laura now, and Papa was in the library with the men. He was explaining how he'd left that editorial with Mr. Baldwin, to be run if just such an emergency arose. And he was telling about the real purpose of the Southern trip. She could hear his voice, as she had so often in the past, responding to Ben's excited questions.

". . . it started on the train, when we overheard a plot to assassinate the President in Baltimore. Then, next day, I happened to meet a Colonel Stone, who was heading the undercover service. He asked me to act as courier for his Baltimore agents. Then, when we were caught in Washington after Sumter, he approached me about going South. Clarissa's relatives there provided a perfect cover."

"Didn't she resent having them used?" Uncle Henry asked dryly.

Mrs. Benson's skirts rustled as she sailed into the library to answer. "I love the South. It was my home. But as my husband always told the children, there has to be one central authority—in governments, as well as families. I'm with Mr. Lincoln!" Carlie knew without looking that Mama's eyes were snapping.

Papa was going on. ". . . only bad thing was the necessity for leaving the children alone. But of course, we never thought it would be for so long."

"They did *all right*," Uncle Henry said, and Carlie could have hugged him.

Papa clapped Ben's shoulder. "I know how hard it must have been, for you and Carlie especially, to be missing all the excitement, stuck up here at home where nothing happens."

Where nothing happens . . . Carlie met Brad's twinkling

eyes and fought back a helpless giggle. Her mind swept back over the turbulent year. Yes, she reflected, at the time none of the things that had happened had seemed exciting. They had seemed like something to be gotten through. Maybe that was the way life was; maybe it was only in looking back that you realized you had been a part of something momentous. And it *had* been momentous, even if on the surface it looked as if she'd only been quietly keeping house.

She saw Brad moving toward her, and she smiled. Mama was speaking now: "What broke my heart was not being able to explain to the children, knowing they were wondering, doubting . . . We did try, once, but we had no way of knowing whether they would understand."

And Papa added quietly, "They just had to take us on trust."

*Trust*. That was it. That was what had brought them safely through the year. That, and the thing Uncle Henry called Dutch stubbornness—only perhaps its other name was faith. They were the reasons she no longer had to run, why she could face the changing future unafraid.

They were why she would be able to say to Brad, "We'll wait and see. We're young, you and I, and we can't foretell the future. But love is strong. And so I'll wear your keepsake—though I don't need to. The real one's in my heart."

She realized that she wouldn't have to put it into words. Brad always knew her thoughts. She held out her hand, the one with the keepsake ring on it, to Brad.